MW00358923

By CATT FORD

NOVELS
The Last Concubine
Lily White, Rose Red
A Strong Hand

Dash and Dingo
(with Sean Kennedy)

NOVELLAS
Extreme Bull
Long Way Home
Murder at the Rocking R
Summer Fever
The Untold Want

Published by DREAMSPINNER PRESS
http://www.dreamspinnerpress.com

The LAST CONCUBINE

Catt Ford

Dreamspinner Press

Published by
Dreamspinner Press
382 NE 191st Street #88329
Miami, FL 33179-3899, USA
http://www.dreamspinnerpress.com/

This is a work of fiction. Names, characters, places, and incidents either are the product of the author's imagination or are used fictitiously, and any resemblance to actual persons, living or dead, business establishments, events, or locales is entirely coincidental.

The Last Concubine
Copyright © 2012 by Catt Ford

Cover Art by Catt Ford

All rights reserved. No part of this book may be reproduced or transmitted in any form or by any means, electronic or mechanical, including photocopying, recording, or by any information storage and retrieval system without the written permission of the Publisher, except where permitted by law. To request permission and all other inquiries, contact Dreamspinner Press, 382 NE 191st Street #88329, Miami, FL 33179-3899, USA
http://www.dreamspinnerpress.com/

ISBN: 978-1-61372-599-3

Printed in the United States of America
First Edition
July 2012

eBook edition available
eBook ISBN: 978-1-61372-600-6

To my Bodie

CHAPTER ONE

AND so it came to pass in the Qing Dynasty during the rule of the Sun Emperor Jun that the Lord Wu Min ordered a caravan to set forth on the dangerous journey to the court of General Qiang Hüi Wei, governor of the states of Yan and Qui, bringing a gift of great value, for he was anxious to win favor and high position with the emperor. Whether he was pleased or disappointed that the designated courtiers and soldiers managed to succeed in reaching the stronghold of Qiang Hüi Wei after passing through hostile territory is lost in the passing of time. History only records that the caravan did indeed arrive in good order, and when news of such was brought to General Hüi Wei, he caused an audience to be granted in order to receive the gifts with all due ceremony in observance of the customs of the day.

"WHAT do you suppose Wu Min has decided would be an appropriate gift, Hüi?" Lord Jiang asked as the two men strode through the halls of the palace on the way to the audience room.

Hüi Wei emitted a short, mirthless laugh. "Bribe, you mean. He yearns for notice from the Son of Heaven and hopes I shall procure it for him."

"You are cynical," Jiang observed.

"And still breathing as a result." Hüi Wei gave his friend a wolfish grin and paused before the door. The two soldiers stationed there raised their lances to let them pass and stood with inscrutable faces, as if they could not hear the comments of the two men. "We shall see what clever lies his envoys try to promote to me."

With that, Hüi Wei nodded and one of the soldiers drew back the curtain to reveal heavy wooden doors with iron hinges. He swung the door back soundlessly, and Hüi Wei preceded his friend and advisor into the room, emerging from behind rich damask curtains upon a dais raised above the gleaming tile floor.

He stood, an imposing figure before the envoys sent to him, muscular and powerful, his impassive face handsome but weathered by his time on the battlefield, his eyes hard as he waited for the company to fall to their knees and bend in obeisance to his commanding presence.

His expression did not change as he took in the incongruous sight of a slender, beautiful girl in the midst of the men, and his gaze moved past her without a flicker of interest. He sat upon his massive throne, rested his hands upon the snarling heads of tigers carved at the ends of the armrests, and waited in silence. As a studied insult to Wu Min's representatives, Hüi Wei had chosen to receive them dressed in rough clothing more suitable for battle, including his leather breastplate, and wearing his sword at his side.

Lord Jiang's voice rang out as he announced, "His imperious person, the governor of Changchun province, including the states of Yan and Qui, oath protector to the Son of Heaven, Emperor Jun, General Qiang Hüi Wei has deigned to receive the representatives of Wu Min, lord of Liaopeh province. Who speaks for Wu Min?"

One of the ornately dressed courtiers bobbed his head while still staring at his reflection in the highly polished floor and answered, "His gracious Lord Wu Min has required me to convey both his respect and a small, meaningless token of his allegiance to Qiang Hüi Wei."

"You will refer to my Lord as the Lord General Qiang Hüi Wei or your master will be pleased to receive you back—cut into a thousand pieces," Jiang rebuked the man sharply, using Hüi's military title rather than his civil one as a subtle reminder.

Hüi Wei tried to keep his lips from twitching. His friend Jiang would certainly never have carried out such a threat personally unless he deemed it necessary for the security of this province, but he had convinced many of his ruthless cruelty by use of utterances such as these. Apparently, this courtier was one of them because he cringed visibly and hurried to correct his address.

"A million apologies, your Honor!" he exclaimed, his voice somewhat muffled by the necessity of speaking directly into the floor. "I meant no offense. It was but my miserable ignorance that caused me to address his Excellency the General incorrectly. I pray you will not visit revenge for my abysmal infamy upon my gracious master."

Hüi Wei dared not glance at Jiang, but he could tell how his friend was enjoying this. "Sit up!" he ordered impatiently. "What does this Wu Min want?"

The courtier sat back upon his heels, red in the face, as if with his girth he was unused to the position of obeisance. None of the rest of his company dared to even look up, but Hüi Wei noticed the four burly soldiers who flanked the girl maintained a tight cluster around her, as if she held some high position and was therefore in constant need of protection.

"Nothing, my Lord! He dares ask nothing of you." The courtier glanced up slyly and then fixed his gaze back at the floor. "If, in some distant future, you should be moved to grant him some small token of your favor—but he is very aware that he deserves less than nothing from you. No, we have come to present you with a gift of great value, merely to express Wu Min's loyalty and allegiance to you, Protector of the North, and to the Son of Heaven, Emperor Jun, and—"

"General Qiang appreciates this gracious gesture, but he is an important man. He has much responsibility in the business of serving the emperor," Jiang interrupted smoothly. "I assure you any gift from Wu Min will be greatly valued."

The courtier seemed to recognize he was being urged to get on with it, although clearly he would have been content to listen to his own eloquence for many hours. He held up one hand. "If I may have permission to direct these miserable servants to approach the most gracious governor—"

Jiang nodded. "You may. To that line and no further." He pointed at a line of black stone set into the floor at least ten feet short of Hüi Wei.

The courtier held up one pinkie and a manservant approached the throne on his knees, holding a small chest. He opened the chest to reveal the gleam of many silver tael piled within.

"A small offering of coin," the courtier said, as if the amount were negligible instead of a small fortune. He lifted the ring finger on the hand still held aloft.

A second servant shuffled forward with another small chest. This time the lid was lifted to reveal the lustrous beauty of pearls of various sizes and colors that ranged from black to pink to purest white.

"Rare pearls harvested from the ocean, at the cost of many lives," the courtier intoned. He added his index finger.

A third servant came forward to unroll a bolt of shimmering silk.

"The finest silk in all of Liaopeh province. Note the subtle beauty of the orchid flower woven into the pattern."

Hüi Wei yawned ostentatiously upon his throne to indicate his boredom with these offerings.

The courtier looked dismayed. "These gifts are mere nothings, not worthy of the governor's greatness. Although garnered through great personal austerity on the part of Wu Min, these tokens are too insignificant to add to your great wealth and consequence. No, the treasure Wu Min wishes to present you with is none of these. It still awaits." Finally, he raised the middle finger on his hand.

The four soldiers got to their feet, and one held out his hand to the lady who was still prostrated in full obeisance. She rested her hand upon his brawny forearm as lightly as a hummingbird in flight and rose gracefully, her gaze properly cast down and veiled by her lashes. The soldiers led her forward and stood ringing her as if guarding her from imminent attack. Her blue cheongsam was embroidered in gold with dragons and phoenixes, and the dark color served to set off her ivory beauty.

In a hushed voice, the courtier spoke as if so impressed with himself he could hardly bear the significance of what he was saying. "Wu Min has made the most profound of sacrifices to offer you his half sister, the Princess Zhen Lan'xiu, to be your wife."

Hüi Wei didn't even glance in the girl's direction. "Thank your master, but I could not accept a gift that would deliver such cruel pain to the giver. The sentiment is gracious, but the sacrifice is unnecessary. I do not need Wu Min to choose my wife for me."

The courtier hurried into flustered speech. "He means no offense! It is known that your Greatness already possesses a wife and several concubines! Wu Min had no thought of the Princess Lan'xiu displacing any of these revered ladies. No! In fact, you may use her as you wish and cast her aside if she displeases you!"

Jiang asked, "Does he undertake to accept this gift back if she is found to be defective?"

Shocked, the courtier said, "She is untouched! Chaste and pure! The most beautiful maiden to be found in all Liaopeh! None who see her fail to fall under the spell of her beauty. Her nature is modest and demure! And she has been most carefully guarded. There have been no sly trysts by moonlight to despoil her purity—"

Hüi Wei said in a bored tone, "You will give Wu Min my thanks for his impressive tributes. I am sure it has cost him much pain to part with his sister."

"Oh, it has, it has," the courtier assured him in an oily voice. "If only you would agree to accept these humble gifts, it would bring him such pleasure as to negate the torment—"

"We will consider these tokens. You have a memorial?" Lord Jiang cut the man off expertly.

"It happens that I do. Wu Min wished to ensure that your graciousness was aware of his loyalty—"

"So you had mentioned." Jiang held out his hand for the scroll.

The courtier got to his feet and approached the dais, withdrawing the scroll from the sleeve of his robe. He winced as Jiang gripped his arm with one hand while he accepted the scroll in the other. He glanced at Hüi Wei's face but could vouchsafe nothing and surrendered the scroll without a struggle.

"The audience is at an end. You may all withdraw," Jiang announced. "The Princess Lan'xiu is to be conveyed to the harem." He snapped his fingers at the general's soldiers, who came forward immediately.

"But—the princess—her guard—she must not be left unprotected!" the courtier sputtered. "Her guards must—"

"I am sure we will be able to protect her adequately. The guards you brought may leave with you, while they still can," Jiang said, his voice implying he would accept no argument.

"Her servant, then. At least permit her servant to bear her company as she makes a new home here—"

For the first time Jiang examined the short, slim manservant with a soft, slightly feminine face. "You are eunuch?"

Blushing, the servant nodded without looking up, taking a tiny step closer to the princess.

The princess's beautiful face showed nothing of the emotion to be expected of a noble girl being delivered into an unknown court and a stranger's bed, but she seemed to sway slightly in the direction of her eunuch servant.

Hüi Wei waved a hand and his soldiers came forward to lead the girl and her servant from the room. The soldiers who had guarded her made no move, as if they had no idea what to do in this unforeseen circumstance.

The courtier's face wore a frustrated expression as he watched the princess disappear, but he seemed to accept his impotence and, once again, pressed his forehead to the floor. "I shall convey to his gracious Lordship Wu Min the fact that the Lord General Qiang Hüi Wei accepted the gifts he chose with much deliberation and thought for the enjoyment and enrichment of your Lordship's house—"

Hüi Wei's shoulders shook as he strode from the room chuckling, accompanied by Jiang. "Do you think he is still speaking?"

"I gave orders to the guards to take note of what he says, but I fear it is in vain to hope for some indiscretion. He is well versed in spewing many words while saying very little. I have no idea what Wu Min hopes to gain with this display."

Hüi's lips tightened into a grim smile as he walked through the halls. "Have you not? And you so long-headed, unless you flatter me by allowing me to be the one to elucidate. Answer me this: how did a man who governs a landlocked province many miles from the sea come by such a quantity of peerless pearls?"

Jiang looked much struck as he hurried to keep up. "That is a very interesting question. It would greatly add to his power and control if he had access to a seaport, but I fail to see how selling his sister would gain this for him."

"At least, not to me. I am well supplied with wives and concubines. One might suppose that another would be a surfeit."

"The emperor is said to have a harem of hundreds of concubines."

"The emperor is the emperor and he does not need to ride to war or put down rebellions from upstart provinces," Hüi Wei snapped. "A plain man like me does not need a different woman to warm his bed every night."

"Speaking of peerless," Jiang said, tactfully turning the conversation, "I have never seen a girl more beautiful than this princess."

"I hadn't noticed," Hüi Wei lied.

"Of course you hadn't, but when you can spare the time, you might have a look at her face." Jiang sighed in admiration. "Such perfection of form. Her skin is as flawless as those pearls delivered with her. Almond eyes as deep as the night sky, a mouth curved like a—"

"Like a snake in its death throes? Enough! I shall take your word for it that she is a paragon of all female graces," Hüi Wei said, laughing. "Take care *you* don't fall under her spell. It is punishable by death to dally with another man's concubine."

"Then you mean to keep her?"

"I have not yet decided," Hüi said coolly.

"But you're not sending her back?"

Hüi opened the door to his private chamber. "Come in with me."

Jiang entered the room, shutting the door behind him. "What game are you playing at? Do not hide your teeth with me."

"What does he say in that scroll?"

Jiang unrolled it. "If I'm reading between the lines correctly, he is hoping to prevent you from invading his province and hopes you will honor your mutual borders. That means he's doing something that he doesn't want you to know about but warrants an invasion. Perhaps he's hoping to distract your attention with her beauty."

Hüi flung himself into a chair with none of the deliberate ceremony he had employed in the audience chamber when taking the throne. He poured both of them a cup of *huáng jiǔ* and took a sip before he spoke. "I shall keep her for a time, if only in order to find out what Wu Min's plan is. He is ambitious and clever but owes allegiance only to himself. He is a careful man. I have fought on the same field with him, and he does not commit to an attack when it will not benefit him personally, no matter what treaty he's signed. He resorts to deceit and trickery to get what he wants."

"And by giving you this girl, he hopes to gain—what? That her beauty will occupy you to the point that he may march past you on the way to the sea?" Jiang laughed at the thought of any woman distracting Hüi Wei to the point of neglecting his sacred, heaven-decreed duty. "He doesn't know you well."

"At the very least, if you had allowed her guard to remain with her, he would have planted some spies in my court. Who knows? Perhaps *she* spies for him." Hüi Wei held the glass up to the light, gazing at the golden liquor. "He judges others to be lesser strategists than himself. That is Wu Min's greatest handicap. No, he has some other reason for sending me this girl. Something he hopes to gain by putting me in possession of her. Perhaps she was born under a curse and brings bad luck to whatever roof she resides under, despite her beauty. The gods sometimes amuse themselves by giving a gift with one hand and taking it back with the other." He laughed. "It must have gone against his grain to give up that tribute of silver, pearls, and silk, simply to disguise his true intent. He must be confident that he will be able to retrieve it all at some point. Wu Min does not open his fist easily."

"He cannot hope that her presence will lead to strife in your household," Jiang mused in a perplexed voice. "A man does not concern himself with the petty squabbles of mere concubines."

"Even Wu Min would not make that mistake," Hüi Wei agreed dryly. "Have her escorted to the seventh house."

"When you do see her, do you think she will tell you why Wu Min sent her?"

"She may not know. And I shall not see her, not at once," Hüi said.

"I thought not," Jiang said in a satisfied tone. "The news will be conveyed to Wu Min that you have ignored his gifts. Leaving them on the floor as you did when you left the audience room was a stroke of genius. Perhaps it might spur him to an incautious action."

"Perhaps," Hüi said. "In any case, have all the tribute cataloged and taken to the strong room."

"With the exception of the Princess Lan'xiu," teased Jiang.

"Find out about that family," Hüi said suddenly. "It must be a most heartless man to send his own sister to endure the fate of becoming a minor concubine in an established household. I could not do it, even if the emperor commanded it. There is something odd behind this whole affair."

"I shall see that the princess is established in the seventh house with her servant, but I shan't make her too comfortable just yet. And perhaps I might arrange a meeting between her and first wife, Lady Mei Ju?"

A slow smile crossed Hüi's lips. "I knew there was some reason I kept a jester in my court."

"Jester! I am no jester!" Jiang exclaimed in pretended outrage. "The joke would be on you if I took that insult to heart and made humor my primary objective in your service."

"I would not insult any but my closest friend so, Jiang." Hüi rose and placed his hand upon Jiang's shoulder. "We shall see this through together as we always have, come what may."

"We shall," Jiang agreed.

CHAPTER TWO

PRINCESS LAN'XIU followed the soldier in the lead, conscious of the
second soldier, sword in hand, trailing her and her servant. She cast
covert glances about her, taking in the strong walls of stone about the
palace, too high to scale and too smoothly fitted to offer a toehold if
one dared to try their luck in climbing them. And beyond that was a
similar wall around the city to be gotten past, if one did manage the
first.

Armed guards patrolled every method of egress to prevent any
intruder from getting in. Great artistry had been employed within the
walls to encourage the inmates to feel they were within some beautiful
park. Trees and bushes had borne flowers in the proper season,
although just now a slight powdering of snow lay upon the ground. In
despair, Lan'xiu noted the footprints left in the mantle of white that
made a stealthy escape impossible.

She followed docilely to another securely guarded square, a sort
of fort within a fortress, and her heart sank when she recognized that
this was the harem. It was walled off with great iron gates always kept
locked. The soldier used a key to permit them entry, and she heard a
bar being lifted from the inside in response to his knock. The soldier
locked the gates again once they were inside. However, instead of one
great building with communal facilities, she saw twelve separate
houses positioned around the square. Bare peach and plum trees stood
within the center of the park, surrounded by brown bushes stripped of
their leaves by the season. Six benches were set out within the open
space.

Each house was identical, save the first. Where the roof tiles on
all the other homes were of cobalt blue, the most splendid home was

crowned with brilliant crimson tiles, to bring auspicious fortune to those residing under it. This house was bigger, more magnificent, with ceramic temple dogs set at each sweeping corner of the roof to guard that the good luck did not escape. A covered walkway led to the front door and light shone from within, giving the red curtains a warm glow. Shadows moving behind the curtains suggested a family within, enjoying an evening's entertainment.

Lan'xiu looked at this house with longing. It was suitable for one of her birth, but her rank accorded her no perquisites any longer. She knew that despite the destiny foretold at her birth, her fortunes had been turned onto a darker, more sinister path.

Each house in the square had a lantern hung to the right of the door. The lantern was lit at only the fifth house, gleaming through the cold blue dusk. As they passed the house where the lantern shone, one of the soldiers grunted.

Correctly assuming this inarticulate commentary had nothing to do with her, the Princess Lan'xiu continued to follow the soldier in silence until he paused in front of the seventh house, producing a huge iron key. The lock screeched in protest when the key turned, and the hinges groaned as the soldier pushed the door open.

Lan'xiu gathered her cloak together to step into the dark, cold hallway, steeling herself for whatever might come next. For all she knew, the soldiers had been given orders to bring her here and execute her. She could feel the warmth of his body as Shu Ning, her eunuch, positioned himself between her and the soldier following them. It did not comfort her to realize he entertained the same suspicions as she.

She controlled her instinctive impulse to jump when the first soldier spoke, not wanting the man to see how frightened she was.

"Your Ladyship, my Lord Jiang extends his apologies. We had no prior knowledge of your coming, and the house is not prepared for you. If your Ladyship will be patient, servants will be here presently to light the fires and the lamps. The house has been kept clean, so it is habitable. Your luggage will be brought to you."

"Jiang? I thought the general's name was Qiang Hüi Wei?" the eunuch questioned the soldier sharply.

"Lord Jiang is the General's second in command. He sees to the smooth running of General Qiang's establishment. It is to him that you would address any complaints or requests."

Lan'xiu waved a graceful hand but did not speak. A lady of her status did not give direct orders to servants. That is what one had eunuchs for.

Once again, Shu Ning spoke. "I am sure the princess will have no cause for complaint. How am I to procure food for her?"

"Food will be brought presently, along with water, tea, and wine." The soldier appeared to have no wish for more conversation. He and his fellow retreated to stand guard at either side of the door.

The shutters were barred from the outside, and dusk had made the shadows within the house grow deeper. Only the faint light of the moon streaming through the circular window over the door silvered the polished floor as Lan'xiu waited anxiously for some sound, a soft footfall or rustle of clothing, to tell her when the attack would begin.

The assault never came, at least not in the form of violence. There was a tap at the door, and one of the soldiers opened it to reveal a veritable army of servants made up of eunuchs and women dressed in plain but well-made clothing. They bore lanterns, covered trays from which tantalizing odors emanated, and lengths of rich fabrics. One carried a brazier of glowing coals, which he took into the sitting chamber. He went to the fireplace and soon coaxed a fire to life.

Other eunuchs scurried about, placing lanterns, hanging curtains at the windows, sweeping sheets off the furniture to reveal chairs and tables of carved rosewood inlaid with mother of pearl designs. In a matter of minutes, they transformed the cold, barren room into one of comfort and warmth.

Shu Ning spoke with the servants, directing several to prepare the largest bedchamber for the princess, another on how to bestow the luggage, and still another to set up a table with the trays bearing food. Then he ordered them all out of the room.

"Come, Princess Zhen Lan'xiu, sit and eat. You must be weary and hungry."

"Ning, why are you talking like that?"

Ning jerked his head to the door and cupped a hand to his ear. "Break your fast, my Lady. And then I will escort you to your bedchamber and put you to bed."

Lan'xiu gave him a rueful smile and sighed. "I fear I am not very hungry."

Ning sniffed at the dishes longingly and insisted, "You must have something to eat." He lifted a cover and said, "Here is rice with bits of golden peach."

"Very well," Lan'xiu said, resigned. "You may serve me some of that." She picked up her chopsticks and ate sparingly. Then she stared hard at Ning, whispering, "Eat, you idiot, don't wait for me. I know you're hungry. Stop pretending."

"Yes, my Lady," Ning said loudly, before hissing, "They must be made to treat you as you have a right by birth."

"Oh, Ning. What would I do without you?" Lan'xiu stretched out a slim hand and patted his arm. "I am so glad you chose to accompany me."

"Nothing could keep me from your side, Lan'xiu," Ning said quietly. Then he began to eat hungrily, choosing pork and rice and vegetables to fill his bowl. When he'd had his fill, he looked up to find Lan'xiu watching him. He placed a finger before his lips. "The bedchamber is upstairs. You need to rest."

He opened the door and peered into the hall. In their absence, the servants had been busy. The rest of the house was warming up and the lanterns were lit. By their light, he could now see the staircase that curved up to the second story landing. Three eunuchs and three women were lined up silently in the hallway, as if awaiting them. "My lady will now retire to her rest," Ning announced.

The oldest female servant clapped her hands and the three eunuchs filed to the door. They went outside and the two soldiers followed them. In the silence, Lan'xiu and Ning could hear the grate of the key in the lock and knew that they were now imprisoned within the luxurious house.

"Show me to the bedchamber," Ning ordered boldly.

The oldest woman dropped into a curtsey and spoke for the first time. "You are her highness's slave?"

"I am her personal *servant*," Ning stressed. "I serve her in all ways."

"Allowances have been made," the woman responded. "No male is permitted to stay the night in any of the houses. However, it is seen that your customs are different. My name is Jia, and I shall be the Princess Lan'xiu's housekeeper. I am at your service. These stupid girls are Din and Miu. You need not concern yourself with them. You will convey any necessary orders to me, and I will have it seen to."

Ning bowed. "I am Shu Ning. You may address me as Ning. And now, Princess Lan'xiu is weary from our journey and would rest."

"Of course. Follow me." Jia flapped her hands at the two younger women, who giggled and fled to the back of the house, peeking back at the princess all the way. "Pay no attention to them, Ning-xiānsheng. They are young and silly, and have never seen a princess before. I, however, have served in the greatest of houses and know how things should be done. Please follow me, Ning-xiānsheng." She turned and led the way upstairs.

Lan'xiu had to smile as Ning puffed out his chest at the title of respect that Jia had conferred upon him, even though she did not feel very merry. However she did let out a small gasp of pleasure at the sight of the beautiful room designated to be hers.

The rosewood bed was massive, standing in the center of the room with a full canopy and corner boards intricately carved with dragons and phoenixes. Enamel paintings of fields and streams decorated the arched canopy boards overhead. Yellow silk bed hangings glowed in the warmth of the oil lanterns and the small ceramic stove. Matching yellow silk swathed the windows, and the puffy down quilt covered in spring green satin made the room seem cozy. Soft, lavender-colored pillows adorned the bed. A dressing table of rosewood with a matching chair with a yellow cushion stood in the bow of one window. A thick carpet of intricate design woven in tones of cream, yellow, and green, with touches here and there of salmon red and cobalt blue covered the wooden floor.

Jia opened the door to a rosewood wardrobe that extended the length of one wall to show that Lan'xiu's clothing had been carefully hung up, while more intimate garments had been folded and placed in drawers.

She went to a door concealed behind drapes on the same wall as the bed and opened it to reveal a large, well-appointed bathing room. "The pump brings the water inside. And if her ladyship wishes for a bath, a fire may be lit under the tub to warm the water." Jia indicated the giant copper vessel. The room was a marvel of ceramic tile and copper, using the most modern of plumbing engineering.

Then she opened another door on the opposite wall that led to a smaller room. "I assume you will wish to sleep within call of her ladyship," she said, addressing Ning. She had still not looked directly at the princess.

"That will do excellently," Ning said. "I am very pleased. You have thought of everything to make the princess comfortable."

"Thank you, sir." Jia dropped a curtsey and stole a glance at Lan'xiu, stifling a gasp at her beauty. Then the housekeeper withdrew, closing the door behind her.

Lan'xiu and Ning stood still, listening intently. Ning tiptoed to the door and opened it. The hallway was empty. He shook his head at the princess. "I will have a look," he said, picking up one of the lanterns. He searched both the bathing room and the room designated for him before issuing forth into the hallway.

Lan'xiu wrapped her arms around her body to still her trembling, waiting for him to return. Or worse, for someone else to enter, perhaps splattered with his blood, to bring her news of his death. She was unaware she'd been holding her breath until the door opened to reveal her faithful servant returning to her.

"We are the only ones on this floor," Ning said quietly. "The attic is empty. I have discovered no way of spying upon us, but we had best be careful."

"Careful!" Lan'xiu laughed bitterly.

"Shhh," Ning warned. "You are tired. You would be better in bed. Shall I contrive a bath?"

"No!" Lan'xiu shuddered. "Not here! Not now. And you must find a way out. If neither of us sleep again, you must escape."

"I will not leave you, my Lady," Ning said in great distress.

"Even though I have been delivered to my death, there is no need for you to share the same fate," Lan'xiu said. "You cannot save me. You must save yourself."

"You never know, this may not lead to your death," Ning said hopefully.

"Always the optimist, my Ning. For you the teapot is always half-full." Lan'xiu gave a shaky laugh. "But you know my brother. It would have suited him to simply throw me off a cliff, but in this way he will attain my death with no visible stain upon his hands. You know he will find some way to use my assassination to his advantage."

"The governor has not chosen to come to you tonight," Ning pointed out. "That is unusual in a warrior accustomed to claiming all he possesses. Perhaps he already has a favorite and isn't much interested in you. You heard him in the audience. He said he had enough wives. He may never come."

"The Lord Qiang Hüi Wei has an intelligent face," Lan'xiu said. "He will show no unseemly haste in claiming his prize. But he is also too intelligent to ignore my brother's overweening ambition. He may slay me out of hand without pausing to inquire whether I know the root of the plot. Between them both, I am not safe, and by virtue of being my servant, you are not safe either, my dear friend. I must get you out of here."

"Perhaps they will let me go out to buy you face powder or some such," Ning suggested.

"Perhaps. And perhaps one of the soldiers is by no means so content with his lot that he would turn down a fortune in jewels. If only I *possessed* a fortune in jewels, I would bribe every last man to get you free."

Ning came to her and sank to his knees, beginning to weep a little. He grabbed her hand and kissed it, unable to speak until he felt her other hand caressing his head. "If you are to die, I will die with you," he declared.

"What have I ever done to deserve a friend as true and loyal as you?" she wondered. "It would make me much happier to know at least that you survived rather than to have you share my fate."

"What would I do? Where would I go?" Ning wailed.

"Who else would put up with you?" Lan said, her voice shaking a little with laughter, even though unshed tears glimmered in her eyes.

Instantly, Ning retorted, "Who would put up with *you*? If Hüi Wei has a brain in his head, he would soon find your beauty conceals the sting of a summer wasp."

Lan laughed. "Honors to both sides, then. We die together."

"Or perhaps we live together." Ning wiped his eyes on his sleeve. "You were an oracle caster, or at least your mother taught you the art. Are you sure we are going to die?"

"You know one cannot read one's own omens," Lan said regretfully. "And since my mother's death, the gods have refused to speak with me, and the way is not clear. Clouds are before my eyes."

Ning sighed. "At least we are away from your brother's minions and we can sleep tonight. We will take turns watching."

"Mind you wake me when you start to nod off," Lan admonished.

"It was only once that I was so tired I could not keep my eyes open," Ning protested.

Lan smiled. "I'll take first watch."

"I cannot sleep in your bed," Ning pointed out.

"There is a lovely window seat with a cushion, just your size," Lan said, pointing at the niche partially hidden behind the curtains. "There seems to be another quilt in your room. You may bring it here and wrap yourself up warmly."

Ning yawned widely like a cat, not bothering to cover his mouth. "I think I will if you're sure."

"I'm sure," Lan said. She watched her friend and servant hurry into the smaller anteroom and murmured, "I shall have plenty of time to sleep when I'm dead."

CHAPTER THREE

LADY MEI JU stood by the window, waiting. At times when the winter snows came or the delicate mists of spring obscured the square, she could pretend that instead of looking across at identical houses, she was still at home with her parents and sisters and brothers, with a view of open rice fields to the mountains beyond.

It had been so long since she had been outside these walls that it made her feel old. Mei Ju sighed and then giggled silently. She *was* old; at least older than the other concubines. And she felt grateful to be. She alone of her family still lived, by virtue of being here when the hordes had overrun her village, razing it to the ground and killing all her family and friends. Those had been terrifying times of rebellion, but her Lord Qiang Hüi Wei had brought stability and peace to the region in the name of the Son of Heaven, emperor of China.

She tried to avoid looking at her reflection in the window as she waited for this new concubine with a heavy heart. Even before she had been designated first wife, she had known that her lord would add concubines to his household, but each time it caused her a pang. For a time, he would be distracted or enthralled with his new possession, and the lantern would not be lit for her. Mei Ju knew her lord's love of conquest, and knowing the other wives, she tortured herself by imagining that each courtship and eventual capitulation had followed a different course than her own. Qiang Hüi Wei was a very clever man, known for his mastery of strategy and love of battle. Each time he had eventually come back to her, but Mei Ju knew well that his heart had never been hers.

Rumor had flown throughout the compound that the seventh concubine was extremely beautiful, and Mei Ju dutifully celebrated that fact on behalf of her beloved Hüi Wei. He deserved only the best. Besides, beauty alone was not enough for Hüi. Although the second and sixth wives were very pretty, they had not managed to hold his interest for very long.

When she caught sight of the small party approaching her home, Mei Ju turned away from the window and clapped her hands twice. Her servant went to the door, and while she listened to the sounds of umbrellas being closed and stood within draining pots, wraps being taken and hung to dry, Mei Ju seated herself before the fire and composed her face to receive her company.

Her maid appeared in the doorway and announced, "The Princess Zhen Lan'xiu begs for the honor of attending your Ladyship."

Mei Ju could not hold back a tiny smile. Her maid always pretended to be so respectful when company came to call upon her. It was quite the contrast from her usual manner when they were alone. "I will be pleased to receive the princess. You may escort her here."

The maid bowed and withdrew.

Mei Ju could not hold back a gasp of astonishment at her first sight of Princess Lan'xiu. If her own skin was white, Lan'xiu's was like burnished ivory. Her face was exquisite: high cheekbones sculpted to perfection, the pure line of her jaw flowing into a long, graceful neck. Her nose was perhaps a bit large, but it suited her face; her lips were pale pink and curved like the wings of a bird in flight. Her eyes were downcast, as was proper, veiled by lush, dark lashes. Her earrings were silver with long, pear-shaped turquoise drops, and a pale green jade bracelet encircled her left wrist.

She was a slender girl who swayed gracefully like the reed that bends to the wind as she walked, but she stood straight and tall. Mei Ju realized that if she stood beside her, she would be looking up at the princess, and that would never do. Lan'xiu's cheongsam of lavender and crimson silk set off her beauty to perfection, while her hands hid inside her sleeves, which were lined in turquoise. The daring color combination made Mei Ju remember that perhaps it really was time to have a new dress made for herself. She had grown comfortable and out of touch with the fashions of the day, despite the entreaties of the third and fifth wives to smarten herself up a bit. She always made the excuse that chasing after the children was dirty work, but now she thought she might need to bespeak a new robe after all.

Princess Lan'xiu prostrated herself on the ground and waited, motionless, her head bowed as if aware she was being inspected.

Despite the fact the princess outranked her in the world beyond the harem, Mei Ju took comfort in the fact that as first wife, her position here was unassailable, and it gave her the confidence to welcome her guest. Suddenly, she noticed Princess Lan'xiu trembling, and the memory of when she was as young and in the same position came over her in a flash. Her natural compassion overrode her sense of formality, and she rose, moving forward to raise Lan'xiu and greet her warmly. Sure enough, Mei Ju found herself looking up at that exquisite face.

"Princess Lan'xiu, it is my pleasure to welcome you here as seventh concubine presumptive. This must be very strange for you." Mei Ju put her hand on Lan'xiu's arm and led her to a chair. "Please, be seated and we shall have a cup of tea."

"After you, Lady First Wife," Lan'xiu said in a soft, musical voice of a low timbre.

Mei Ju seated herself and watched Lan'xiu sink onto the facing chair, her eyes still fixed on the floor. "Our customs must seem strange to you, coming from the north."

"They are somewhat different," Lan'xiu admitted. "I do not wish to offend through ignorance."

Leaning forward, Mei Ju touched Lan'xiu's sleeve. "Look at me, my dear."

Startled, Lan'xiu looked up and Mei Ju gasped again at the lovely, deep, almond-shaped eyes. Such a beauty! And then she forgot her own pain and was filled with pity. This poor girl was terrified and suffering some untold agony. Mei Ju knew she would not get to the bottom of it upon a first meeting, but perhaps she could allay at least some of the fear.

"How old are you, Princess?"

"I am almost eighteen," Lan'xiu responded. "Please, call me Lan'xiu. I am no princess outside my own province, and I miss hearing my name."

"You are pure and chaste," Mei Ju said shrewdly, "but you must not fear my Lord Qiang Hüi Wei. He is a skilled and gentle lover. When he takes you, he will cause as little pain as possible."

Lan'xiu went white to the lips, turning so pale Mei Ju feared she might faint and wondered if she had been too forthright. But the girl was a concubine; this was her fate and it would come to pass, like it or not. Men were weak, and Mei Ju could not imagine any man would have the fortitude to resist the temptation of being the first to pluck such a perfect blossom, no matter what his head or heart had to say about the matter.

"He is my lord and master," Lan'xiu said miserably and bowed her head. "It will be as he wills."

"You must forgive me for being so personal, but you are the most exquisite creature I have ever seen," Mei Ju burst forth. "Such perfection has never rejoiced my eyes before. You are flawless, like the summer sky." She was relieved to see a tiny smile hover over Lan'xiu's curved lips. She had begun to fear the girl could not smile, and yet with regret she noticed the smile only rendered her even more beautiful. Her teeth were like a set of perfectly matched pearls.

"I am far from flawless. I have learned to hide my faults."

"I cannot discern a single blemish," Mei Ju said in wonderment.

Lan'xiu sighed. "I have always regretted my hair."

Mei Ju examined the tightly smoothed hair, piled high and secured with a silver and turquoise enameled slide. "Your hair is perfectly lovely."

"Unless my servant irons it straight, it is rather wavy, especially when the weather is damp," Lan'xiu admitted. "Some women of the north are afflicted with this condition."

"Your maid must slave to disguise it," Mei Ju said flatly. "Take it down, please, that I may see it."

Lan'xiu turned her head and called out, "Shu Ning!"

A short, clever-looking eunuch bustled into the room and came to her side before prostrating himself to Mei Ju. Then he sat back on his heels. "Princess."

"Lady First Wife wishes to see my hair down," Lan'xiu said in a resigned tone.

Against protocol, Shu Ning shot a sharp glance at Mei Ju. She was amused to see he seemed to be assessing her intent toward his mistress. Apparently, he was able to discern that she harbored no ill will, because with nimble hands he took down Lan'xiu's hair and coaxed it into curl.

Mei Ju cocked her head to one side. She found the curls ugly but endlessly fascinating, so different from her own smooth locks. Without being pulled back, Lan'xiu's dark hair rippled wildly, taking on a glint of reddish chestnut, but perhaps it was just the warmth from the dancing flames of the fire. Then Mei Ju sighed. Nothing, *nothing*, seemed to mar this girl's perfection, not even the ugliness of curls. The masses of wavy hair served only to accentuate the delicacy of her features. "Thank you for indulging my curiosity. Shu Ning, you may restore her highness's hair to the usual dress."

Shu Ning yanked at the princess's hair with an ivory comb. Lan'xiu showed no pain on her face; she merely endured until her hair was neatly piled up again.

"Thank you, Ning. You may go," Lan'xiu said. Then she put a hand over her mouth and glanced at Mei Ju in dismay for the insolence of having given an order within the first wife's home.

Mei Ju laughed as Ning fled the room, no doubt in fear that his mistress would be punished for this presumption. "Allowances will be made for you. Hüi Wei will not resent your giving your servant an order, even in his presence. You have been used to being a princess."

"I humbly apologize for this transgression."

When it seemed that Lan'xiu meant to prostrate herself on the floor again, Mei Ju stopped her. "I mean you no harm, child. We are sister wives. You are one of us now, and it is my responsibility as first wife to make you welcome and educate you to our customs."

"I thank you," Lan'xiu said, her voice shaking and her eyes downcast.

"Do not be so humble when you meet the other wives. Second Wife Ci'an should have been named 'Shark'. Weakness is like blood in the water to her, and she will hunt you down ruthlessly if she senses any vulnerability."

Lan'xiu looked alarmed but said, "How would she manage that, guarded and hemmed in as we are?"

"She would find a way, have no fear, or she would if Hüi Wei did not take care to have our doors locked at night." Mei Ju clapped her hands. "I have sent for tea and cakes. It is cold without, but we sit by a nice warm fire within and should enjoy ourselves. You will address me as first wife before others, particularly my husband, Hüi Wei, but my name is Mei Ju and I would like you to call me that."

"Beautiful chrysanthemum," Lan'xiu murmured. "That is a lovely name."

Mei Ju sighed. "Yes, named after a common chrysanthemum that may be found anywhere. And round like the flower." She patted her curved hips with regret.

"But chrysanthemums are cheerful and bring much happiness. Forgive so forward a comment in one who does not know you, but comfort clings to you like a silken garment. It is impossible to feel unhappy in your presence."

Mei Ju stared at Lan'xiu in astonishment once again. She could see no guile in the girl's face; in fact, she did indeed look a bit happier than she had when she first came in. "How very odd," she said.

"That was an odd thing to say?" Lan'xiu asked anxiously.

"No, it was a beautiful compliment and gracefully said. The odd thing is, that is precisely what my husband tells me," Mei Ju said softly.

A welcome diversion came in the shape of five children who burst into the room. "Mama! Mama! Where are our cakes?" they shrieked.

"Quiet, you bad children, you must be patient and wait to be invited," Mei Ju scolded with no real expectation of being taken seriously.

The three boys immediately tumbled over the long divan, wrestling their way onto the floor while two little girls came to Mei Ju's chair and snuggled into her embrace, one on each side.

Lan'xiu laughed with delight at their antics, and Mei Ju beamed at her. "You like children?"

"I love them," Lan'xiu said, chuckling at the boys' exploits.

"I hope the gods grant you many," Mei Ju said formally.

A flicker of pain crossed Lan'xiu's face, and after a slight pause, she replied, "That is very kind of you. I hope so too."

A servant arrived just then, bearing a tray with a steaming pot of tea, cups, and several plates with a variety of cakes.

"Red bean cakes," the plumper of the two girls said in a pleased voice. "And sesame!"

"You may each have one, but you will need to wait for Princess Zhen Lan'xiu to make her selection first," Mei Ju instructed.

"A really, truly princess?" the other girl asked, staring at Lan'xiu.

"Yes," Mei Ju said, forestalling Lan'xiu. "She is the new wife to your father. She has just come to us. You may get your tea and your cake and then return to the playroom."

"Must they leave?" Lan'xiu asked.

"They must if we do not care to wear our tea rather than drink it," Mei Ju said firmly.

Lan'xiu smiled as she watched the children fall upon the tray like ravening vultures and then tear out of the room clutching their cakes. When the sound of the childish voices faded, her smile did as well. "They are all so beautiful. Are they all yours?"

"I have six still living," Mei Ju said with understandable pride. "My eldest son trains to be a soldier and diplomat, like his father. All my sons stand in line to carry on Governor Qiang's noble heritage and serve the emperor as he does."

"You have indeed been blessed," Lan'xiu said.

Mei Ju looked at the beautiful face. This girl was intelligent, that was clear. In fact, being a gambling woman, Mei Ju was almost ready to back her against the machinations of Second Wife Ci'an already, without even knowing how this girl might think. With all her intelligence, an innate sweetness radiated from Lan'xiu. Despite her apparent misery at being consigned to the lowly position of seventh concubine of a man with whom she had never yet exchanged a word, Lan'xiu seemed genuinely happy that she, Mei Ju, first wife, had supplied their lord and master with four fine, healthy sons and two beautiful daughters.

Lady Mei Ju was also willing to wager that when Lan'xiu bore her own sons, she would accept their position as lesser sons and would not lift one of her slender fingers to advance them within the household, although she had no doubt that Lan'xiu could do so if she chose.

Only the fact that Second Wife Ci'an had borne just one daughter, and a sickly one at that, had enabled Mei Ju to allow her children out of her sight for even a minute. If Ci'an had managed to produce a boy, all bets would have been off.

She poured a cup of tea and offered it to Lan'xiu. "Jasmine. I hope you like it."

Lan'xiu reached for it, sniffing delicately. "The fragrance is lovely. Like a flower."

Mei Ju looked down at her own plump, but shapely hands. Lan'xiu's hands were a bit large for so delicate a girl, and she displayed unfortunate calluses at the base of her right thumb and fingers. Another of her flaws, and Mei Ju reproached herself for being glad to see it. "Do you like needlework?"

Lan'xiu immediately set down her cup and slid her hands within her sleeves. "Alas, I have no talent for it."

"I only wondered because of your hand. You should use a pad to guard against the needle," Mei Ju said.

A blush colored Lan'xiu's face like a rose. "I do not sew well."

"Third Wife Fen, although of noble lineage, was forced to work in the fields before she came here," Mei Ju said, hoping it would lead to a confidence from the princess.

"She must enjoy her life here in contrast," Lan'xiu said.

Mei Ju took pity upon her evident discomfort. "Forgive my curiosity. It was not to pry that I invited you here. Instead, I will tell you about the household and your position within it."

"I know that I am the seventh and most humble concubine," Lan'xiu said, her voice giving away nothing.

"I am first wife, as I told you. I lived here as Hüi Wei's wife for ten years before he took another."

"That would be Ci'an, second wife, if I recall," Lan'xiu said, with an adorable tiny wrinkle between her arched brows.

"When Hüi Wei first achieved success on the field of battle, nobles of neighboring states who did not wish to take their chances meeting him in war sent concubines as a peace offering. Ci'an, Fen, and Huan all arrived at nearly the same time, and as a gesture of welcome and courtesy, I permitted them to be called wives. They are in reality only concubines. I am the only wife Hüi has married."

With a deep sigh, Mei Ju added, "I will be frank with you and take my chances on your discretion. Ci'an was a mistake. Hüi Wei conquered a province to the northeast ruled by a barbarian. It was a hard battle and many lives were lost. Hüi Wei judged it to be better to come to terms and stem the flow of blood. Her father, the king Daji, was to stay within certain boundaries, and the emperor would allow him to rampage as he would there. But Daji's terms were that the emperor, or failing that, Hüi Wei himself, must take his daughter to wed."

"So Ci'an was foisted upon my Lord Qiang Hüi Wei," Lan'xiu asked, properly using his entire title.

Mei Ju cleared her voice. "Hüi was a very young man then, with a fire in his loins. Ci'an is very pretty; make no mistake. It was not entirely a diplomatic decision that he accepted her. But he soon realized his mistake. She shares her father's ambition and ruthless personality. In fact, it is entirely possible that her father was only too glad to rid himself of her combative and competitive nature. She might even have succeeded in deposing him if she'd lived there any longer. Hüi actually found it necessary to forcibly explain to her that he would not permit her to dispose of any who stood in the way of her becoming first wife."

Shocked, Lan'xiu gasped, "She tried to harm you?"

Nodding, Mei Ju answered, "Yes, she did."

After a short silence, Lan'xiu reached forward to touch Mei Ju's sleeve for the first time. "I am glad she did not succeed."

Pleased that Lan'xiu had come out of her shell enough to make even such a tenuous connection, Mei Ju said, "Hüi was very displeased with her. I do not think her lantern has been lit since then. In fact...." She drew a deep breath before continuing, ashamed that the thought of Ci'an's punishment still caused her such pleasure. "He beat her. With a whip."

Lan'xiu went pale again.

Taking pity upon her, Mei Ju said, "He will never treat you thusly. You are a lady. He said that if one acts like a mule, one must be treated like one. He is a very loyal and honorable man and cannot abide treachery." She watched Lan'xiu closely to see her reaction.

Another flicker of inscrutable pain crossed the ravishing face, but then the princess said, "Then my lord repays your loyalty with his own."

"Although I can no longer bear Hüi any more children, my lantern is still lit one night each week," Mei Ju said softly.

"This lantern you speak of. Is this a metaphor for something?" Lan'xiu blushed in embarrassment.

"When Qiang Hüi Wei chooses to visit the household, the lantern is lit beside the door of the chosen one. It allows whichever wife to make ready to receive him and forestalls inopportune visitors."

"I see." Lan'xiu shivered slightly and took a sip of her tea.

"Hüi Wei will send a servant to light the lantern during the day. That is how you will know when he chooses to come to you," Mei Ju explained. "You are so lovely, I would be surprised if your lantern were not lit before the stars have faded from the sky too many more nights."

"It will be an undeserved honor when that happy day arrives," Lan'xiu said, not entirely suppressing the dread in her voice.

Mei Ju was troubled. She did not know how to comfort this girl. She seemed even more fearful than any of the other wives, and all had been virgins when they came—with the possible exception of Ci'an, second concubine. One never knew about her. "You are seventh concubine presumptive. If Hüi never chooses to come to you, that is what your title will remain. If he accepts you, then you will be seventh concubine or seventh wife, by my grace. Hüi Wei is a very important man. There are times when he has to be away or has no time for us. "

"And you remain waiting always within these walls," Lan'xiu stated rather than asked.

"As first wife, I have on various occasions accompanied Hüi Wei to the outside world," Mei Ju said with pride. "All the wives see each other, and our children play together until the boys are of age to go into training and school. It is a very pleasant life. Every comfort is provided for. And I am very fond of a good game of cards or mah-jongg."

"But we are prisoners within these walls."

"No more a prisoner than Hüi Wei." Mei Ju could see her words meant nothing to the girl. "We all have our own burdens to bear in this world and the one to come. Men are just as much a prisoner of their destiny as any woman."

"Perhaps." Lan'xiu didn't seem to entirely believe that. "When you get together, is Second Wife Ci'an included?"

"She is. She is one of us, even though she still schemes and strategizes to win favor from Hüi Wei. In vain, but it amuses us both. The other wives don't regard her very much as she outranks them."

"Why is that?"

"I shall have to explain them to you. Ci'an, as I said, is a bitter, warped soul. If anyone holds her prisoner, it is her own ambition. She cannot learn to be content with her lot." Mei Ju watched to see what reaction her veiled words of advice elicited from the princess, but the girl kept her face an inscrutable mask. "Third wife is Fen and fourth wife is Huan. They are never apart."

"Close friends then."

"Very close." Mei Ju nodded, pleased that Lan'xiu seemed to understand the situation without having it spelled out for her. "If you cannot find one of them at home, chances are that she will be at the other's house and—occupied.

"Sixth Wife Alute is like a perfect piece of carved jade. Beautiful to look at, but the lanterns are not lit upstairs. At least she is of an accepting nature. She would eat whatever you put in front of her."

"And fifth wife?" Lan'xiu asked.

Mei Ju's face relaxed into amusement. "I suspect you will like her. We all do. Bai is her name. She is very charming and funny, always up to some prank or joke. She keeps us all laughing, even with the short winter days and cold outside."

"I shall look forward to meeting them all," Lan'xiu said.

"Just be sure you hide a dagger up your sleeve when you meet Ci'an. I suspect that she will not take to you at all."

"I shall be careful," Lan'xiu assured Mei Ju. "I thank you for sharing your wisdom with me. It is most generous of you to condescend to welcome a mere seventh concubine."

"I was not always first wife, my dear. I know how you feel."

It was Lan'xiu's turn to look at the older woman with astonishment. "But... how can that be? You *are* first wife. And you are so kind. I cannot believe you killed off six or seven previous wives as Ci'an aspires to."

Mei Ju looked down at her hands, still smooth at her age, with the polished nails showing the half moons at the bases. "I am older than my husband, Hüi Wei. I was once a concubine to his older brother. I bore him children as well, but they were sickly, and none of them survived infancy. I did not love him, but I did my duty. And then, he was killed in battle."

"I am sorry," Lan'xiu said in her soft voice.

"If Hüi Wei were not the man he is, he could have had me thrown from the ramparts or returned to my village in shame or sold to pleasure the troops. Instead, he came to see me when his brother died and he succeeded to his position. And then, he married me. I have been a good wife to him and borne him six healthy children. I have given him the sons I could not give his brother."

"He sounds like a fine man, but why are you telling me this?" Lan'xiu wondered.

"I don't quite know." Mei Ju gave a tinkling laugh. "I wish to offer you comfort. I have been in even more uncertain of a position than you are, but my lord is a kind man. Whatever your brother plotted by sending you here, you need not fear that Hüi will punish you for his transgression. He will be patient with you."

Lan'xiu wrinkled her brow again and blinked rapidly. "Thank you for all your kindness to me, First Wife. I thought that luck had turned her back on me, but surely she shines upon me in guiding me to you. I shall never forget your compassion."

Mei Ju stood up, briskly saying, "I should hope not. After all, we shall see each other every day from now to the end of our lives. I welcome you to the court of Lord General Qiang Hüi Wei and to the household, Princess Lan'xiu, seventh wife presumptive."

CHAPTER FOUR

AFTER the Princess Zhen Lan'xiu was helped into her cloak and Ning had opened an umbrella to hold over her (even though he had to stretch his arm to full length to ensure that it covered her and was left all in the wet himself due to the differences in their stature), Mei Ju watched the small procession move out of sight toward the seventh house.

She waited by the window in the gathering dusk until she saw another servant approach under an umbrella, carrying a lit torch. As always, she held her breath, *willing* the servant to light the lantern by her door. A little bubble of jubilation erupted within her when the servant approached her house and her lantern began to glow.

Although they no longer shared a bed, Mei Ju hurried upstairs to prepare for Hüi's arrival. After seeing the fine cheongsam Lan'xiu wore, Mei Ju ordered her maid to fetch her best hanfu out of the wardrobe.

"But it is not a festival day or your husband's birthday," the maid objected.

"Do as I say, you silly wench," Mei Ju snapped. "And find my jade drop earrings. And dress my hair again. My lord visits me tonight."

"As you wish, Madame Wife." The maid dropped a sketchy curtsey, and it was clear she thought Mei Ju's hopes were in vain.

Mei Ju resolved to set her maid to polish the household bronzes on the morrow to pay her out for that disrespect, but she would not stoop to argue with her now. Although Lan'xiu was without doubt the loveliest girl she had ever set eyes on, between Mei Ju and Hüi Wei resided the comfort and respect of a long, intimate relationship. She would have to place her faith in that.

When she came downstairs to await his pleasure, she was powdered and scented. She had reddened her lips and pinched her cheeks to make them pink, but she did not realize how the anticipation of seeing her love made her eyes glow. Mei Ju remembered gratefully that she'd been very pretty as a girl, but time and bearing children had lined her pleasant face and made her once slim figure rounder. She smoothed her dress over her hips, pleased that at least she wasn't fat yet. Although she loved sweets, she ate of them sparingly, wishing to remain pleasing in her lord's eyes.

She had her reward when he came into the sitting chamber and his face lit up at the sight of her.

"Mei Ju, as pretty as ever. It is good to see you."

"And you, my Lord." She sank to her knees and bowed.

"So formal after all these years," he teased, extending his hand to help her up. He kissed both her cheeks and then her lips. "Mei Ju." He sighed contentedly and sat down in the large chair, stretching his hands to the fire.

"You still find me pretty, Hüi?" she asked anxiously.

"I could never find you anything but pleasing to look at. You are the mother of my children. You have given me fine sons and daughters as pretty as you." Hüi looked at her with a troubled expression. "You need not fear the loss of my regard, no matter how many concubines join this household."

"I miss going upstairs with you," Mei Ju said.

He got up and came to her, brushing a tear from her cheek and putting his arms around her. "I miss that too, but you know we must not."

"It would be worth death to feel you bearing me down into the mattress once more," she whispered, clinging to him.

"It would not be worth it to me," Hüi said firmly. "I cannot lose you, and my children need their mother. The doctor said you cannot take the chance of another pregnancy, and I will not put you at risk, no matter how much I may desire you."

"It is my fault that you took Ci'an into this household," Mei Ju said mournfully.

"Let us not speak of her," Hüi said. "It was never your fault. I need you here to rule my household. Do you think I don't know that you are mother to *all* my children, no matter which wife bore them? Besides, I need your counsel and the security of your loyalty. I have no one else I can trust."

"Except Lord Jiang," Mei Ju reminded him.

"A very different thing. He doesn't think as you do, being male." Hüi drew her to the divan and put his arm around her. "Tell me everything."

"I hope you know that I did not need Jiang to remind me to welcome the Princess Zhen Lan'xiu to the household," Mei Ju started.

"I hope he did not *remind* you. I merely requested him to ask you to find out a specific bit of information; that was all. I meant no offense by sending him rather than coming myself."

"I understand." And Mei Ju did. Whatever Hüi did was noticed and commented upon. Despite Lan'xiu's obvious allure, Hüi would wait a judicious amount of time before taking notice of her existence because news of his visit would be instantly broadcast far and wide. "Whatever her brother, Wu Min, intended by sending her here, the princess is not privy to the plot."

"You're sure," Hüi asked.

"She is terrified and knows not what to expect. I imagine that before she came here, she had no thought of being a mere seventh concubine—"

"Of a minor official," Hüi put in dryly.

Mei Ju slapped his arm playfully. "Nonsense. There is nothing minor about you. Princess Lan'xiu does not speak much about herself. I could not even find out whether she likes to sew!"

"Surely you found out something."

"Of course, although not from her lips. My maid has spoken with her eunuch. He keeps the hand of discretion before his mouth, but she knows how to gossip and drew him out. Eunuchs love intrigue."

"Which is why I keep them below stairs," Hüi agreed.

"The northern province of Liaopeh was once ruled by Wu Chao, who sired both Wu Min and Lan'xiu, but they were born of different mothers. He had only the two children: Wu Min, his son, who inherited his rule, and this daughter who is much younger. Wu Min's mother died young in childbirth with a stillborn male, so when Wu Chao took another woman, she became first wife. When Wu Chao died, there was a period of unrest within the court. Apparently Lan'xiu's mother died of a sudden and mysterious illness. The eunuch believes Wu Min caused her to be poisoned, and that the same fate awaited Lan'xiu. He is fiercely protective of her.

"There was some sort of disturbance within the women's quarters at some point before the mother's death, but Lan'xiu was not harmed. It was then that Wu Min started a campaign to get her wed, shopping her to any official who could render him aid."

"I would not think that would have been a difficult task to marry her off. She seems a pretty enough girl." Hüi shrugged.

"Are you blind?" Mei Ju demanded. "I have never seen a more beautiful girl in my life, and I have lived longer than you!"

"Always rubbing that in," Hüi joked.

"Respect your elders," she reminded him. "Have you looked at her?"

"Only a glance when she was first presented," Hüi said. "I would not give Wu Min's envoy the pleasure of my reaction to report. I left the other gifts on the floor where the servants set them."

Mei Ju giggled. "I hope that rankled with him. Well, when you *do* find the time to look her over, I think you will be pleased. She is an exquisite jewel."

"I am far more interested in what dark reason Wu Min had for sending her here. Most men would care a bit more for their sister's happiness than their own ambition."

"From what you have told me of Wu Min, I would wager that he does indeed have some plan, but Lan'xiu is not party to it. And if what my maid has gleaned from her eunuch is true, Wu Min hates Lan'xiu and would prefer to see her dead. Perhaps this is his way of heaping dishonor upon her."

Hüi thought about that for a minute. "What is she like?"

Mei Ju stared at him while she thought it over. "Clever. Polite. She likes children. She is… very sweet."

"Sweet?" Hüi exclaimed. "Not much like her brother, then. What makes you say she is sweet?"

"She thanked me for my kindness and compassion," Mei Ju said slowly.

"I see," Hüi said with quick comprehension. "We always compliment in others what we value in ourselves, whether we are aware of it or not. You see? It would be difficult for anyone to speak with you and reveal nothing of themselves."

Mei Ju smiled, remembering their discussion of Lan'xiu's flaws, but that was not something she would share with Hüi. She would never want him to find her petty in pointing out the faults of another wife. "She has no false pride in her rank. Lan'xiu will fit into the household without creating any trouble."

"Mei Ju, I apologize to you once again for foisting Ci'an upon you. Your life should be comfortable and luxurious, and instead you live beside a poisonous viper," Hüi said with regret.

"Hush. It is not your fault, my love." Mei Ju held her finger to his lips, pleased when he kissed the tip. "In your position, you had to make that marriage of convenience. And your prominence is owed the status of many wives. I have made my peace with it."

"You are indeed kind and generous. What would I do without you?" Hüi asked. He tightened his arms around her.

Hours later when he took his leave of her, Mei Ju waited by the window to watch him walk away. Hüi's heart was not yet engaged by Lan'xiu, but Mei Ju knew his tastes. She had been pretty enough to hold his attention when they first married, but she knew she had not captured his heart. The only comfort was that she knew he did not love any of his other wives, either. And then she had been brought to the birthing bed so often, she could not deny his right to pleasure when she could not provide it.

From the news her maid had brought her after Ci'an was added to the harem, Mei Ju knew that Hüi's relationship with her had been stormy but passionate. It was not until Ci'an showed her true colors in an abortive attack upon Mei Ju that Hüi had come to his senses. He never shared a bed with Ci'an again, but by then she was already pregnant with his daughter. If not for Mei Ju, that sickly daughter would have died immediately of a neglectful death for want of a mother's care, but Mei Ju had taken the baby into her own home and nursed her lovingly until she passed away.

For political reasons, Hüi had accepted as concubines the daughters of highly placed nobles ruling provinces that bordered upon his. Even with the acquisition of these other wives, Hüi had always come back to her, but Mei Ju knew he loved her only as a valued and trusted friend. He might have deceived himself into thinking it was a warmer emotion, but he could not fool her. She sighed with the torment of her fate to love a man who did not love her in return although truly, her marriage was luckier than most.

And now at last, Hüi had met the woman he would love so deeply and truly that their passion would become legend. At least Mei Ju would still retain a small corner of his soul to call her own. No matter how powerful the bonds of attraction, Hüi would never banish her from his life.

She shivered and came back to herself. She had no psychic gifts, but her love made her acutely sensitive to any subject concerning her husband, and she knew him well. Lan'xiu could not know and Hüi Wei could deny it, but in that moment, Mei Ju saw the future with clear eyes and she *knew* it in the depths of her bones. "I would put money on it if I had anyone to bet with," she muttered. Her smile was mischievous as she wondered if Jiang would be up for a little wager.

CHAPTER FIVE

IN THE week that followed, Hüi Wei deliberately had the lanterns lit at each house of his harem save two. He was not yet ready to confront Lan'xiu. And Ci'an could rot for all he cared, and the sooner the better. After her attack upon Mei Ju, he had ordered bars installed on the windows of Ci'an's house and her door was kept locked. When she was permitted to go out, Ci'an was accompanied by an armed guard.

The other wives kindly continued to include Ci'an in their parties, but Hüi Wei gave orders that soldiers of the household guard keep her under observation at all times. Despite changing her servants regularly, she had still somehow managed to procure poison and attempted to smuggle it into Fen's tea when Third Wife first joined the household.

The court physician was the only person admitted to Ci'an's home, and only when she was ill. Otherwise she was kept secluded, even from her own daughter until the child had died.

Hüi continued to enjoy the company of his other wives at intervals while still ignoring the existence of Princess Lan'xiu. And he hoped that point was clearly evident to all observers. He would be naïve to ignore the fact that spies were everywhere—even within his court—and bribes or enough beer could persuade a man of utmost loyalty to pass on what seemed to him an innocuous bit of gossip. So Hüi felt he could be certain Wu Min was completely aware that the gift of his sister had been ignored.

Hüi was determined to allow at least two weeks to pass before he went to the seventh house, although he was curious about Lan'xiu. Her image remained burned into his mind, though he had barely given her a glance at their meeting. He wondered what her voice sounded like and if her skin felt like silk—

Whenever he found his thoughts drifting to her, Hüi admonished himself and reapplied himself strictly to his responsibilities with determined vigor.

He heard gossip of her from his other wives when he went to them, although they had as yet not met her. Hüi deduced that not only had Mei Ju been talking of Lan'xiu, but that the other wives must have spent some time watching her from their windows when she was permitted to walk in the square to get some air. Fen and Huan were taken with her beauty and could speak of nothing else. Alute said in her placid way that Lan'xiu wore pretty clothes, and Bai admired her laugh. But then Bai was a bit of a loon. She had also said that Lan'xiu had twin pixies that sat upon her shoulders, one that made her sad and one that made her smile.

It amused Hüi to think what Ci'an might have to say about Lan'xiu, but considering he refused to see the second concubine, chances were he would never know.

Just when he had decided the time was auspicious, an uprising to the west called him away from home. After a hard fought but short campaign, the rebellious king's head adorned a spike at the gate to his city, a new functionary had been installed to rule and left with enough soldiers to motivate him to a proper sense of loyalty to the emperor, and Hüi was able to return home. Hüi had entertained suspicions that Lan'xiu's brother, Wu Min, might have had a finger in the plot, but the erring king had refused to confess to anything before he lost his head. Perhaps Hüi Wei's strategy of ignoring the girl was making Wu Min impatient, and he had always been one to hide his moves upon the chessboard of power behind some gullible pawn.

Of course, Hüi's first visit upon his return must be to Mei Ju, who clung to him and examined him for injuries whenever he returned from war. Then protocol demanded he visit each wife in turn, to give each the relief of seeing him unharmed.

Therefore it was a full month after the princess's arrival before he sent a servant to light the lantern that hung beside the door of the seventh house.

"Finally you go to sample the beauty of the princess," Jiang teased him at luncheon. "Perhaps you will remain to devour after the first nibble."

"Have you seen her since the audience?" Hüi asked in a dangerous tone.

"Only in my imagination, where I often go to spend time these days." Jiang heaved a ridiculous sigh and assumed a dreamy expression. "I should not dare to enter the household without your permission. The last time I went there, it was at your behest to converse with First Wife."

"I know," Hüi apologized. "I did not truly doubt you. This princess is a thorn in my side, and the sooner she is extracted, the better. I wonder how much of an insult Wu Min would take if I sent her back now."

"Without going to see her?" Jiang's face lit up in glee. "I cannot imagine worse. Unless you sent bits of her back in different trunks. But that would be a tragic waste of all that beauty. If I know you, you will find a way to use her *and* insult her brother."

"Everyone keeps saying how beautiful she is," Hüi said impatiently. "Ci'an is beautiful but dangerous. She would have killed me if she could."

"Did she try?" Jiang asked with interest.

"Yes," Hüi snapped.

"Why did you never tell me?"

"Because you would have killed her, and if you recall, we need her alive so that her father will remain docile."

"How did she do it?"

"She threw a vase at me and then tried to stab me," Hüi said. "When she found out that I did not approve of her attempts to assassinate my other wives, I told her I would not have her lantern lit again and she flew into a temper."

"Did she hit you?"

"Of course not. I stood still. Women can't hit what they aim at. And she didn't have much of an arm for stabbing, either." Hüi's lips curled in satisfaction. "I'm afraid the physician was necessary when I got through with her."

"Well, you will not experience that with Princess Lan'xiu," Jiang said.

"How do you know if you haven't seen her?" Hüi asked curiously.

"Ever since Ci'an's little tantrum with Mei Ju, I have kept tabs on what happens in the household," Jiang said. "I have a responsibility to First Wife and your children."

"And I thank you for that," Hüi said.

"And you must let me know how it goes when you exercise your latest mount," Jiang continued without acknowledging the thanks he deemed unnecessary.

"It is unseemly to speak of the princess as if she were a horse," Hüi said, getting a little hot under the collar.

"I meant your horse," Jiang said with innocent surprise. "That new yearling that was brought up from the farms last week. She's a beauty."

"You meant nothing of the sort," Hüi snapped. Then he wondered why he was so on edge. It could have nothing to do with a new concubine. Women were all the same, barring a few details of coloring and suchlike, and he had been through new acquisitions before. There was no possible reason for him to be anxious. That was for the women. It was their job to please *him*, not the other way around.

"Sadly, you have caught me out," Jiang agreed. "But what is a ribald joke or two on the eve of claiming the most beautiful wife you have ever managed to acquire?"

Hüi's lips relaxed into a grin and he sniggered. "I must admit, I am a bit curious to find out what she has been thinking all this time. Perhaps she has been relieved to be left alone."

"Do you think she will tell you?"

"No, she seems to be a quiet girl. Even Mei Ju cannot draw her out, and apparently she likes Mei Ju and holds her in respect."

"As she should." Jiang nodded approvingly and then leaned over to brush his fingertips over Hüi's cheek lightly. "You need to shave. You don't want to scratch the poor girl to death. She won't be able to be seen in public for days if you go to her like that."

Hüi rubbed a hand over his whiskers, which were heavy for a man of his land. He had always secretly enjoyed that he could grow a beard where most could not. "I suppose it would be a minimum of courtesy to her."

"Go clean up, for the gods' blessings," Jiang ordered. "And then I want to hear every detail." He rubbed his hands lasciviously. "The most beautiful girl I have ever seen."

Hüi found himself on the edge of losing his temper again but said nothing. He stood up and retired to his chambers to shave. And perhaps he might change to a more attractive robe. He wondered if Lan'xiu might have liked his hair better in a braid, but he kept it short for battle, to give his enemies no handle to grab onto. If long, it tumbled to his shoulders in unruly waves, and he rather thought it made him look fierce and imposing like a lion.

Again, he had to call himself to order. He was getting hard simply by thinking of her. The one glance of her stunning beauty had started to haunt him, and the flame of desire curled into his belly, sparking his manhood as none of his other wives ever had. During the recent campaign, he had pleasured himself until he was sore, dreaming of her beauty.

There was something so alluring and fascinating about her that it went beyond mere beauty. He wanted to gaze into her eyes and see his passion reflected back at him. Hüi became startled when he realized he wanted her love, and he didn't know her yet or even love her himself.

There was something special about this girl, and Hüi wondered if perhaps she was a witch who had put a spell on him during the brief moments they were in the same room. He feared the powerful attraction he felt to her, but he reveled in it.

It made him feel like a man. A man of conquest.

She was his now, and he would possess her, claim her, and master her so that she would bend to his will.

In this mood, it was all he could do to wait until after dark. It was unseemly for the master and lord to display any eagerness for the company of a mere woman, and a concubine at that. He knew all eyes would be upon him when he went to her house, and he had to force himself to saunter when he longed to race there, knock down the door, and sweep her into his arms.

He rapped upon the door three times and waited until it was opened to him by a young maid who bowed deeply, backing away to allow him entry.

"Thank you," Hüi said courteously. It did not do to neglect these simple acts of courtesy, and it won him the loyalty of most of his dependents.

The woman bowed again but remained silent.

Hüi's attention was drawn by the eunuch who came down the stairs before bowing deeply. In his light voice, the eunuch said, "General Qiang, my mistress awaits you in the bedchamber."

"Thank you," Hüi said. "You may go."

The maid hurried to the back of the house without comment, but the eunuch looked miserable as he withdrew more slowly. If this had been any other situation, Hüi might have wondered about that, but all his attention was fixed on the girl awaiting him upstairs.

With each step his tension grew. Every step closer to her made him more nervous than facing a horde of barbarians sweeping in from the north, although why, he could not tell. He was in the position of power here. If she did not like him, it would make no difference. He would possess her against her will as often as he pleased. He *owned* her.

The upper hall was darkened, and only one door stood open. A warm glow emanated from within, and Hüi went toward it.

He gasped soundlessly when he caught sight of the girl. She stood with her eyes downcast, her hands hidden within the sleeves of her hanfu, fear etched in every line of her body. However, there was something courageous about the way she waited for him when clearly she was terrified, and that roused a little feeling of tenderness within that surprised him. He'd expected passion, and she did indeed arouse within him an almost frighteningly violent wish to rend her clothing and throw her upon the bed and ravish her, but there was something more complex than mere sexual attraction in his reaction to her.

It was as if his heart were soaring with happiness that he had finally found the mate to his soul and would ever be as one with her. Nothing like the calm content he felt with Mei Ju. This emotion was new and powerful and unsettling. But his happiness struck a stark contrast to the girl's misery, and it compelled him to try to comfort her. He closed the door behind him.

"Princess Zhen Lan'xiu," he said.

"My Lord Qiang Hüi Wei," she responded properly, although her voice trembled.

He could see her entire body shaking, but the sound of her voice was like music to his ears. Unlike the shrill tones of most of his wives, Lan'xiu's voice was low and melodic, and she spoke his name softly.

Her lashes swept her cheeks like the wings of a butterfly, and he wished to look into her hidden eyes. "Look at me," he commanded.

Startled, she looked up, and he felt his soul fly out of his body to meet hers when their eyes met. She seemed to feel it as well, because a small wrinkle appeared between her brows, as if she was perplexed by some new emotion that she did not expect. "My Lord?"

"You belong to me. Do you admit that you belong to me?" he demanded.

"I belong to you," she agreed softly. The corners of her mouth turned down, and her eyes filled with a curious mixture of sadness and longing although a fire burned deep within them.

Hüi could have sworn she wanted nothing more than what he did, to join their bodies together and experience the rapture of their melding. Doubt and fear showed in her eyes while her beautiful face remained impassive.

"I have never seen so exquisite a creature," he murmured. He drew nearer and put his hand on her cheek.

Lan'xiu closed her eyes and rubbed her cheek against his hand like a kitten, still trembling.

"I will not hurt you," Hüi said, looking down at her.

She didn't answer but raised one hand to touch his. Contrary to the soft touch he expected, the roughness of a hardened palm rasped against his skin, a callus that ought not be found on any woman's hand. He stared at the sword callus on his own, making a connection that seemed impossible. His eyes narrowed with suspicion as he searched the beautiful face. It couldn't be possible that a woman....

Instantly he sprang away from her, gripping her wrist hard enough to elicit a cry of pain from her. "What treachery is this?" he snarled, shaking her hand and pointing at the calluses on her palm.

"I am party to no treachery, my Lord!" Lan'xiu exclaimed in fear. She tried to draw her hand away from his, but he was too strong for her.

Hüi pulled her flat against him, imprisoning both hands behind her back in one of his. She did not resist him as he roughly felt her chest. He found no familiar, round softness there. He groped between her legs and found hardness there as well. Disgusted, he flung her from him, staring down at where she fell to the floor. "No treachery you say!" he said with contempt. "You are no woman!"

Lan'xiu shakily got to his feet and stared at him proudly. "I am no woman, but the treachery was not mine. It was not my wish to sell myself into a slavery I did not want. My brother betrayed me and is using me to betray you."

Hüi drew the sword he was never without. "I should kill you here and now."

"You will do as you deem best, my Lord," Lan'xiu said. He folded his hands, bowed his head, and waited.

Hüi raised the sword and advanced upon the beautiful girl—boy—and grasped his hair, pulling his head back to expose the long, slender throat. He rested the sharp edge of the blade against Lan'xiu's skin, causing a line of crimson drops to form, but the boy uttered no sound of protest. He merely waited, watching Hüi with his liquid eyes.

Something in his expression caused Hüi to release Lan'xiu's hair, noting the softness against his palm like a caress as it tumbled free from the clasp to fall in a cloud around the boy's face. He pushed the boy away. "Sit there!" he ordered, pointing at a chair. He began to pace, keeping a close eye on the boy as he obediently went to the chair and sat.

"I can kill you now or five minutes from now. I don't suppose it will make much difference," Hüi muttered. The battle raging within almost immobilized him. Clearly, Wu Min had sent a boy in the guise of a woman to make a fool of him, but that mattered little. What bothered him more was his reaction to the boy. Even more so than when he thought him a woman, he urgently desired to tear the boy's clothing from his body and carry out his previous plan of ravishment, and he could not understand what dark forces drove him.

"Who—what *are* you?" he demanded finally.

"My name is Lan'xiu," the boy said.

At last Hüi understood the intriguing timbre of the girl's—boy's voice. "Beautiful orchid," he said scornfully. "A female's name."

"That is the name given to me by my mother," Lan'xiu insisted. "My brother, Wu Min, was already seventeen when I was born. She knew if he found out I was male, he would have dashed my brains out with a rock and left my body on the mountain for wild beasts. He was intent upon my father's throne and could brook no competition."

"But you were the younger son. There was no danger to him," Hüi said. "What woman would shame her son by forcing him into skirts, even to save his life? That is what puzzles me."

"She did not force me," Lan'xiu said quietly. He stroked the silk of his cheongsam with one finger. "I like dressing like this."

"You are trying to fool me. You wish to be a woman," Hüi spat.

"I do not wish to be a woman," Lan'xiu exclaimed in a frustrated voice. "You do not understand. I like dressing this way. I feel pretty like this."

"Well, you're certainly pretty," Hüi said sarcastically. "Pretty enough to fool anyone into thinking you a woman. So your brother believes that you are a girl and sends you to occupy my attention while he plans some assault against me."

Lan'xiu started to shake again. "He found out that I am not a girl. He was enraged at being so deceived and killed my mother. He planned to kill me also, until he thought of this scheme."

"I do not wonder that he was outraged," Hüi shouted. "I share his sentiment and I do not take kindly to those who mistake me for a fool!"

The door opened, and the eunuch stood upon the threshold, looking worried.

"Ning! You may go! Shut the door behind you and go downstairs!"

Hüi started at Lan'xiu's sharp tone of command. Although the eunuch hesitated for a moment, his eyes fixed upon the line of blood on Lan'xiu's throat, he obeyed the order. "Yes, my Lady." Still eyeing the general belligerently, he backed slowly from the room and shut the door.

"Born to command, eh?"

"Ning has been with me since I was a child and he would prefer that I didn't die," Lan'xiu said wryly. "And he prefers not to die either. But we have accepted our fate." He folded his hands in his lap, the picture of resignation.

Hüi continued to pace. "I should kill you here and now to avenge this insult. I can have it put about that I found you had betrayed me before I claimed you."

"That would play into my brother's hands," Lan'xiu said. In a calm voice, he explained, "I have had much time to consider this. If you slay me for betraying you, you hold yourself up to ridicule as a cuckold. If you cast me from your door in disgust, my brother will take care to spread the news that I am male and that he was able to fool you into taking me as a concubine. If you kill me, the stain of guilt is upon your hands rather than his and he is provided with all the excuse he needs to launch an attack to avenge my death. Once he disposes of you, he will carve a path to the sea. He believes that you are the only thing that stands in the way of his seizing all of China."

"The emperor might take issue with his opinion on the point. I am not the only barrier that stands between Wu Min and the sea," Hüi said. He found his anger draining away and sat down at a safe distance from the girl—boy. "You appear intelligent enough. Why did you lend yourself to this plot?"

"Lend myself? What choice did I have? A certain death awaits me either way, but I would extend my time in this world as long as possible. At home I was closely guarded. If I had tried to run away, my brother would have killed me then and enjoyed it." Lan'xiu shuddered. "I should prefer a clean, swift death by your sword to enduring the long, painful tortures he tells me he has devised for me."

"And those calluses on your hand?"

"My eunuch, Ning, is a sword master. He thought I should learn to defend myself."

"Or assassinate me?"

"The swords are not within this room, my Lord. You may search if you choose, but you will not find any weapon here."

"So, you smuggled them in when you arrived." Hüi arose and strode to the door, bellowing, "Ning!"

The eunuch appeared so promptly, it was evident he had not followed the orders to retreat.

"I thought I told you to go downstairs." Lan glared at him.

"I was still on the stairs, on my way down," Ning said defensively, glaring back.

"As slow as a tortoise in winter."

"You didn't give me a specific time by which I had to arrive downstairs."

"You should have been a lawyer," Lan said.

Hüi's lips twitched at the interplay between the two. Evidently, even imminent death couldn't seem to interrupt their accustomed bickering. "Bring her—her Ladyship's sword, Ning, if you please."

Ning's mouth dropped open in alarm, and he glanced at Lan'xiu for guidance.

"You heard my Lord. He gave you an order," Lan'xiu said.

Ning went and returned quickly, holding a delicately engraved sword with both hands.

"Give it to he—him," Hüi ordered.

Lan stood up and held out his hand. Ning put the sword into it and then wheeled to face Hüi. "You'll have to go through me to get to her!" he said defiantly, clenching his fists.

"Ning, you fool," Lan said, his voice exasperated but fond at the same time.

"That will present no difficulty, seeing as I am holding a sword and you are not," Hüi pointed out.

"Ning, go away!" Lan put his hand on Ning's shoulder. "If the fates intend me to die tonight, then let me die with honor. I will not hide behind you."

"Oh, Lan'xiu!" The misery in the eunuch's voice touched Hüi, and pity moved within him as Ning sank down on his knees to kiss Lan's hand. Then the eunuch stood up and cleared his throat, saying, "Fight well as I taught you. Don't let him have it all his own way. Let your sword taste his blood even if he kills you at the last!"

"Get out of here, you bloodthirsty little demon," Lan said. He gave Ning a push. "Go now. Go quickly. *All* the way downstairs."

Glaring at Hüi, Ning circled him and left the room, closing the door.

Both Lan and Hüi waited for the sound of his footsteps on the stairs to fade away.

"My Lord, grant me one wish whether you slay me or not?" Lan'xiu asked anxiously.

"What is it?" Hüi asked a little impatiently.

"When you kill me, I beg of you, let Shu Ning live. He is a mere eunuch. He can do you no harm. He came here to serve me, knowing it would mean his death as well as mine. However much I value his faithfulness, death would be a poor reward for his loyalty."

Hüi considered for a moment. "Very well. I will not guarantee that he may remain here in my city, but I will spare him as a boon to you." Then Hüi raised his sword. "At your pleasure."

"I will be yours in a moment."

Unaccountably, Hüi found himself wishing that could be true, and he watched as Lan set down his sword and tied his hair back before tucking the hem of his hanfu into his sash to free his legs. Then the boy picked up the sword as if he was familiar with its heft in his hand.

They both knew Hüi would inevitably win. He was taller, broader, more muscular; but evidently Lan had some iron in his soul, despite his wearing women's clothing.

He circled Hüi cautiously, and Hüi had to laugh when he realized Lan was trying to get him into position so the light of the fire would be in his eyes. He interrupted that plan with a feint only to be surprised and pleased to feel the strong parry of Lan's sword.

The joy of the fight was upon Lan's face, making it much more beautiful than when pinched with fear. Even though he knew he would die, it was apparent he meant to put up a good fight first.

Hüi delivered a thrust in good earnest and drove Lan back. The boy had been well taught, and cleverly managed to parry or evade the majority of the blows, but Hüi was simply too strong for him. At one point Lan stumbled over a footstool and overturned it, distracted by Hüi's sword passing through the silk of his sleeve without harming him, but he managed to find his balance again.

Hüi drove him steadily back until Lan was fighting for his life, his back pressed up against the wall. With a trick double parry, Hüi flicked the sword from the boy's hand and pressed his body against Lan's, pinning him to the wall, holding the point of his sword to his chin. "I think I won this fight, don't you?"

Lan smiled valiantly. "My life is forfeit to your superior skill, my Lord. You have beaten me fair and square. Thank you for giving me a chance to earn my freedom."

Hüi strained forward, relishing the firmness of the slight body trapped beneath his, becoming aware that he was rubbing his manhood against another answering hardness. "I wanted to test my sword against yours," he muttered.

"I would have your sword pressed against mine," Lan answered huskily, his breath coming faster, staring up into Hüi's eyes. "I have dreamed of—" He broke off and turned his head away, saying harshly, "If you must kill me, I beg of you, do it quickly."

Hüi glanced at the sword in his hand, bemused as to why he was holding it. "I do not wish to kill you." The sword fell to the carpet with a thud.

Lan was gasping for air, Hüi was pressing so hard against him. "What do you wish to do, my Lord?"

"I wish to take what is mine!" Hüi shouted hoarsely. He swept the slender boy off his feet and carried him to the bed, tossing him upon it.

Lan lay there quiescent, awaiting whatever Hüi would choose to do to him next. His breath quickened while both fear and desire showed in his eyes as Hüi retrieved his sword and stood over him, looking down at the exquisite boy trembling on the bed.

Lan flinched but didn't pull away as Hüi slid the flat of the sword under the sash of his hanfu. With a sudden movement, Hüi ripped the sword upward, slashing through the silk. The edges of the hanfu slid away with a whisper, exposing the traditional silk corselet, embroidered with scarlet thread upon jade green fabric. Lan shuddered when Hüi slowly inched the sword under the thin covering, slicing it apart to reveal large brown nipples on the flat plane of Lan's chest. Hüi set down the sword to take each nipple between thumb and fingers, rubbing them to hard little peaks.

Hüi ran his hands along Lan's skin, down his smooth, hairless chest and belly, under the waistband of the silk undertrousers where a bulge distended the front. Lan cried out in surprise when Hüi grasped the waist and ripped the trousers in two. When he had laid Lan'xiu completely bare he took in a deep breath and examined the beauty on display for him. Long limbs splayed gracefully, exposing the hard sex nestled in the curly hair between Lan's legs, and angular shoulders tapered to a slim waist and even slimmer hips. "You are so beautiful."

"And yours, my Lord," Lan whispered. He held out his arms invitingly, a yearning expression in his eyes.

Hüi kicked his sword aside to divest himself of his own clothing in haste. He fell upon Lan, taking his mouth in a deep kiss, driving his tongue inside the parted lips, exploring, tasting, conquering. He could feel Lan spread his legs to let Hüi's hips rest within their embrace.

He rocked his groin urgently against Lan's, feeling their erections rubbing hard against each other. He could not bear to end the kiss, drinking in the infinite sweetness of Lan's mouth. The kiss went on and on while Hüi could feel Lan's arms around him, holding him with a strength and eagerness he had never felt from any of his wives.

The slim naked body arched up beneath his, straining to meet his every thrust. If he could have stopped himself, Hüi would have preferred to be inside Lan, but it was not possible. It was as if every unfulfilled desire of his soul poured out in one earth-shattering explosion as he reached orgasm too soon. He tore his mouth away and looked down to see Lan's face transformed with ecstasy as they shared the same moment of exquisite pleasure, liquid heat spilling between them.

His chest heaving in a quest for air, Hüi eventually was able to lower himself to blanket Lan's body completely. He became aware of Lan's hands roaming up and down his back and the murmur of Lan's voice in his ear.

"What are you saying?"

"Only that I am yours and I belong to you, my Lord," Lan answered. His eyes were shining with happiness when Hüi looked at him. "I can die content now."

Hüi chuckled. "I didn't put enough effort into it to kill you yet. That was just the opening engagement upon the field of battle."

"It was very well fought, my Lord," Lan said demurely. "I surrender."

"You haven't yet, but you will, I can assure you of that," Hüi promised, his voice silky with seductive threat. He rolled off the boy and traced the line of dried blood on his throat with one finger. "I am sorry about that. You may have a scar."

"It doesn't matter," Lan said.

Hüi was amused. The boy was more ethereally beautiful than any woman he had ever seen, and—for some reason incomprehensible to him—enjoyed dressing and living as a woman, but that one offhand comment revealed him as the male he truly was. Any woman would have dreaded a scar to mar her beauty. Lan'xiu truly didn't care, and it made Hüi even more curious. "Tell me what you thought your life would be."

"My mother was under no illusions about my half brother," Lan said with reticent sadness. "She had planned to get me to a monastery before she died, where I might live out my days under another name. I had no other hope than that, but at least it would be freedom of a sort."

"But you had nothing else that you dreamed of," Hüi persisted, drawing his fingertips over Lan's naked body. He circled one nipple and watched the rise and fall of Lan's chest quicken in response.

"I wanted to belong to someone, to be loved," Lan said. "Someone like you."

"You are attracted to men?" Hüi had certainly witnessed men loving men in times of war, but the wise commander turned a blind eye to such behavior. After all, a man had needs, even when women were scarce.

"Yes," Lan said tranquilly. "But I never thought this dream would come to pass."

Hüi's hand traveled lower, caressing the defined line along the top of Lan's thigh, skirting the genitals to stroke his leg. "It hasn't come to pass yet."

"I suppose it was presumptuous of me, considering how many wives you have. But when I was sent here, I never thought to have even this much before I died." Lan tried to sound cheerful. "I suppose you will kill me now."

"I don't think I will," Hüi said thoughtfully. "I have not yet ravished you, and I believe I promised to do so. I *will* possess you before this night is done and claim you so that you never dream of another man." He cupped Lan's balls firmly in his hand and squeezed gently, watching the young man's hips start their movement in response.

Stars shone in Lan's eyes and he only said, "I think I would like that."

CHAPTER SIX

LAN rolled onto his side to watch Hüi's face while he dozed. From the depths of despair to the heights of happiness was a dizzying climb in just a few hours. After enduring an entire day of dread after his lantern was lit, Lan'xiu had begun the evening hoping for nothing more than a mercifully swift death. Now, it seemed the heavens had opened for him and the good luck he had never known shone down upon him.

To be held in Hüi's strong arms and kissed until his senses were spinning, to feel that powerful muscular body pressing him into the mattress were things he had only dreamed of, and his dreams were but a pale imitation of what the reality had turned out to be.

One of the benefits of long lashes was that even with one's eyes lowered, one could obtain surreptitious glimpses through them, and Lan had been enthralled with Hüi from the moment he first saw him. The General Lord Qiang Hüi Wei was the biggest man Lan had ever seen, with powerful thighs and broad shoulders. He had the face of a conqueror and eyes that hid many secrets. His careless confidence proclaimed that Hüi was the victor of many battles, not only upon the field, and Lan had dared to hope that perhaps his brother, Wu Min, might yet be vanquished.

Of course, Lan would not be alive to witness the defeat, but it gave him comfort to think of it after the havoc Wu Min had wreaked upon his family and his province. At least Lan's death would not be in vain if it motivated Hüi Wei to exact revenge for the deception practiced upon him.

And now… Lan sighed happily and ran his hand over the muscular shoulder and down Hüi's arm, gently squeezing the hard bicep of the man lying next to him. Unthinkable that this man should desire him, too, but there was no mistaking the passion that had ignited between them. Perhaps for a time, Hüi would be intrigued, and then possibly he might get used to Lan with the sort of vague fondness one has for one's pets and possessions. Of course, he would eventually return to his proper wives when the novelty wore off, but he might yet let Lan live, out of kindness.

"And I will have this memory for the rest of my life," Lan whispered.

"Better wait until I've given you something more to remember," Hüi growled, flipping Lan onto his back and pinning his wrists to the bed.

Lan widened his thighs, enjoying the feeling of Hüi's strong legs between his, the hard manhood stabbing his belly, his vision swirling as once again Hüi kissed him breathless.

Helplessly, Lan arched up, trying to ensure that all of his naked body was pressed against Hüi's. He had not much enjoyed being held a prisoner of his brother's. It was better being one of the household here. Even though the women had treated him kindly for the most part, he had longed for nothing more than to make his escape and take Ning with him.

But this experience was different from anything he had ever imagined. What he enjoyed most was Hüi's weight trapping him, holding him prisoner to be used at his lord's pleasure. He liked being helpless with Hüi. He enjoyed Hüi's hands restraining him, exploring him, touching him at will without inquiring whether he enjoyed it. He knew Hüi had enslaved him with this new pleasure, and Lan could deny him nothing. Even when Hüi's teeth nipped a bit too sharply at his nipple, the pain was a gift from his lord, to be suffered and enjoyed if it gave Hüi pleasure.

Evidently, it did, for Hüi alternated sucking at the hardened nub of flesh with tiny stinging bites. Lan squirmed under the attention, feeling his cock grow harder despite the pain.

While Hüi's mouth pressed to his nipple, Lan felt Hüi's hand move firmly down his body, over his hip, squeezing the roundness of his buttocks until the fingers slid within the dark valley, finding and caressing his most private spot. Tingles of pleasure flowed from his entrance over his body, and he spread his legs to give Hüi greater access.

Grinning, Hüi raised his head. "You like that, do you?" He stroked more firmly over the furled opening, gloating over the gasps of pleasure Lan could not hold inside.

"Yes! Yes, I like it!" Lan panted. He moaned in disappointment when Hüi moved his hand and then his entire body, missing the intimate contact. He heard the sound of a drawer opening and then Hüi lay upon him once more.

He startled at the feeling of a slick finger being pushed inside his nether opening and could not help letting out a small yelp of pain.

Hüi kissed his throat. "This will hurt a little just at first. But when I take you, you will belong to me fully. You will be mine."

The feeling of the finger moving within him was strange, and yet Lan liked it after the initial shock. However, the feeling he'd experienced of wanting to do whatever would please this man who owned him—heart, body, and soul—would have made him agree even if it meant being split in two. "I am yours," he assured Hüi. "I want to be yours."

Lan's hips flew up and he arched off the bed as Hüi's finger stroked over hidden pleasure deep within him. A startling burst of pleasure rippled outward, shaking him to his toes. He thought nothing could feel better, and then Hüi did it again.

Lan knew Hüi was watching him, but he was lost in pleasure. He knew his eyes were unfocused and his mouth hung open, and he could only hope that Hüi enjoyed the sight. It was as if his lord had demanded not only possession of his body, but also the opening of his innermost soul, and he was powerless to resist.

He felt his knees being pressed back to his chest and knew himself to be exposed and open to Hüi. His legs were lifted to Hüi's broad shoulders, and he felt the fingers leave him empty and yearning to be filled, then the nudge of something large and blunt at his opening. His eyes flew open in protest, but Hüi bent his head to take his mouth in a deep kiss and smother any cry of pain.

Lan moaned into the kiss as he felt the ring of muscle tighten and then yield under the assault of Hüi's cock. It burned and hurt as Hüi slid his cock home in one smooth thrust. Lan's muscles clenched helplessly, but now he knew what it meant to be a slave to another's pleasure. He was helpless, impaled to the hilt, squirming under the weight of his master, unable to do anything about the giant intruder within.

He looked up to catch Hüi watching him closely and realized his face was contorted with pain. He tried to smile to reassure the other man, but Hüi shook his head, smiling as he said, "We will wait. It will get better, I assure you. Let me know."

Lan felt his muscles begin to relax and the pain melted away, leaving him feeling pleasantly full. Experimentally, he reached down to feel where Hüi's cock penetrated him, enjoying the tingles that radiated outward from his hole and the sensation of the firm shaft filling it.

Then Hüi moved his hips, sliding his cock out of the narrow passage before gliding back in, and Lan ringed Hüi's shaft with his fingers, with wonder feeling himself impaled. This time Lan felt it when Hüi's cock massaged the walls of his passage, and pleasure blossomed within him.

Once again Hüi withdrew and slid home, the movements of his hips getting faster as he thrust deeper. Lan let his legs slide off Hüi's shoulders to wrap them around his waist, hanging on for dear life. Hüi lowered his body, trapping Lan's rigid cock.

Between the driving of the cock deep within and the rubbing of their bellies against his erection, Lan was transported upon the wings of rapture. Hüi was slamming into him now, their flesh making an occasional slapping sound on contact, drowning out Lan's moans and gasps of pleasure.

He squirmed and tried to reach his own cock, but Hüi slapped his hand away. "Not until I permit you to come," he said.

"Yes, my Lord," Lan answered, although he knew he would not be able to control himself. The feeling of Hüi's cock inside him, rubbing and stretching him made him feel like he might actually be split in two, but he liked it. He arched in ecstasy when Hüi's cock slid within him, heightening pleasure to the edge of pain.

Then the thrusts grew shorter and more erratic. Hüi raised himself from Lan's body and his hips snapped in short, uneven strokes until he froze for a second. Lan cried out when Hüi's hand found his cock. Two strokes and he spilled between them, making Hüi's belly slide against his.

Hüi rammed home even deeper with a hoarse cry of triumph before pouring his essence within the narrow channel. Then he lowered himself to lie completely atop Lan.

Lan could feel his nerveless legs slide down to the mattress and turned his head into the crook of Hüi's neck and shoulder. A feeling of contentment and peace came over him such as he had never felt before.

"Now you belong to me." Hüi's voice was muffled in the pillow.

"I do," Lan agreed.

"And I will never let you go," Hüi said.

Lan had never felt happier. His ass was a bit sore and Hüi's cock was still buried inside him. Hüi's weight also curtailed his breathing, but Lan never wanted to move from this position. This was the pinnacle he had yearned for. If Hüi felt impelled to kill him when he awoke, Lan knew he would sacrifice himself happily to pay for having this dream come true.

LAN'XIU lay awake most of the night, dozing now and then, but determined to enjoy the feel of naked skin against his for the first, and possibly last, time in his life. Lying on his side, curled into the sheltering bulk of his lord's body, the dim light allowed him to see the strong sinew of the arm that encircled him, and Hüi's breath blew warm over his shoulder. The occasional snore made Lan want to laugh, but he didn't wish to wake Hüi and hasten his leaving. As intimate as their lovemaking had been, being held in Hüi's embrace while lying together naked sparked some long suppressed emotion that overwhelmed Lan, like a tidal wave sweeping over him. He longed to drown in the pleasure of belonging to this man for the few hours of respite he had been given.

There was no doubt in his mind that by the light of day, Hüi Wei would return to his senses and recoil from him, put him to death for being the means of his humiliation. No man could endure the thought that others knew his household sheltered a man in the guise of a woman, and Wu Min would most certainly use that fact to his advantage when it came to light. Therefore, when he had time to consider, Hüi Wei would be forced to put Lan'xiu to death. Whatever steps Hüi took to silence Wu Min would naturally mean nothing to Lan'xiu, as he would be dead. The strain of his existence within the household and the day spent awaiting his inevitable death at the discovery of his secret with as graceful a resignation he could muster had taken its toll, however, and eventually Lan'xiu nodded off.

He awoke to the feeling of soft lips nibbling at his neck and a hard cock sliding within the valley between his cheeks, rubbing insistently over his hole. Sleepily he pushed back, signifying his willingness.

Slick fingers prepared him hastily, and Lan moaned when Hüi's erection took their place, entering him ruthlessly enough to make his sore muscles protest the burning stretch.

Hüi remained still until Lan let out a breath and said, "Take me, my Lord."

An inarticulate but possessive growl was his only answer as a hand slid under Lan's thigh and lifted it, spreading him even more widely open to receive his lord's pleasure. The feeling of the hard cock surging within him in the rhythmic dance of possession made him feel happy to be able to give Hüi something he obviously wanted. Hüi let Lan's thigh rest on his forearm and reached between his legs to grasp his cock and stroke it. Only one specter lingered to distract Lan'xiu from the pleasure of being so thoroughly fucked.

"Are you going to put me to death this morning?" Lan gasped, snuggling within the circle of his lover's arms.

Hüi stopped thrusting. "Will you cease asking me that?" Hüi exclaimed. "I assure you, I will give you plenty of notice if I decide to kill you. I am the master here, not you." He drove his hips forward, causing his hard shaft to impale Lan's ass even deeper.

"Yes, my Lord," Lan said meekly, if a bit breathlessly.

CHAPTER SEVEN

THIS time when Lan'xiu ordered Ning to go downstairs, he followed instructions to the letter. He found Jia, the housekeeper, lurking in the hallway below, listening to the sounds coming from upstairs and giggling with her hands covering her mouth. "At last! The Master is taking the princess! A fine time she will have being blooded for the first time!"

In a fury, Ning turned on her, snapping that she should remain in the kitchen if she couldn't find a nearby barnyard where by rights she would fit in very nicely indeed! Preferably she might lie down in the sty with the hogs!

Jia was very understanding and did not take offense easily. "This is only to be expected when a young girl is as beautiful as the princess and untouched. It rouses the beast in the best of men. You have served her for a long time, but you mustn't worry. She is young and she can take a good pounding." Jia made the symbol for fucking with both hands clasped together, her palms making a rude noise when the air was squeezed out. "It is good luck for this house that he is between her thighs at last. I wondered why he delayed taking her for so long. She is as juicy as a ripe peach."

"You are disgusting!" Ning spat.

"Don't be silly! We are a robust people here and enjoy sex as a gift from the gods." The sound of some piece of furniture toppling over interrupted her. Ning started toward the stairs but she caught him by the sleeve. "Begging your pardon, Ning-xiānsheng, but it is not your place to come between the master and his concubine."

A faint cry sounded, and the lines around Jia's eyes crinkled in mirth as she giggled again. "Ah! The princess has a bit more spark in her than I suspected. A lady in the sitting room but a tiger in the bedroom; the men always appreciate that. She is giving him a fine chase before she lets him catch her."

"What if he hurts her?"

"He will not hurt her—much. A man always enjoys the kill more after a good hunt."

Ning shut his eyes in horror. Jia could not know how truly she spoke. Even now Hüi might be sheathing the sharp blade of his sword within Lan'xiu's body, watching the crimson lifeblood ebb away. And next it would be his turn. Hüi could not afford to let him live with the knowledge he kept locked within his skull. A high-pitched giggle made him open his eyes and glare at Jia.

"For all that she is a virgin, the princess seems to know how to excite a man. Her ladyship will most likely need a day or two to recover from the fine ride the master will be giving her. Ah well, she will soon learn to like it."

"Get out of my sight before I do something we both should regret!" Ning hissed.

With another giggle, Jia followed Ning's advice and returned to her kitchen, although possibly her step was quickened by his raised hand and the anger snapping in his eyes.

He had thought that nothing could be worse than to stand here helplessly listening to his precious Lan'xiu being murdered by that irate soldier, but that damned Jia had managed to increase the torment he suffered. Qiang Hüi Wei was so very large and strong compared to the slender princess; Ning could only imagine the violence being visited upon her person. Knowing how to use a sword could only take one so far. Lan'xiu had little experience of a real fight after only sparring with him, and he had always taken good care not to give her so much as a nick. Of course, Ning knew that a man of the governor's position could not stomach having such a trick being played upon him, but he had hoped for some measure of mercy when Hüi Wei found out the truth.

Surely, *surely*, he would understand Lan'xiu was no party to this deceit perpetrated by her brother.

When they had first arrived in this strange land and entered the audience room, ostensibly as guests but in truth prisoners of their seeming guard, Ning had examined the new lord's face, knowing that nobody looked at a eunuch to see what they were doing. He could see the man was shrewd and strong, a man of innate power whether the emperor backed him or not, but the lines beside his mouth betrayed that he had a sense of humor. He had begun to hope Hüi Wei might yet forgive Lan'xiu and give her leave to immure herself within a monastery, but now all hope was gone.

If Lan'xiu had not said she would not hide behind him, Ning would have braved any fate to rush to her aid, no matter that he would die with her. He paced impotently, his fists clenched, biting his lips to keep silent whenever he heard another faint cry.

It suddenly occurred to him that although she had commanded him to go downstairs, she had not forbidden him to come *back upstairs*! To think was to act, and Ning charged up the stairs to his room where he had hidden his own sword, a heavier one than Lan'xiu used. He crept to the adjoining door and placed his ear upon it to listen.

He almost dropped his sword when he heard Hüi Wei's voice! He could not make out the words, but surely the tone was that of a man speaking endearments to one beloved of him, rather than the anger of a man bent on wreaking justice and death.

Ning placed his sword on the floor and bent to look through the keyhole. He could not see much but what he did see made him fall to his knees with a thud, he was so surprised. Luckily, his room also boasted a carpet that muffled the sound. After listening for any reaction from the next room, he concluded that the combatants were too occupied with each other to notice outside distractions.

Cautiously, he approached the keyhole on his knees, peering through it. He glimpsed a pile of clothing on the floor beside the bed, and the bed itself seemed to be moving or shaking.

Soft murmurs, rustling sounds, and a cry from the princess that could have been pain but sounded suspiciously more like ecstasy left Ning completely confused.

He pressed his ear to the door again. Hüi Wei raised his voice in a triumphant shout that mingled with breathy moans in the princess's familiar voice. It did not sound much to Ning as if she was in dire need of rescue.

But perhaps he was not interpreting what he heard correctly. Perhaps Hüi Wei was torturing her as a prelude to killing her. The general might simply have stripped her to verify his guess as to her gender, resulting in the clothing left on the floor. If so, it was clearly his duty to come to her rescue. Now it sounded a bit like she was crying. Ning felt for his sword in the dark but froze when he heard her laugh.

Hüi Wei's voice again, sounding rather threatening this time. Lan'xiu's voice raised enough for Ning to make out that she was agreeing to obey some order.

Should he go in? Should he not? If he were wrong, Lan'xiu would be angry with him and that would be bad. If she were angry, how much angrier might Hüi Wei be, perhaps angry enough to have him killed! That would be bad too. Then Lan'xiu would be left all alone here in a strange land, perhaps to die alone, which would be much worse. Ning had always meant to beg that she be killed first so that at least she would have his friendly face to look upon when she died. But it sounded like she might actually be enjoying whatever was happening within.

The unmistakable squeak of the wooden bed frame under stress stopped Ning's ruminations and he grinned in the dark. Lan'xiu was right; he would have been an excellent lawyer. Here he was, sitting in the dark, arguing all around the issue while in the meantime, she and her new master seemed to be entertaining each other very well.

Ning sat with his back to the door and leaned his head against it to enjoy a silent laugh. Whether Hüi Wei had ever enjoyed the company of a man in his bed before this, clearly Lan'xiu's beauty was enough to seduce the most committed lover of females into testing strange waters.

Without a thought to the fact that he was intruding upon their privacy, Ning stayed where he was, enjoying the sounds of a passion he would never know. Even if Hüi Wei decided in the morning that his pride had been so compromised that he could not allow the princess and her servant to live, at least Lan'xiu's last night on this earth might give her a taste of the kind of love she had dreamed of. For her sake, Ning was happy this had come to pass.

"Sheathing his sword indeed." Ning smiled and closed his eyes, filled with contentment, at least for the moment.

THE sound of the bed squeaking again jerked Ning from a sound sleep. He made a mental note to mend the frame for the princess. At the rate they were going, it sounded like her bed would be getting quite a workout, at least if Hüi Wei decided to permit them to live.

The sky was still dark, but the dawn was approaching. Ning could hear the song of a few birds outside. Apparently the general was an early riser—Ning covered his mouth and giggled at his inadvertent pun—and had decided to put in a little exercise before breakfast.

This time the murmurs and cries sounded soft and sleepy, and quite soon silence had fallen again within the room next door. Ning stretched his stiff neck from side to side, making another mental note to refrain from sleeping while leaning against a door in the future. If he had a future. He gazed out the window, and when a line of pale yellow stole across the horizon beyond the houses opposite, he knew he could delay no longer. It was time for Hüi Wei to go. It would be unseemly for his dependents to know the general had spent an entire night in the company of any of his concubines. That was simply not done.

Ning stood up and knocked quietly at the door. There was no response from within. He knocked a little louder. Still nothing.

Finally, he turned the knob and eased the door open. He paused then, not knowing precisely what to do in this situation. Nothing had fitted him for this in his training. Then he found himself wishing that he knew how to paint so that he would have a tangible image to look at for all his days to remember the scene of the two lovers lying together.

Hüi Wei slept on his back, holding Lan'xiu close so his head was nestled upon his muscular shoulder. Their legs twined together, the darker skin of Hüi Wei's thighs making Lan'xiu's gleam ivory in contrast. Lan's long hair covered his face and his naked body was relaxed, the elegant line of his spine leading to the curve of his buttocks.

Ning realized that Hüi Wei had opened his eyes and was looking at him, moving one hand to caress Lan'xiu's naked shoulder as if protecting him from harm.

"My Lord, it is almost dawn," Ning whispered.

"Thank you." With infinite care, Hüi eased himself away from Lan'xiu, positioning a pillow for support in his place. He climbed out of the bed and stretched with no apparent worry for his display of nakedness. Then he stooped to retrieve his clothing, sorting them from where they lay upon the floor mingled with Lan'xiu's ruined hanfu. When he was dressed, he bent over the sleeping young man and pressed a kiss to the tumbled hair.

He came toward Ning with an intent look in his eyes.

Ning held up a hand to stop him. "Your sword, my Lord."

Hüi nodded and looked vaguely about for it. Ning came forward silently and drew it out from under the bed where it had landed, handing it to the general. Hüi Wei led the way out of the room, and Ning closed the door softly.

"This way, my Lord," Ning said. He led the way downstairs through the sleeping house. He went to open the front door, but Hüi Wei stopped him.

"I have decided not to execute the princess for the time being," he announced.

Ning had to force down his untimely laughter. It would never do to offend the man at such a delicate moment, but after having witnessed the tender kiss Hüi Wei had bestowed upon the sleeping princess, Ning would have placed bets that the general was more likely to declare his undying love for her than to kill her. "Princess Lan'xiu will be most grateful to receive this auspicious news when she awakes, I am sure. I thank you humbly on her behalf."

Hüi Wei peered sharply at the smooth, impassive face. His lips twitched as if he noticed Ning's suppressed mirth and might have joined in, if it had not been unseemly to indulge a servant in this way. "You do know that the princess is not—"

Ning raised a finger in front of his mouth and gave a quick wink. "I know everything there is to know about Princess Lan'xiu."

"You call her 'she'."

"It is safer for all concerned," Ning answered. "Did you hear that? The first cock begins to crow." Again he had to resist the urge to cackle at his own lewd wit.

"Thank you, Ning." Hüi Wei rested his hand on the eunuch's shoulder for a moment and then was gone.

Ning shut the door and rubbed his hands together in glee. "I know not how long we have left to live, but at last, it is my turn to poke fun at Lan'xiu! I thought the day would never come! I wager she will be eating her dinner standing up for a day or two!" Then he composed his face, thinking of the tasks at hand. "First, I must discover where these people keep their chickens. And I am sure Lan'xiu will enjoy a bath when she awakes." Chuckling to himself, Ning went to the back of the house and down the stairs to find Jia.

CHAPTER EIGHT

HÜI WEI hurried to put the harem square behind him before the sky grew light. He had never yet been spied having lingered so long in one of the houses. As a soldier, one did not wish to give the curious reason to suppose one could be seduced from one's duty by the pleasures of the flesh. Hüi made it his custom to be sparing in all things in the name of discipline. Besides, if only to save Mei Ju pain, he would prefer to be gone before she took her accustomed place at her window.

He had seen her watching for him before when he visited other houses, and he schooled his face to be serious and thoughtful, although he wanted nothing more than to shout his triumph from the rooftops. Never with any woman he had deflowered had he experienced the thrill of conquest so strongly as when he had taken Lan'xiu.

The beautiful young man's responses had been artlessly genuine; he had never experienced the tender touch of a lover before. He had come to their bed pure, Hüi Wei was positive. Taking his virginity and giving him pleasure in the same night made him feel proud. He, an accomplished lover, had only taken Lan'xiu on the first of many steps to discovering a universe of untapped pleasure together, and it made him feel dangerously adventurous. His cock felt heavy and a burst of adrenaline made the prospect of a bath and breakfast seem tame.

He turned his steps toward the stable. The stablemaster was not yet about, and the stable boys were still cleaning out the stalls. When they saw him, they stood with their mouths hanging open, not knowing enough even to bow. Ordinarily, he might have voiced a few sharp words to school them, but he was anxious to be off and away. He had much to think about. Instead of exhorting one of the stunned lads to do it, he saddled his own horse and trotted to the city gates.

His soldiers were alert and on guard, he was glad to see. One of them sprang forward to open the gate for him with a sharp salute. The clatter of his horse's hooves on the stones of the street echoed against the walls of the tightly packed houses. Hüi Wei permitted himself a smile at the thought of some sleepy merchant opening his window to shout his irritation out into the street and retreating when he saw it was the lord governor making the untimely row.

He turned his mount east, heading toward the rising sun. In that direction lay a hill where he went often to look down upon the city and province he guarded in the name of the emperor. There were times when a man needed to be alone to think.

When he reached the apex of the tallest hill, Hüi Wei dismounted and allowed his horse to graze in the grass. The horse was well trained for war; he would not run away and leave his rider behind.

Looking down upon the fortress of his palace, Hüi Wei was able to pick out the seventh house of his harem, gilded by the light of the rising sun. He wondered if Lan'xiu was awake yet and if he would wake thinking of him. Hüi chuckled with pride at the thought that he had certainly given Lan'xiu enough to make him remember, even if it was only a sore ass.

It had been some years since Hüi Wei had had sex more than one time in a single night, and the score of three in itself was a source of pride for him. There was something about Lan'xiu—of course he had submitted to Hüi's desires most properly, denying him nothing he had demanded, but there was something secret and intriguing about him.

His head was filled with the novelty of making love to another man, feeling again the firmness of Lan's muscles rather than yielding womanly softness, Lan's resilience no matter how hard Hüi had fucked him, the eagerness with which he responded, the astonished gratitude at the pleasure Hüi had given him—

Hüi Wei closed his eyes to better savor the vision of the lushly rounded bottom he had taken, the only softness of the finely muscled body. His hand strayed to the bulge in his trousers and he rubbed himself. If only Lan'xiu had been there, by the gods' pleasure, Hüi would have taken him again!

His eyes flew open at the thought. Already all thoughts of killing Lan'xiu or sending him away had flown from his mind. Hüi could barely wait to see Lan again.

And yet….

He remembered his conversation with Ning. How difficult would it be to continue to keep Lan'xiu in his harem and prevent anyone from finding out? Would he need to school his tongue to refer to him as her? What about children? If he continued to have her lantern lit, it would soon become obvious to everyone that Lan'xiu was unable to bear children. How would he explain that? Not that he needed more children; he had been blessed with many, but a man had his reputation to think of. If he could not get his youngest wife with child, some might question his potency, a dangerous position to be in when one was a general and governor and entrusted with keeping the emperor's northern border safe.

The difficulty of how to keep Lan'xiu's secret and still get what he wanted consumed Hüi's brain. All his life he had punctiliously made his responsibility to the emperor his first priority—now his entire being cried to him to grab what he wanted! He realized that before this, doing his duty had been easy. Lying with women had been a pleasurable diversion in his busy schedule; making love to Lan'xiu was a sublime experience, one he feared he might never tire of.

It was not that the act of a man loving a man was thought to be immoral in his society. Taking a male lover if he so chose, seeing as he had discharged his duties to emperor and ancestors by siring male children to carry his name forward, would occasion no censure or even comment. In fact, for the first time, it dawned on Hüi that many might well believe he had taken Jiang as a lover, for they were often together.

But the exigencies of his life might not permit him to do just as he liked without consideration of his responsibilities. He had always been a private man, and flaunting a male lover was not like him. It would give his enemies ammunition and another avenue of vulnerability to pursue. Besides, it seemed that Lan'xiu preferred to dress and live as a woman, although Hüi did not understand that impulse at all. That in itself created what seemed an insurmountable difficulty.

Happiness drained away from Hüi Wei, and he groaned in misery. What he ought to do is carry out Lan'xiu's wish and send him to live in a monastery.

"One cannot fall in love in a single night!" he cried out in rebuke of himself. "You are infatuated, nothing more. This isn't real. It will pass."

But he knew that was not true. The arrival of Lan'xiu had proved more momentous than even his brother, Wu Min, could have hoped. Taking Lan'xiu had thrown Hüi Wei's entire life into turmoil, and for the first time, his future was not clear to him. He did not know what to do.

CAPTAIN WEN was waiting impatiently for his rotation assignment as commander of the household guard to come to an end so he could once again take up the real work of a soldier. Guarding the harem was not precisely challenging work. Located within a fortress city, within the walls that surrounded the palace of General Qiang, within yet another set of walls made of stone and barred with iron, it would have taken a determined man and an army to make it within to carry off any of the wives, who presumably would have proved an unwilling hostage and therefore not easy to handle.

Seeing as no outsider ever received permission to see the concubines, there could be nothing to motivate such an attack, unless an enemy sought to undo the general with emotional distress. Captain Wen permitted himself a small smile at the thought. General Hüi Wei was a disciplined man, a hardened soldier. He couldn't imagine the man would show distress even if one of his wives was to be killed. To watch him enter the walls of the household, one would have thought he was there to inspect the barracks. Besides, there were easier ways to get his attention than through the wives.

Being as he was captain of the guard, Wen knew the true reason his men were stationed there. It was not so much to keep people out as to keep the people inside *in*. In particular, they were there to keep Second Wife from escaping or hurting any of the other women.

Being a careful man, Captain Wen had made his observations of Second Wife in the spirit of knowing his enemy. For his taste, her beauty was too obvious, but he had noticed that some of his men were susceptible to the sexual snares she set for them. When Lord Jiang had posted Wen, he had suggested strongly that he change the men's assignments weekly so that none would have time to fall under Second Wife's spell and possibly be lured into complicity to enable one of her plots. It puzzled Wen that his men did not respond to the sweeter beauty of some of the other wives, but instead were entranced by the unstable but fascinating Second Wife.

Therefore Wen found Jiang's advice to be wise and followed it. To his credit, Second Wife's schemes had been frustrated at almost every turn, but he found it fatiguing to always try to anticipate the machinations of a woman with nothing but revenge to occupy her clever brain and many empty hours to fill. Wen would welcome a posting to a front line somewhere after this. He needed a nice, relaxing war for a holiday.

He was usually up before dawn, patrolling the square for signs of activity on the off chance Second Wife managed to find someone to carry out her errands of evil. Wen had already frustrated the attempt of one maid to smuggle a weapon in to Second Wife, so he had found it profitable to be on the alert in the small hours.

It was thus that he was entertained and puzzled by the strange activities of last night.

First General Hüi Wei had entered the compound. Wen had noticed the twitch of a curtain at First Wife's windows; it was known that she always watched when Hüi Wei was within the walls to see where he went.

Hüi Wei had seemed hesitant, which surprised Wen, as his leader was a decisive man in general. Finally Hüi went completely around the square, as if he knew not which house he planned to visit although the lantern burned brightly at the seventh.

After Hüi Wei was admitted, Wen expected nothing further of note and had returned to his quarters to nap, rising again after the midnight bell was struck to witness Hüi Wei leave as was his habit. The moon was high, although a mere crescent in the sky, but the stars were bright enough to see by had there been anything to see.

Hüi Wei lingered within the seventh house. At least, so Captain Wen surmised. It was possible that Hüi Wei had merely paid a short courtesy call and left promptly, but Wen had observed the Princess Lan'xiu when she walked in the square or visited with First Wife. She was one of the few women whose beauty he could appreciate. Like Second Wife, Lan'xiu was quite lovely, but despite her beautifully sculpted face, a softer quality seemed to shine from within. Despite her obvious unhappiness, there was no hardness in her expression.

Therefore Wen assumed that Hüi Wei had found good reasons to remain within the seventh house. Captain Wen returned to his quarters to take another nap because it was not part of his job to record Hüi Wei's comings and goings. When he arose to make his first patrol at dawn, the sky was just welcoming the sun, but it was still mostly dark. A movement caught his eyes and he was astonished to see Hüi Wei hurrying across the square. His soldiers opened the gate for the general, and he slipped away before the first rosy fingers of dawn could reach into the square.

That was very interesting indeed.

Slivers of light at two windows told Wen that several other occupants of the household also found the general's activities of interest.

No light burned in the second story windows of Lan'xiu's house, but naturally the lamps burned in the kitchens as breakfast was being prepared. Wen was about to turn away when a rectangle of gold caught his eye and the princess's eunuch emerged from the kitchen door, looking about the square in a suspicious manner. This was just the sort of activity Wen was trained to watch for.

Accordingly, he kept his eyes trained on the slim man, expecting to see him slip away to another house, perhaps with a message or even a weapon. Being as the princess and her retainer were new, there was no telling what mischief they meant to get up to, not that Wen was unequal to the task. And the eunuch was rather attractive, so it didn't hurt the eyes to watch him.

Of all the lurid possibilities that occurred to Wen, he never expected to witness the retainer of a princess steal to the communal kitchen gardens, take a guarded glance around and then sneak into the hen house! When the eunuch emerged, holding a lifeless chicken by the head, the body dangling from his hand, Wen almost laughed out loud. He reproved himself, for it was possible this was some poison plot, but then he laughed again as the eunuch scuttled back into the seventh house, trying to stuff the chicken inside his robe.

He would have to inquire of the cook later. Perhaps this plot was nothing more than the princess expressing a desire for chicken soup, but he would need to make sure. Wen laughed quietly to himself and then sighed. It would be good to get back to border patrol.

CHAPTER NINE

"WILL you wear the primrose or the jade green?" Ning asked, hovering at the wardrobe.

"I will wear the silver." Lan'xiu said listlessly, watching the rain obscure the view across the square as it streamed down her window.

"First Wife has invited you to meet the other wives formally for the first time. You must look your best," Ning scolded. "That gray is dull, fit for sitting by the window on a rainy day, that's all. Or scrubbing the floor. You should give it to one of the maids. The idea of you going about in the color of mud or sand!"

"It has a purple lining," Lan'xiu said.

"Brilliant!" Ning said, sarcasm heavy in his voice. "You can wear it turned, inside to the outside. What is amiss with you? You are a princess; you *must* put on a show worthy of your rank!"

"I am no princess here," Lan'xiu said.

The desolation in her voice made Ning's heart ache for her. He knew however much she might dread meeting the other wives, it was the fact that her lantern had remained dark in the weeks that followed Hüi Wei's first visit that made her so sad. However, no matter how closely their lives were entwined, this was not a subject he could discuss openly. Any servant would be forbidden from speaking freely about the master. "Lan'xiu, you are the most beautiful princess in all of China. If you dressed in a rice sack and bare feet you would outshine all of those women anyway."

"Then it doesn't really matter what I wear, does it?" Lan'xiu pointed out waspishly. "And have you checked every princess personally by way of comparison?"

In an odd way, Ning rejoiced to hear her snap; at least she was not sinking into the slough of despond if she was still able to ignite a spark of anger. "You do no honor to your husband if you dress like a servant. Nor to your hostess. First Wife has been very gracious to you and she is not required to treat you well. Besides, you do yourself no honor to wear your emotions on your sleeve in public. That is not how you were brought up."

"You are right, First Wife has been most kind," Lan'xiu said, bowing her head. The fact that Mei Ju could have treated her cruelly with impunity was true; as first wife, not even Hüi Wei would have rebuked her if she had ignored, mistreated, or even struck Lan'xiu. "It was wrong of me to give way. I will wear the turquoise robe with the chrysanthemums in her honor."

"A very auspicious choice, Lan'xiu. And a delicate compliment for First Wife," Ning approved. Although he would never call her by name, he knew well Mei Ju was named for the flower. He withdrew the hanfu in question, a shimmering turquoise silk heavily embroidered with gold chrysanthemums at the neckline, hem, and sleeves. He selected a black under-tunic with gold and green designs to peek out at the neckline.

Lan'xiu stood patiently as Ning arranged her green satin sash, embroidered with cranes of good luck, and hung the ornaments of silver coins and carved jade beads from the buckle attached to the sash. She sat before her mirror so Ning could place jeweled sticks in her hair; her favorites, topped with cloisonné butterflies enameled in rainbow colors. Delicate antenna of wire quivered with every movement, making the pearl tips move gracefully as she inclined her head.

The same long silver earrings dangling with the turquoise drops adorned her ears. Ning slid a ring that had belonged to Lan's mother on the middle finger of her left hand. It was shaped like a dragonfly and the body was studded with gems. The wings were almost transparent, woven of thin wire into lacy swirling patterns to resemble the actual wings of the insect, and large enough to extend over the back of her hand.

He stood back to assess her appearance and smoothed back a stray hair. Then he powdered her face one last time and touched up her already reddened lips. "You look beautiful, as always, Lan'xiu. The gods will make the other wives turn jade green with envy."

Lan'xiu gave a sigh but her lips curved into a smile that hurt Ning to witness, although he would not burden her with his feelings. He could not know how she felt after her one night with the general, but if only as a matter of pride, it had to gall that her lantern had remained dark and her nights cold and lonely. And she went now to face the very women who knew better than anyone that she had been left alone since Hüi's first visit.

"Do not let them see how you feel," Ning said quietly, his mouth near her ear in case of eavesdroppers. "It would not be seemly in a princess."

"Thank you, Ning," the princess said in her lovely voice. "You do well to remind me of how one must behave."

He patted her shoulder. "You will make me proud. You always do."

Lan'xiu stood up and smoothed her skirts. She took one last look in the mirror and scrutinized her appearance. "You've made me as presentable as can be. I am ready."

Ning followed her down the stairs to where soldiers stood ready as porters. It was not fitting that Princess Lan'xiu walk through the pouring rain in her embroidered slippers, so they would carry her to First Wife's house in a covered chair. Ning unfurled an umbrella, resigned to following behind on foot.

It was a short trip across the square, but for such an occasion, the soldiers bore the princess around the park upon the stone pavement, rather than through it. Ning was secretly grateful for this attention to formality. He was getting wet enough and did not relish sinking ankle deep into the mud so plentiful in the park. He hoped that First Wife would allow him and the other servants to descend to the kitchen to warm themselves rather than make them shiver in the hallway.

After he had helped the princess out of the chair under the covered walkway, escorted her into the house, and taken her cloak, Ning bowed deeply, hoping to convey to her without words that she should disport herself like a princess and not let the other women outshine her. Then he gratefully followed a maid who showed him the way downstairs to the kitchen.

LAN'XIU paused in the doorway, her heart beating so hard she was afraid the other women would hear it and know how frightened she was. She had visited Mei Ju since the first time they had met but had spent most of her time playing with the children, who accepted her uncritically as a large but amusing playmate. The other wives would be sure to examine her person, dress, and jewels with sharp eyes, and they might not be so kind. When she walked into the sitting room, she forced herself to smile and bow deeply, as befitted the seventh and lowliest of the concubines gathered there.

She remained bent low until she heard Mei Ju's voice, admonishing her to come in.

"My dear Lan'xiu, don't stand there like a ninny. We observe no ceremony here. Come in and meet the other wives."

Lan'xiu straightened up and advanced into the room, which seemed filled with beautiful women, although there were only five and one was Mei Ju, with whom she was already familiar. She was glad she had worn a pretty dress instead of the drab one Ning had despised, for they were all beautifully attired in brilliant silk robes.

"Lady First Wife," she said, going to her knees to kiss the gold ring on Mei Ju's hand, a symbol of her higher status.

Mei Ju smiled at this show of respect. "Please, be seated here at my right, Princess Lan'xiu. I will pour you some tea to warm you up. It is terrible weather, is it not?"

One of the concubines spoke up. "It is good for the farmers."

Another girl laughed. "You make it easy for us to remember you were a farmer's daughter, Fen."

"Second Wife Ci'an has been unfortunately taken ill and could not attend this day," Mei Ju explained. "Fen, who speaks often of the farmers, is third wife; Huan is fourth." The two women sat together upon the divan, close enough together to wreath their arms about each other's waists.

Lan'xiu bowed to them from her chair. They nodded back to her in return.

Then Mei Ju indicated a pretty woman with a round moon face and tranquil expression. "That is Alute, sixth wife, and the most restful creature." She indicated the last woman, slim as a sprite and fairly quivering with energy. "And Bai is fifth wife, completely the opposite. She lives with the faeries conversing in her skull and is off with the pixies most nights. But she makes us all laugh."

"Even Ci'an," Bai piped up. Her face was like that of a pixie, full of mischief and light—not precisely pretty but very engaging. "You must forgive me for saying so right out loud, Princess, but you are so very beautiful! I have never seen a girl as lovely as you are!"

"And Bai is not much for proper manners," Huan said officiously. "I hope you will forgive her."

"Oh, Huan, you are not my mother!" Bai rolled her eyes comically.

"There is nothing to forgive," Lan'xiu said in her soft voice. "I take no offense."

"I'm sure you must be used to being stared at," Fen said enviously.

"Where I come from, the women live apart. I usually saw only my mother and my servant," Lan'xiu said. "It is you who must forgive me. I fear I am not very clever in conversation. I've not been in a room with so many people often."

"The household did not meet as we do?" Fen asked. "That is barbaric!"

Huan interjected, "Fen has advanced ideas on the subject of rights."

"The… household there… was… different." Lan'xiu did not wish to explain any of the details of her old home. It had been a relief when she was able to shake the dust of her homeland from her shoes, even if it meant facing an almost certain death in a strange land.

"If I looked like you, I would dance and sing all the day long," Bai said. "But your eyes are full of sadness. And yet your smile says there is happiness inside. What magic would it take to coax your joy to come out to play?"

"You already dance and sing all the day long, Bai," Mei Ju said affectionately. "I can't think of a single thing that could elevate your spirits even more."

"Well, it would be nice to be so beautiful," Alute put in placidly. "And a princess. Did you wear a crown?"

Lan'xiu squirmed uncomfortably. "No, I usually dressed much plainer than I am today, especially when I was riding my horse—" She put a hand up to cover her mouth in dismay. She had not meant to reveal even that much.

"I used to ride," Fen said. "But only to the fields. And I led the horse home at the end of the day, because it had worked so hard and was as tired as I."

"It seems you might have liked a ride home yourself after a day's work in the fields," Huan said, staring intensely at her friend. "This life is more fitting for someone as pretty as you."

"Once I learned the rules here," Fen said with an answering smile. "At first it seemed strange not to go to the fields, and to dress in one's best every day." She gazed admiringly at her hands, which were slim and shapely. "And now my hands are soft, not hard from work. And I am able to grow my nails long."

Lan'xiu noted with interest that Fen alone of the women wore jeweled nail guards on each finger, which unfortunately made her pretty hands look a bit like claws. With a little trepidation, she asked, "What rules must I follow here? I would cause no offense through my ignorance."

Fen and Huan looked at each other and giggled while Mei Ju looked both pained and embarrassed at their response. Alute seemed to feel she was not required to answer any question as long as the others were there to do so, but Bai knew no such shyness.

"First Wife takes precedence in all matters and governs within the household. She settles any disagreement. Treat the other wives as you would be treated, except for Ci'an. It is not permitted to sneak outside and quench the flame that burns in another wife's lantern—"

"Bai!" Mei Ju exclaimed in protest. "No one has ever—"

"Ci'an has thought about it. You know she has," Bai said. "It is only her locked door that prevents her from doing it."

"I am sure the Princess Lan'xiu would never consider doing anything so ill-bred," Mei Ju said, still shocked.

Bai pointed to Lan'xiu, who had covered her smile. "See! A little bit of the happiness has leaked out! It was only a jest, Princess. I would never suggest that you would do such a thing—"

"I wouldn't," Lan'xiu retorted and giggled again.

"I just wanted to see you laugh." Bai folded her hands with a satisfied smile.

"You are a mischievous imp," Mei Ju scolded, but then she smiled. "But I cannot be angry with one who always manages to make me laugh. Just take care you are on good behavior when my husband lights your lantern."

"He likes it when I misbehave," Bai said with a sly smile. "He spanks me. I like it, so I am very bad sometimes. He says he knows just how to make me behave myself."

Aghast, Mei Ju turned to Lan'xiu. "Don't listen to her, Lan'xiu. Bai is just teasing you. Hüi Wei would never strike a woman—"

"Oh ho! He wouldn't?" Bai chortled, delighting in the shocked look Alute was giving her. Fen and Huan were pointedly ignoring her, their faces flushed with embarrassment.

"He is too gentle and kind. He is master here and we all strive to please him. There is no need for him to use force," Mei Ju said sternly.

"I hope not," Lan'xiu said faintly. She was no longer sure who to believe. It seemed that each wife saw a very different man through the prism of her own experience with Hüi Wei. She dared to sneak a look at Bai, who gave her a knowing smile when their eyes met and rubbed her bottom with one hand as if it were still smarting.

"Please have some more tea, Princess," Mei Ju said, desperately trying to restore decorum.

"Please, call me Lan'xiu," Lan said. "I am no princess here, only the humblest concubine."

"Well, at least one person mouths the truth at this celebration of prevarication and lies," a harsh voice said.

Lan'xiu jumped and turned to see who had spoken.

"Oh gods, Ci'an has made a miraculous recovery and just in time to join us," Bai groaned.

A woman posed in the doorway, as dramatically beautiful as Lan'xiu, although in a completely different manner. Her hair was coal black and shiny as a panther, her skin was dead white, which made her crimson lips gleam like cherries against the snow. Her eyes were long and dark and glittered like black ice in winter. Her face had a hard look, as if there wasn't an ounce of extra flesh on her body, none of the comforting roundness of Mei Ju or the softness of Alute. She was handsome rather than beautiful and almost masculine in her features. While still youthful and attractive, Ci'an looked as if she would not age well. She wore a black cheongsam embroidered in red with a patterned white sash and large gold earrings hanging nearly to her shoulders. There was no ring on any of her fingers.

Lan'xiu stood up and found they were of equal height, which evidently did not please Ci'an. Lan'xiu bowed low, as befitted the last concubine giving respect to the second.

"Yes, just in time to bring this party to life. I have heard much about your arrival, Princess of Nothing," Ci'an said. Her voice simmered with rage, and she looked daggers at Lan'xiu. "A pretty enough bit of fluff, but you have no rank here and your lantern was lit only once. I know you spread your legs for my husband, but he has not returned to give you a second jab. He must have been disappointed with your performance. What a great pity for you. I fear you cannot be the new favorite." She waved a hand at Alute. "The stupid little pigeon here currently bears that title. My husband greatly prefers an empty hole with nothing much to say."

Lan'xiu felt her face flush and wondered how this woman could know that it rankled so to see the other lanterns lit while hers remained dark. It would not do to reveal how she longed for her lord to visit her again, to be held once more in those strong arms, to feel the weight of his body bearing down upon hers. She had thought that perhaps Hüi Wei had truly been as captivated with her as she had been with him, but alas, it seemed not to be so. She wanted to look away from Ci'an's cold, triumphant eyes, but Princess of Nothing or not, she was still a princess, and she was not going to let this woman stare her down. She bowed punctiliously before she sat down again. "Greetings, Second Wife Ci'an."

Mei Ju spoke up sharply. "Hüi Wei is *my* husband, *Second Concubine*! You will refer to him as our husband as befits a mere third-rank concubine! It is by my forbearance alone that you bear the title of second *wife* at all!"

Surprised to hear such an authoritative tone from so gentle a woman, Lan'xiu kept her eyes on Ci'an to watch her response.

"Yes, Lady First Wife. I dared to forget my lowly, ignominious place here for a moment." Ci'an bit her words off as if sinking her teeth into raw meat and spat them at Mei Ju.

In the silent battle of stares that followed, it was Ci'an who dropped her eyes first and Lan'xiu had an inkling of how much it enraged the woman to submit. The needs of safety in her own home had honed Lan'xiu's skills at lip reading, and she was able to discern the words that Ci'an muttered to herself. "If I had but borne a son...."

A movement at the door drew Lan'xiu's attention. Two soldiers came to stand inside the threshold, their watchful gaze fixed on Second Wife. Ci'an noticed them as well and went to a chair opposite Mei Ju's and sat down, waving her hand at the soldiers as if to dismiss them.

"Be at ease, my handsome young prison-keepers. I promise I have not brought my poison or dagger with me. I am not in the mood for murder today." Ci'an's teeth were sharp and pointed when she smiled. "I came only to get a glimpse of the new acquisition. I can hardly wait until Mei Ju invites us all to pat your swollen belly when you increase." She leaned forward as if to speak confidentially, but her loud voice ensured that all could hear. "They tell me your sheets didn't show much blood the morning after. Who knows how many chickens have lost their lives in the name of virginity? Rumor has it one disappeared the next morning from the kitchen gardens."

Her cheeks flaming, Lan'xiu sat up even straighter. She opened her mouth to retort and then closed it. Just because Ci'an seemed incapable of following the rules of polite society, it was no good reason for her to sink to the same depth. Instead she managed to reply calmly, "I am fond of chicken dumplings."

Bai burst into laughter. "I like a good chicken dinner myself. With rice and cashews! What is your favorite nut, Lan'xiu?"

"I am partial to almonds," Lan'xiu said, turning to Bai with a slight smile of relief.

"No, the right answer should have been me, Bai!" Fifth Wife giggled at her own wit.

"Almond milk is good for the skin," Alute piped up. She stroked her fingers over one of her own smooth cheeks with pleasure.

Ci'an rolled her eyes. "Always the bright one, isn't she? And Bai will now tell us how *her* favorite nuts are the ones within the nutsack that hangs between the legs of *our* husband, and Fen will lecture us on how the peasants put nuts by for the winter and give us recipes that substitute nuts for meat as if we were ever expected to cook a meal ourselves, and then Huan will applaud her and tell us *again* how brilliant and forward thinking her *dear* friend Fen is."

"When did you start to study gastronomy?" Bai inquired. "But then, you have so *much* time on your hands to study." She fluttered her lashes while giving Ci'an a disingenuous smile.

Lan'xiu had to admire Bai's imperviousness to Ci'an's venom. Nothing seemed to daunt her, and it seemed a good habit to acquire if one were forced to consort with Second Wife.

Ci'an appeared to be simmering with rage, but then she laughed instead of lashing out. "Bai, I vow you alone know how to spike my guns. If only the others were smart enough to learn from you." With exaggerated courtesy she bowed to Lan'xiu. "It was my most humble honor to meet you, Princess Lan'xiu. I hope you will be as happy a captive here as I within this gilded cage." With that she swept from the room, knocking over a small table bearing her teacup as she went, not even reacting when it shattered on the floor, splashing the tea everywhere.

The two soldiers fell in beside her and presently Lan'xiu caught sight of them carrying umbrellas to shield Second Wife as she returned to her home next door.

"Lan'xiu, I apologize on Second Wife's behalf for that extremely vulgar display." Mei Ju gave a delicate shiver. "If only Ci'an could find some comfort in the company of the rest of the wives. I fear she is a very miserable woman."

"Or deranged," Huan snapped.

"In which case there should be some provision made for her. Perhaps she should be removed to a home for lunatics," Fen said seriously. "What do you think, Alute?"

"Oh yes," Alute agreed vaguely. She had been looking at her reflection in the shiny silver tray on the table.

"*What* a party!" Bai crowed. "Fen, have I ever told you about the time—"

Lan'xiu stifled a giggle. Despite the disagreeable way Ci'an had expressed herself, she seemed to be sadly correct about the predictable dullness of the household parties.

CHAPTER TEN

LAN'XIU tried not to be obvious about it, but he had taken to standing at his window, watching for the servant who lit the lanterns. He had not seen Hüi Wei nor had any message from him since their first and only night together, when Hüi had taken his flower. This night no torch had been borne into the harem square and no lantern had been lit. He sighed with disappointment mixed with a tiny bit of relief. At least he would not have to watch Hüi Wei enter the house of another wife and torture himself with thoughts of Hüi making love to anyone but him.

He wondered if, after all, Hüi had found him revolting and resolved never to return to him. Perhaps death would be preferable to rejection. To have known physical love for the first time, to have felt that powerful body against his, taking him… he shivered as a thrill went through him. Their one night together had been heaven. If that night were all he would ever have to remember, it would have to do. It was more than he had ever hoped for in his life, even if he was destined to spend the remainder of it sequestered behind these prison walls, alone, but somehow the memory didn't seem very comforting in the face of his yearning.

Alone except for Ning, of course. Ning was a comfort but also a goad, pushing, chattering, wondering, and gossiping.

Earlier that day Ning had decided that Lan'xiu needed to brush up on his swordplay and made him breathless in their practice session.

"Is it I or you who needs to practice?" Lan'xiu had asked tartly.

"Perhaps both. I do not wish to get fat," Ning said complacently. "Eunuchs are prone to gain weight, you know."

"And so you torment me to achieve your own ends," Lan'xiu grumbled.

Ning merely grinned at him, making a hole between his thumb and forefinger and sliding his other thumb in and out. "Not all exercise is the same, is it? It takes two to—"

"Shut up!" Lan ordered crossly. "Go away. I want a bath. Prepare hot water for me."

"Very well. I will have the fires lit."

Ning left the room, and Lan'xiu was able to put off his false smile. He hoped that even Ning could not guess what terrible thoughts haunted him. In his own home, before his mother had died, Lan had been permitted to ride his horse free through the long grasses, the wind in his hair, going where he pleased. Slowly the nets of intrigue had been drawn more closely about him, and he realized too late what fate his brother planned for him. And now here he was, trapped in a harem where, if the truth were known, he had no right to be, waiting for a man who likely had never given him a second thought. Lan had worn his chosen disguise for so long that until Hüi had ripped it off, Lan had almost forgotten who he truly was. Now his body was alive with need and want, and his soul craved the love he thought he had felt in Hüi's arms.

It was a poor comfort to rejoice that no other wife enjoyed Hüi Wei's company tonight either, but it was all he had to cling to. Lan wondered where Hüi was and what he was doing, envying the freedom that allowed him to come and go at whim.

The door opened, and expecting Ning's return, Lan'xiu did not turn around. Terror flared within him when hands larger than Ning's grabbed him roughly, squeezing his shoulders so hard they hurt.

He was spun violently to face his captor, struggling feebly to free himself until he saw it was Hüi Wei. A welcoming smile died on his lips at the intent look in Hüi's eyes.

Hüi ripped the hanfu down, trapping Lan'xiu's arms and baring his throat and shoulders. Then he bent his head and bit sharply into the crook on Lan's neck, soothing the sting an instant later with his tongue.

Then Hüi drove his tongue so deep into Lan's mouth, he thought he might suffocate. Lan breathed hard through his nose, allowing Hüi to ravage his mouth, bite his lips, suck his tongue so hard it hurt.

"On your knees!" Hüi ordered in a deep, thick voice when he ended the kiss. He forced Lan down.

Lan swayed, his arms still trapped in his hanfu, his face inches from the bulge Hüi was struggling to free from his trousers. Lan could smell the musky scent of arousal. He could feel the heat on his cheek.

Hüi succeeded in freeing his cock and pushed it against Lan's lips. Obediently, Lan opened his mouth. He felt a hand on the back of his head, forcing him to take in the hard shaft. He relaxed his throat, breathing through his nose so as not to gag, afraid that Hüi would push his cock right down.

Hüi set up a rhythm, pushing his cock between Lan's lips, forcing the young man to swallow it all. Lan tried desperately to give pressure with his lips and tongue, instinctively divining what his master desired. Some demon of lust seemed to be driving Hüi, and Lan didn't understand it, but it made him happy to feel so desired.

Abruptly, Hüi withdrew from Lan's mouth and gave another order. "Bend over. Stick your ass in the air."

Lan struggled to free his arms but felt his face pushed into the carpet and his hips lifted. Hüi lifted the skirts of his hanfu, and there was a ripping sound as he rent the silken panties Lan wore. Lan flinched when a hand landed hard on his ass, and the sound of the slap was sharp in the quiet room.

He gasped at the feel of something hot and wet against his hole. He was in no position to look, but it had to be Hüi's tongue, licking at him, pushing inside him. He had never felt anything like it. Hüi's hands and cock were hard; this invasion was soft and velvet, setting up soft waves of unknown pleasure. Soft lips applied suction and the humming started. The vibration nearly drove him mad with arousal. Lan became aware that his cock was hard and aching, dripping. He wanted to be fucked so badly, but Hüi seemed intent on teasing him. His tongue danced over Lan's throbbing hole, licking, then stabbing at it, sliding inside. Finally, he added two fingers, driving them in and out in a steady rhythm.

Lan gasped for breath at this sudden assault, but he loved every minute of it. He would gladly pay with his imprisonment to be held captive by his lover in such a fashion.

The fingers were withdrawn and he felt Hüi's thighs pressed against his. Lan braced himself and felt his entire body rocked forward as Hüi roughly pushed his cock all the way inside Lan's clenching channel. Lan let out a cry at the burning pain and moaned when Hüi pulled out all the way, dragging the biggest part of the head out of Lan's hole with excruciating slowness.

Lan gasped once more at the exquisite pain when Hüi penetrated him again, entering him with equal force. Then Hüi began to pound him, hard and fast, chasing his own orgasm with no thought to Lan's pleasure. Lan tried to work a hand free to touch himself; his cock ached and he needed to come so badly.

Hüi stopped his fucking and used Lan's sash to bind his hands behind him. "Not until I permit you." Then he began thrusting again, holding Lan's slim hips in place.

Each thrust rocked Lan's whole body, and he was helpless to resist the movement. He enjoyed the pummeling, each stroke ravishing him with pleasure, Hüi's cock filling him and making him quiver with sensation.

Hard fingers dug into his hips and Lan knew he would have bruises tomorrow, but he wanted them. Any mark to remember this and to remind him of who he belonged to. Hüi's strokes grew shorter but harder, and with one last thrust, he buried himself to the balls.

Lan could feel the fire of Hüi's release fill him inside and rejoiced that he had served his lover's needs in this new mood. After a moment, Hüi grunted and, still embedded within Lan's ass, rolled onto his side on the carpet, pulling Lan with him, keeping him impaled on his still hard and throbbing cock.

With one hand he pulled Lan's chin to turn his head and ravaged his mouth again. When he released Lan, his hand wandered down to pinch and twist at one of Lan's nipples, sending a frisson of pleasure straight to his groin. Lan groaned in frustration and struggled in his bonds.

Hüi's hand roamed still farther down, and finally he wrapped his fingers around Lan's straining cock.

"Yes," Lan hissed.

He felt Hüi's chest move and heard the rumble of laughter, but Hüi merely spat on his hand and stroked Lan's cock, rubbing his thumb in the fluid at the tip to tickle the head and ridge.

Lan's hips were moving urgently. Hüi held him imprisoned against his chest with one arm while he stroked with the other. Lan arched his neck and felt teeth nipping at his throat. Hüi moved his hips, reminding Lan that he still had a cock up his ass, adding to his pleasure. Finally, with a hoarse cry, Lan erupted like a fireworks display, sending pearly drops of liquid over Hüi's hand. He was panting when he came to rest.

"Hello, my little Lan'xiu," Hüi said softly into the skin of Lan's throat. "I missed you."

"And I you, my Lord," Lan breathed. "You forgot to light the lantern. I wasn't expecting you."

"I didn't forget. I snuck in," Hüi said, sounding pleased with himself. "It was more fun that way."

"Do you—" Lan stopped short. He would not ask anything about what Hüi did with the others.

"Only with you. Everything is different with you."

Lan felt the bonds around his wrists loosen and stretched his arms. "You will soon need to buy me a new wardrobe. This is the second hanfu you have ruined."

"And well worth it. I will buy you a thousand robes if I must, for the pleasure of tearing them off you." Hüi kissed Lan's bare shoulder before letting his cock slide free. "I wish we could have a bath."

"I sent Ning to prepare one for me. Perhaps the water is ready," Lan said hopefully.

"Shall we go see?" Hüi got to his feet and helped Lan up. In contrast to his previous roughness, he undressed Lan gently, kissing the satin skin as he exposed it. When he came to a scar, white against the skin of Lan's back, he traced over it with a fingertip. "What is this scar from?"

"A knife went in, wide but not deep enough."

For the second time there was steel in Lan's voice. Hüi turned Lan to face him. "Who did this to you?"

"My brother, Wu Min."

Lan'xiu did not wish to speak of it, and Hüi seemed to respect his reticence. "I am sorry," he said.

"It doesn't bother me anymore," Lan'xiu said, and then he claimed the right to undress Hüi in his turn, running his hands over firm biceps, hard chest, and rippling stomach muscles.

Then Hüi took Lan's hand, and they went together into the bathing room. "Did you like it?" he asked almost shyly.

Lan smiled. "I enjoyed it very much. Feel free to announce yourself that way anytime."

"I also like it slow and gentle at times," Hüi said, taking Lan's lips in a soft kiss.

"I like that too," Lan whispered, his lips resting against Hüi's.

Soaping and rinsing before entering the bath turned into a pleasurable ritual as Lan'xiu was permitted to explore the general's muscular body. He shivered as Hüi did the same for him, cleansing him with tender wonder.

Gently, Hüi picked Lan up, lifted him into the steaming bath, and then stepped in himself. He slid down to rest against the sloped back and pulled Lan to sit between his legs, leaning back against his chest.

Lan'xiu relaxed against the warmth of Hüi's body, watching the ripples of water lap at his thighs. He could feel Hüi's chest lifting him out of the water slightly with each breath. He was sleepy, and he listened to Hüi's voice as if in a dream.

"Have you cast a spell over me?" Hüi asked softly, as if lost in the same dream. "Are you some sorceress sent to steal my soul? For I feel that I am only half a man when I am apart from you. When I sleep you enter my dreams, but I cannot grasp hold of you. I reach for you and you disappear like the early morning mist, a beautiful phantom, and then gone in the golden sunlight."

"I am no phantasm, my Lord. Wrap your arms around me, feel my flesh pressed against yours. I am real."

"Tell me, do you love me as I love you?"

"I cannot say, for I know not how you feel about me. For myself, I can only say that I am but half-alive when you are not here with me." Lan'xiu reached up to touch Hüi's cheek and found it damp with tears. "I never knew I could feel so much love."

"Nor I," Hüi murmured. "If you are not a witch or a dream, then I must thank the gods for sending you to me, a treasure I did not know I wanted." He tightened his arms about Lan'xiu suddenly. "Oh, Lan'xiu, somehow I must engineer events so that we can be together more often. Can you be patient with me? When I have the lanterns lit elsewhere, I feel I am betraying you, but we must be careful."

"Because of Wu Min?"

"He is but one obstacle. I have always been careful not to show a preference for any of my wives," Hüi said. "Lest some scoundrel scheme to slay one of them to wound me. If I should lose you now, having just found you—"

Lan'xiu laughed joyously. "You will not, my Lord. I have a stake in this matter too. I will take great care to keep on living." He startled when Hüi Wei stood up, lifting him with him, but turned to wrap his arms about Hüi, looking at him questioningly.

Hüi got out of the bath, holding out his hand to assist Lan'xiu as if he were a delicate maiden. They stood dripping with their naked bodies pressed together. Hüi kissed Lan gently and reached for a cloth to dry him.

Lan'xiu accepted the attention and then took the cloth from Hüi to dry him in turn.

Holding Lan's hand, Hüi led him to the bed, laying him down and staring at him in silence. He reached for the oil, and Lan spread his legs wide. Hüi stroked over Lan's hole, teasing the tight entrance until he placed the tip of his finger against the opening and pushed slowly inside.

Lan gasped and arched as the finger penetrated him. Stroking his finger in and out, Hüi watched Lan's face for signs of discomfort, but there was none, only an expression of blissful pleasure.

When Hüi bent to suck first one nipple and then the other to a point, Lan'xiu writhed on the bed in ecstasy. The sensation seemed to go right to his cock, and added to the finger up his ass, he was in heaven.

Hüi withdrew his finger and crawled between Lan's thighs, stroking them with his palms. He bent and took Lan'xiu's cock in his mouth, clumsily, as if he'd never done this before. Lan put his forearm over his mouth to prevent the rather loud scream of pleasure from breaking loose. He really didn't require Ning's assistance at this point of the proceedings and didn't want to scare his servant with his enthusiastic expression of the pleasure the hot wet mouth was giving him. Suddenly he understood Hüi's earlier need for this service from him.

Hüi released him and wiped his mouth, grinning down at him. "I guess you liked that."

Lan moaned and held out his arms, fearing that later he would be embarrassed by the abandoned whimpers of need issuing from him, but right now he needed more.

He could feel his hole flex hungrily as Hüi rubbed the tip of his hard cock over it. Lan widened his legs even more, letting out a deep groan when Hüi pushed inside him. Hüi was still on his knees, edging closer to slide a little deeper with short thrusts. Lan couldn't wait to be filled, even though the stretching hurt him again.

Something about being so filled made him feel utterly owned and possessed. When Hüi was buried as deeply as he could be, he inched forward, kissing Lan's chest, throat, and face, until he was stretched full length on top of him.

Lan wrapped his legs around Hüi's, feeling a hand circle around his shoulders and cradle his head. Hüi couldn't seem to stop kissing his throat, even while his thrusts became longer and deeper. They moved as one, and Lan felt as if he were soaring amongst the clouds, propelled to even greater heights of pleasure with each stroke as their bodies moved together. Lan felt Hüi's grip tighten upon him. He couldn't move his arms, he was so wrapped up in the other man's embrace.

And then Hüi's tongue was in his mouth, plundering the depths in time with the cock plundering his ass. Lan writhed beneath his weight, feeling the spurt of his release as he convulsed with a powerful orgasm.

Then he was filled again with the wonderful hot essence of Hüi's orgasm and heard the other man's groan of release.

Together they drifted in a dream-like state of lazy surfeit, their bodies pressed so close they almost felt as one.

Gradually, their bodies relaxed, and inevitably they separated. Hüi pulled Lan to him, bringing him close so his head rested upon Hüi's shoulder. They lay together, their breathing synchronized, almost not daring to speak lest they break the mood.

Finally, Hüi sighed again. "Why do you enjoy wearing the dress of a woman?"

Lan'xiu gave him a secretive smile. "They are much nicer to the touch, the silks and satins. There is more to choose from, and they are made in pretty colors. The softness next to my skin gives me pleasure." He drew his hand along his inner thigh, rejoicing to see Hüi's eyes widen as they tracked his caress. "Besides, I simply… feel pretty dressed like that. I like it."

"You can handle a sword. Against an opponent more your size and strength, I would back you for the win," Hüi mused in a wondering voice. "You have been well taught."

"I shall remember to tell Ning you said so," Lan'xiu said. "He will appreciate the compliment."

"When I took you before, I would never have been as rough with any of my other wives, but you were fine with as hard a pounding as I have dealt."

"More than fine," Lan'xiu said. "Can't you accept that, with you, in bed, I am a man as much as you, but when I go out, I enjoy the thrill of wearing pretty silk dresses and hiding behind a fan?"

Hüi rolled atop Lan, looking down into his laughing eyes. "And I enjoy looking at you and knowing that under those dresses are silken underthings—"

"That you enjoy ripping off me—"

"Very much," Hüi agreed, lowering his head to mouth one dark nipple, enjoying feeling the nub of flesh harden again under his lips and tongue.

Rather breathlessly, Lan said, "The budget for upkeep of the household will increase if you keep spoiling my clothes."

"Maybe you should wear the ones you like least when I light your lantern," Hüi murmured. "You may count upon a certain amount of damage, I fear. When I first see you—" He dropped his head to bite sharply at Lan's nipple, enjoying the jerk and cry that followed and then licking the sting away with the sweep of his tongue.

"Again, please, my Lord."

"Again," Hüi said in a proud voice, rubbing his growing cock over Lan's smooth thigh.

CHAPTER ELEVEN

CAPTAIN WEN had noticed that both the eunuch, Ning, and his mistress, the Princess Lan'xiu, seemed to be much addicted to keeping fit. Ning and the princess did early morning exercises in the courtyard behind the seventh house and often walked together around the inner square, sometimes for an hour at a time.

They were almost always together, but Wen had noticed that sometimes Ning would run behind the houses by himself. Naturally, Wen would never have committed the solecism of approaching a concubine belonging to the general, so he had to wait to catch Ning alone, especially as it was Ning in particular he wished to speak with.

And so when Ning began to trot behind the houses one crisp morning, Wen was able to surprise him when he stepped out from behind the corner of the last house.

"Greetings, Eunuch Ning. I am Captain Wen, of the household guard."

Ning was panting from his exertions, but he hid his surprise. "Greetings, Captain Wen. What business have you with a mere eunuch, a servant such as I?"

Wen was amused that Ning seemed a bit guarded and unconsciously let his hand rest over an imaginary hilt, even though he wore no sword. "I merely wondered if your mistress was partial to chicken."

Ning's face became more guarded, even hostile. "And if she is?"

"I only wondered why you did not order the kitchen maid to go to the henhouse."

Ning was caught without an answer. "I am new here and...." His voice faded away.

"You need not fear any indiscretion. I haven't written all my observations in my reports," Wen said.

"Then why challenge me in the street?" Ning looked about, as if realizing they were not exactly in the street.

"I have noticed your habit of exercise. I admire that." Wen bowed.

"As a eunuch—" Ning began.

"I know," Wen said with an understanding smile. "I fear I am interrupting, but you are in no danger of encroaching plumpness if you forego a quarter of an hour to speak with me."

"What do you want of me?" Ning's voice was sharp.

"I want nothing. I do not even want the price of the chicken you, er, borrowed." Wen seemed a bit embarrassed. "I came to announce that I am—ahem—partial to the third sex," he said, as if only then realizing how awkward an approach this was.

Ning's wrath died down, and he looked perplexed. "A eunuch is not adept at the usual sexual practices."

"If you will forgive me for being rudely direct, it depends on how one was cut," Wen said. "I have had many a pleasurable afternoon in bed with a eunuch."

"Pleasurable for you, no doubt," Ning said irritably.

"It would not please me if I could not please my partner as well," Wen said. "I had wondered if you had ever considered...." He looked questioningly at Ning. "Of course, we should have to get to know each other a bit better first. Perhaps I could help educate you with some of our more customary chicken acquisition methods."

"I see! Blackmail?" Ning exclaimed wrathfully.

"Calm yourself. I am merely teasing you. I shall never let you live that down, no matter what your reason was for that clandestine poultry rendezvous. I go off duty at four in the afternoon, if you would care to have tea with me."

"I shall consider it," Ning said with great dignity but a gleam lighting his eyes. Then he abandoned dignity for practicality. "Where do you go to drink tea?"

"I am permitted outside these gates, but as you are not, I suggest we have our tea in your kitchen."

"But Jia—"

"Jia is an old friend of mine. She may laugh at us, but she will not begrudge us the tea or the space," Wen said.

"She will most definitely laugh," Ning said gloomily.

JIANG had spent the past two weeks without success trying to corner Hüi Wei for some private conversation. He had heard the clop of hooves before dawn on the day after Hüi had gone to see Lan'xiu and looked out his window to see something he had never witnessed before: Hüi Wei fleeing the city as if from a rout. He wondered if the princess had anything wrong with her, or worse, if Hüi had failed in his manly duty. Or even whether he had forced the princess to reveal some plot so dastardly it shocked him into flight. For some time Jiang had wondered whether Princess Lan'xiu's lifeless body lay within her house, not that he cared about her death if she had threatened his friend. Within the day, however, he ascertained that she still lived, which confused him even more.

He alone was privy to details of Hüi's relationships with his many women—although the stories were few because his friend was a gentleman—but usually there was some small anecdote to be shared. Never had Hüi avoided him so comprehensively. Therefore, he had taken to watching Hüi, trying to decipher what was in the general's mind. His initial thought that Hüi might be planning a new campaign or had received a secret missive from the emperor was dismissed. For too long Hüi had relied on Jiang for strategy, be it political or military, and he had done nothing to warrant changing that.

Then it occurred to him that perhaps Hüi was spending time elsewhere in the household, although the idea puzzled him. Hüi had always been disciplined about his bodily pleasures; he never drank to excess, nor ate too many sweets. And Jiang had never observed that Hüi was especially lustful; he seemed motivated more by affection and the need for heirs in his visits to the household, except for that fiery infatuation with Ci'an, which lasted only long enough to produce one sickly daughter. With her alone the flame of desire had burned hot for a short time, but the embers were long since cold.

Mere beauty could not hold Hüi for long. Ci'an was stunning, but her underhanded scheming disgusted him. Mei Ju had an affectionate nature, but although warm and welcoming, she was not interesting enough to hold his attention for long. After the disaster of Ci'an, Hüi had shrewdly taken concubines for political reasons alone. Jiang would not have been surprised to learn, if Hüi had had the bad manners to confide in him, that he visited their houses only for reasons of etiquette and ceremony. Hüi would not want to fall prey to the sexual power of any woman again.

Hating himself for doing so, Jiang had begun to follow Hüi. He had to know what was going on with his friend. Of course, with a soldier as alert and well trained as Hüi, it was not easy to maintain surveillance on him without being obvious, so there were times when Hüi Wei managed to evade him. It took a full week before any light dawned to elucidate the problem, and that came when Jiang trailed Hüi to the jeweler's shop in the city that lay within the fortress.

When he noticed Hüi disappear within the doors, Jiang racked his brain to think of a reason why Hüi might be patronizing the goldsmith. When it finally occurred to him, he started to shake with laughter.

Not the most gallant of men, Hüi had not been in the habit of giving jewelry to his wives. He tended toward more domestic sorts of gifts, like tea services or furniture. Therefore, something must have happened to change his usual habit of thought. Jiang took the chance of being observed and edged closer to the door, trying to overhear what was being said.

Apparently, five gifts had already been selected, but Hüi was indecisively wavering between the comparative merits of emeralds or rubies. Jiang retreated, wondering if he should return to the palace immediately or keep watching his friend.

Jiang began to have a glimmering of which way the wind was blowing when he next followed Hüi Wei to the silk shops, where he chose several items of women's clothing.

He calculated that the only new variable that had entered the equation was the Princess Lan'xiu. Then he shook his head in confusion once more as he watched Hüi go to the ironmongers that made weapons. Now nothing about this shopping trip made sense to him.

AS ALWAYS, Lan'xiu braced herself before she went to sit with the other wives. She knew they watched as avidly as she when the servant who bore the torch came to the square and that they knew well that her lantern had not been lit again. The competitive nature of the household guaranteed that some would slyly jibe at her with her lack of fortune in order to point out their own good fortune. She dared not let slip that Hüi had come to her without the formality of the usual public announcement.

If they had but known it, Lan was certain jealousy would be immediate, and in Ci'an's case, potentially violent. If the other wives were privy to all he had said to her, it would have been even worse.

The smooth running of this household was based upon a certain uneasy openness, and now the secret she must keep from them wasn't only about who she was, but also that Hüi had come to see her on the sly. If he was not ready to accept her as she was, it made her sad, but she understood. She could not turn her face away from him, because she knew how it felt to feel lost and unsure. How ironic would it be to have miraculously found Hüi ready to embrace her despite her deficiencies, only to then be cast out by his outraged wives.

She was used to keeping her own secret, but now that she was responsible for keeping Hüi's as well, it made her timid in their gatherings. Lan'xiu had gained the reputation of being a shy, quiet girl, even though she would have loved to chatter and giggle with the rest of them, discussing clothing, cosmetics, and possibly even foolish little secrets about how to please their husband.

Only Ning could steel her to face her sister wives, although she often told him she went only to get away from his constant ragging.

Lan'xiu had taken to wearing her plainest robes when she went to consort with the others, hoping to downplay her looks so as not to excite their envy or attention. Her excuse was that she loved playing with the children. Being a modest girl, she could not know that nothing could make her look ugly; in fact, the plain hanfu of amber silk she wore today only emphasized the burnished satin of her skin.

As usual, Mei Ju called out to her in welcome when Lan'xiu entered her home. "Come here, Lan'xiu, sit by me and tell me what you think of the new dress I had made."

Lan'xiu gave one of her rare but lovely smiles. "You look very smart, First Wife. That rose is a pretty color for you." It was, but the cheongsam was so over-embellished and ornamented that it made Mei Ju look rather unfortunately wide.

"Look at what my husband gave to me," Mei Ju said, holding out her chubby wrist.

"It is very beautiful," Lan'xiu said, dutifully admiring the bracelet with a little sigh. She was wearing her only pair of earrings, as usual, and her plain jade bracelet. She had put away the ring that belonged to her mother, not caring to hear Ci'an's comments on it.

The new bracelet was made of curved pieces of jade in varying shades of green, rose, and white linked together with silver good luck charms between them. Mei Ju looked at the bracelet and stroked a finger over one of the pieces of jade. "Hüi has given me many things, but I value this bracelet above all others. See, there is a charm here for each of the children I have borne him."

Her words stabbed Lan'xiu in the heart like a knife, for she would never bear her lord any children, and her barrenness would be held against her—and him. Now it was her turn to be disappointed that Hüi had not come to her again, but a lady did not visit her own disappointments upon another, especially the woman who had been so kind to her.

"Your husband has great love for you, Mei Ju, that is clear. It is a beautiful bracelet and a beautiful sentiment."

Mei Ju touched Lan'xiu's sleeve. "Thank you, my dear, I know—" But her words, whatever they were, were destined to remain unspoken when the third, fourth, and sixth wives came in together.

Lan'xiu rose and bowed, remaining standing as befitted her lowest rank, while Mei Ju stayed seated to receive the other ladies, all of whom kissed her hand and bowed. Lan'xiu was pushed aside as Fifth Wife Bai bounced into the room with her usual merry smile.

"Oh, am I late? I am late, aren't I?" She gave a high-pitched laugh. "I am always late!"

"But you always bring the sunshine with you, my dear," Mei Ju said, with an answering smile.

The words gave Lan'xiu a pang; Mei Ju was always kind to her, but she was not amusing like Bai, or good-natured like Alute, or contented like Fen and Huan. She was conscious that guarding her secret had consumed her to the point that she offered the other wives little in return for their friendship, however shallow it might be. So anxious not to offend, she had become little more than wallpaper, attractive but not precisely scintillating.

Isolation had bound the wives of the household together into a unit, however uneasy, and she was the odd one out, just as much as Ci'an was, despite their efforts to include her. As Lan'xiu was resolving to try to exert herself a bit more to make herself agreeable, a silence fell over the chattering women. She looked up from her reverie as they all turned to face the doorway.

It was Second Wife Ci'an, whose preferred manner of arrival seemed to be coming late and sneaking in to eavesdrop.

Her hands were hidden in her sleeves when she entered and her lips curled sarcastically. "Greetings, sister wives. It is *so* good to see you all again."

"Second Wife Ci'an," Mei Ju said, welcoming her formally. "I trust I see you well. I am anxious for you, the physician is so often at your house."

"What of it?" Ci'an snapped.

"I was merely expressing the wish that you were enjoying a period of good health," Mei Ju said gently.

Lan'xiu wondered how she could be so gracious with this arrogant woman.

"Oh, you needn't start planning my funeral yet," Ci'an smirked. "I intend to outlive you yet, *First* Wife."

Where they sat together on the divan, Fen and Huan looked away pointedly. Mei Ju's wise face remained inscrutable, but Alute looked distressed at the insult.

Bai came to the rescue, cheerfully saying, "Ci'an, you are too beautiful and evil to die soon. You must have made a pact with the demons to look so lovely when you suffer from strange maladies so often."

Lan'xiu was cautiously amused to see that Bai's forthright statement stymied Ci'an and even caused her to laugh.

Second Wife Ci'an moved into the room. On this occasion she was dressed in a robe of the finest mulberry silk with a broad embroidered panel that crossed her bosom and edged the length of the dress to the hem. The sleeves were similarly decorated, as was the little stand-up collar. Real pearls had been used for buttons, and a tall headdress of rich golden ornaments of flowers and birds crowned her hair, which was dressed high, towering at least eight inches over her head. It seemed almost a pity that she had chosen that day to outshine Lan'xiu, dressed in her plainest robe.

"If I had to choose one of you to slay upon this day, I vow you would be the last to go, Bai. You amuse me. You insult me with one tongue and call me beautiful with the other," said Ci'an.

"I was born with Gemini rising in my stars." Bai held out both hands at her sides and swayed first to her right and then to her left. "The twin natures possess my soul and balance each other. I am sometimes good and sometimes very, very bad." She gave a giggle that all the other wives understood to indicate that it was with their husband she chose to be very bad. "Our Lord Hüi Wei has said he does not know whether to beat me or...." She gave a wicked smile and then turned to Lan'xiu. "Come sit by me, Princess Lan'xiu."

"Yes, do go sit with crazy Bai, Princess of Nothing," Ci'an concurred. "Of course, she may simply be asking to you to sit with her because her lovely cheongsam outshines your rather plain and drab one."

"Don't listen to her, Lan'xiu," Bai said, chuckling. "Last time I wore this dress, Ci'an informed me it was an ugly rag."

Lan'xiu went to the divan where Bai sat, settling next her. "I think it is a very pretty dress."

"Clearly, you are no judge of fashion, judging by what you are wearing. Bai, I misspoke when I told you that. I think Lan'xiu's dress makes yours look like the height of fashion." Ci'an smirked, her eyes fixed upon Lan'xiu's earlobes. "You must love those turquoise earrings. You wear them so often."

"I do like them." Lan'xiu put her hand up to touch one of the turquoise drops. She had almost made the mistake of admitting they were the only pair she owned. "They belonged to my mother."

"They're simple. And therefore appropriate for *you*." Ci'an waited for Lan'xiu to realize the insult, but when she made no reply, she continued. "Rather boring with that dress, perhaps, but when one hasn't much to boast of except a spurious title…." She shrugged, peering superciliously at Lan'xiu. "If you play your cards right, perhaps one day someone might give you a nice little lacquer comb out of pity."

"It wasn't pity that got Lady Mei Ju her new bracelet!" Bai said with a laugh. "Nor her lovely dress."

"Ah, yes, the fecundity bracelet. Not as elegant as one might have wished for. Quite the popular sentimental purchase amongst the merchant classes, or so I hear." Ci'an gave an exaggerated yawn and sat down, drawing her chair uncomfortably close to Lan'xiu. "Certainly fitting for one who has borne a litter of little bastards."

Mei Ju grew angry and lashed out at Ci'an. "This bracelet means much to me and to my husband, Second Concubine. It celebrates the many healthy children we have created between us. *More* than *you* managed to produce."

Ci'an reddened at this reminder of her sonless state. Perhaps she remembered the rebuke Mei Ju had given at the previous party and didn't want to run the risk of another, or perhaps she wasn't finished with the other wives, but she bit her lip silently before turning again to

Lan'xiu, leaning forward to elbow her in the ribs. "You simple innocents have no idea how to keep a man interested. If you liked, I could share some secrets of how to fan the flames with Hüi. The first night after he left me, I couldn't sit down the day after. My sheets were red with blood." She looked meaningfully at Lan'xiu and winked as she said it.

Ci'an's laugh made Lan'xiu want to take a bath.

"I've noticed it remains *quite dark* on your side of the square. Now that Hüi has made the ritual visit out of politeness, he obviously plans to have no more to do with you. I'm sure you could settle for a nice little flirtation to fill your time, like Fen and Huan have." Ci'an waved a hand at the chair where the two girls sat together as usual. "You can only plead innocence for so long, or perhaps you're too stupid to see which way the sun sets? Choose a nice young man from the guard. Some of the soldiers set to watch us are quite virile and not so focused on their responsibilities that they can't put those assault skills to use closer to home. Isn't that so, Liang?"

One of the pair of soldiers who accompanied Ci'an everywhere flushed red but continued to stare into space without comment.

"Or perhaps you prefer the company of eunuchs? I see you have a tame one of your very own."

"Most eunuchs are very good company," Lan'xiu said. She could not defend Ning by boasting of his prowess with a sword, but she was tiring of Ci'an's unending stream of malice. "Perhaps you might find it profitable to make the acquaintance of one or two before you insult them."

"Oh no, my sweet innocent. They are very well to serve brainless consorts, content to lie upon their backs and spread their legs—"

"Second Concubine!" Mei Ju rose to her full height, which wasn't very tall at all, but she was impressive in her indignation. "You shame only yourself with your vulgar ramblings. I order you to leave my house at once! You! Guards! Make yourself useful and escort this woman to her home. Ci'an, I hope a period of solitary reflection may restore your humor!"

Ci'an gave Lan'xiu a wink and hauled herself up out of her chair. "Get your eunuch to procure you some porn, *with* illustrations, Princess of Stupid. You have much to learn if you wish to hold the attention of our husband. You would look lovely with your heels over your head, all red in the face while he pumps away at you, I'm sure."

Lan'xiu felt the color mount to her cheeks, humiliated that Ci'an would plant such images in the minds of the soldiers who stood there listening, but she made no reply, deeming it useless to involve herself in a verbal brawl. When she replied with a dagger, Ci'an beat her down with a battle-axe.

Even Bai did not care to answer that parting jibe, and Ci'an was escorted out in a chilly silence. Her dismissal did not seem to discompose her; in fact she appeared rather amused to be shunned by the other wives, as if it gave her some advantage.

Mei Ju seated herself and leaned forward to touch Lan'xiu's sleeve. "My dear, don't let that witch bother you. Your earrings are very pretty."

For some reason that comment made Lan'xiu want to laugh when she had been holding back her tears, but she couldn't appear to make fun of First Wife. Mei Ju was a tender soul, and Lan could tell it cost her to stand up to Ci'an. "I am very fond of these earrings."

Bai put in, "It really doesn't matter what you wear. You could wear the poorest cotton cheongsam and no jewelry at all, and you would still outshine the lot of us."

"I have no desire to—" Lan'xiu started to exclaim.

"You cannot help your face. You are as the stars and gods made you," Bai said, sounding serious for once. "Unearthly in your beauty, like a star shining in the night sky."

"I think you are quite pretty and your earrings too," Alute said placidly. "Ci'an is just mean."

"Thank you," Lan said, blinking rapidly at the tears that threatened to fall. For the first time she felt like one of them, even though she couldn't have been further from them.

Mei Ju lifted the teapot. "May I give you tea, my dears?"

CHAPTER TWELVE

JIANG sat down at the general's breakfast table and poured himself a cup of tea, intending to waylay him. The glutinous rice and fruit appeared particularly tasty this morning, but perhaps that was only because he was so relishing the opportunity to tease Hüi Wei about his new acquisition.

His commander, Captain Wen, had reported on Hüi Wei's visit to Princess Lan'xiu the previous night, perhaps not realizing it had been a clandestine assignation. Hüi had not had her lantern lit, so perhaps he had not gone to feast on her body. Perhaps she had confessed to him some plot.

When Hüi failed to show up to break his fast, Jiang knew his friend was most definitely still avoiding him and decided he would have to confront him in a place where Hüi could not retreat from him.

He knew just where to start looking and ordered his horse to be saddled. Once he was outside the border of the city, he was able to spy Hüi in the distance atop his favorite hill. Evidently, he was not hurt, but he was pacing in a way that spoke of deep confusion.

Because a warrior like Hüi would be difficult to surprise, Jiang did not even try. He made the obvious frontal approach up the hill and greeted his friend. "Good morning, Hüi."

"Jiang. You should not have come here," Hüi snapped.

"If not I, then who?" Jiang dismounted and tied the reins of his horse to the nearest tree. "Come, Hüi. You look as if you had been tortured last night instead of enjoying the charms of the most beautiful creature you own."

"My horse is indeed comely," Hüi said, patting the horse's neck, perhaps as an excuse to turn his face away.

"I did not mean your horse," Jiang said sternly. "I would have expected you to be happy, content, triumphant, or excited after bedding the princess. Instead you steal to her side in secret, and now you are alone on top of this hill, moping. What went wrong?"

"Nothing at all." Hüi began to pace nervously.

"Did the princess deny you?"

"She could not," Hüi said. "She is a concubine. It is her lot to obey."

"Was the princess not pure when you first took her?"

"Untouched," Hüi answered tersely.

"Then what happened? Is Lan'xiu stupid or deformed or disgusting or venal—"

"He is none of those!" Hüi roared and then stopped, his face shocked and dismayed that he had betrayed himself so easily. "I mean 'she'."

"You meant 'he'," Jiang said calmly.

"Do not let me believe that you knew—you *knew*—this princess is a... a...."

"Male. Yes, I suspected, from the first."

Hüi sat down hard upon the ground. In a wounded voice he asked, "Why did you not tell me? You are my friend, why did you not warn me?"

Jiang sat beside him. "I could not. What if I were wrong? You might have killed that unfortunate girl, if she had been a girl, and all for a mere guess? I could not do it."

Hüi shook his head. "I don't understand. I don't understand anything. Why should I, after all the women I have tumbled, why should I feel attraction to one of my own sex now?"

"Why not?" Jiang shrugged.

"Just that easy?"

"Just that easy. He is very beautiful. I've never seen anyone to compare. He would tempt anyone."

Again, Hüi was angry. "Did you come to taunt me that I have had a male foisted upon me to play the part of a concubine?"

"I came because I know you are troubled and I want to help you." Jiang paused, regarding the angry lines etched in the mask of Hüi's face. "Because you are my friend."

"And what, precisely, do you think troubles me?" Hüi demanded with a sneer.

"How to guard his secret. You want to keep Lan'xiu, but you do not want any gossip about you and your affairs."

Hüi seemed to slump as the anger drained from him once again. Jiang knew the signs.

"The worst was trying to think how to keep this from you. We have always shared everything." He noticed a look of embarrassed regret upon Jiang's face. "We have, have we not?"

Jiang averted his face. "It is my shame to admit to you now that there is one thing I have kept from you. Why do you not ask how I knew that the Princess Lan'xiu isn't what she seems?"

"How *did* you know? She is perfection: in form, in face, in manner, in carriage! She has Mei Ju believing she is a woman, and that is not easy—" Hüi paused when a realization suddenly struck him. "You are—that way—too?"

"I have never cared for women," Jiang said softly. "I follow the passions of the cut sleeve."

"Is that why you never married?"

"I have never married a woman. I have a comrade—a partner. We have loved each other for ten years now."

"Do I know this man?"

Jiang laughed. "You should. He is one of your highest-ranked commanders, Zheng Guofang."

"It is like you to praise him, but he ranks after you, my friend." Hüi clapped Jiang on the shoulder. "A good man! You have chosen well, my friend. I'd wondered—but never mind that!"

Soberly, Jiang looked at Hüi. "The one regret of my life is that I have had to keep this secret from you, my closest friend."

Hüi made a pained sound. "You didn't trust me?"

"You didn't trust *me*!" Jiang pointed out. Then he sighed. "It was not simply a question of trust. When I discovered the truth about myself, I dared not tell you. I fell in love—with someone completely unsuitable—"

"It was with me," Hüi said in a flash of insight. He covered his eyes with his hand. "Oh Jiang. I am so sorry."

"Don't be. It was only puppy love. I got over it," Jiang said. "It would never have worked."

"Not that. What a tragedy that you have had to hide this secret from me all these years," Hüi said sorrowfully. "This is my failure. I was not a good enough friend for you to trust me with your true self."

"We were both too reticent. Perhaps we both had much to learn before we could speak freely," Jiang suggested. "We have shared our secrets now." He grasped Hüi's hand and their fingers tightened in a strong clasp. "Now to the matter at hand. Do you love him?"

Hüi shook his head in bewilderment. "I don't know. I think so. Perhaps it is too soon, just a novelty that will wear off."

"You need time to get to know him better," Jiang said.

"Ning said we must call him 'her'—"

"Who is Ning?"

"Lan'xiu's eunuch, her servant. Ning refers to Lan'xiu always in the feminine. He says that it is safer."

"Very well, no doubt he has long experience in guarding her secret. We will call her 'she'."

"Thank you," Hüi sighed.

"First of all, what are you going to do about her brother?"

"Last night—"

"Can't resist giving me a blow by blow, eh, dear friend?" Jiang jabbed Hüi in the ribs with his elbow, relieved when his friend's expression lightened.

"I was not going to share what passed between me and Lan'xiu," Hüi announced with great dignity. A beatific smile spread over his face as he looked down upon his palace fortress to the inner household square, picking out the seventh house once again.

"I'll bet much passed between you." Jiang snorted with ribald laughter.

"Have your joke, you deserve it." Hüi chuckled too.

"I have never seen you react to a night of pleasure with any of your other wives this way," Jiang observed.

"That is partly what troubles me," Hüi confessed. "When I first discovered she was a boy, I threatened her with death. It was then Lan'xiu informed me that if I put it about that I had killed her in a righteous rage after finding her with a man, it would provide her brother with an excuse to attack. If I send her back, Wu Min will kill her in the slowest, most tortuous way possible. He enjoys that sort of thing. If I simply throw her out, her brother will make it his business to inform the emperor that I was fooled by a man dressed as a woman. None of these options redound to my credit, and I would avoid them if I could."

"It is rare that a pawn is aware of the possibilities of which it may be put to use," Jiang said. "Of course, no doubt, she also wishes to keep on living, so it is in her best interest to point that out to you. Are you sure she is not here as his spy?"

"One day you must speak with her," Hüi said with a faraway expression. "She waited for me, thinking that I would kill her when I discovered her secret. I admired her courage when she faced me and admitted the truth."

Curiously, Jiang asked, "How did she convince you to spare her?"

"We fought," Hüi said, chuckling at Jiang's doubtful expression. "With swords. She has been well taught."

"I assume you won, as you are not dead."

"Naturally. Even though she fights well, I am stronger and have more experience."

"It is not merely her beauty that attracts you?"

"Age steals beauty from youth, and one day that may be gone. There is another beauty and innocence within her that makes my soul long for her. When you meet her, you must look into her eyes and tell me what you think."

Satisfied, Jiang nodded. "As to her future, have either of you considered that if you keep her as your seventh concubine, you have stolen the ammunition from Wu Min's cannons. He will be nonplussed with your lack of reaction if she continues to abide within the household without any comment."

"That is very clever of you, Jiang."

"And *that* is why you keep me as court jester."

"You won't let the water flow over that dam either, I see," Hüi said, then exclaimed, "If I do that, he will know that I—I bedded a man!"

"Or that you accepted her into your household but are ignoring her, a studied insult to him if you resist that beauty," Jiang pointed out. "You may allow her or any other concubine to live within the harem without using her."

"You know as well as I do that spies are everywhere. Even in innocent conversation, the maid tells the laundress, who tells the butcher, who tells the peddler, and the news comes to Wu Min's court whenever I have the lantern lit at Lan'xiu's house."

"Perhaps you could mention to me in public how you enjoy playing games of chance with her," Jiang suggested. "Give the impression she does not attract you, although that might be beyond your powers of dissimulation, as besotted as you are. You don't want the entire court laughing behind their sleeves at your lies. How often do you plan to light her lantern?"

A slow, lustful smile spread over Hüi Wei's face. "How high can you count?"

Jiang laughed. "Not as high as you, my friend. Now, tell me about all this jewelry you ordered. Is it all for Lan'xiu?"

CHAPTER THIRTEEN

"LAN'XIU!"

"What is it, Ning?" Lan asked, looking up from his book.

"The general has sent his servant. Your lantern has been lit."

Setting the book down, Lan rushed to his window to peer down toward the door, but the tiled roof blocked his view. "Really?"

Ning stood in his path but grinned at him. "Do not betray your eagerness by rushing downstairs to check. I would not tease you about such a thing. And Jia already makes me suffer enough with her ribald jests about Hüi's first visit; if you run down like a child about to get her first horse ride, I will need to gag her."

"What should I wear? My hair! It's so untidy! And Hüi Wei said—" Lan stopped himself, realizing the infelicitous nature of the admission he had almost made.

"Ahem, considering the recent wear and tear upon your clothing, I would suggest the pale blue damask hanfu with cranes embroidered in turquoise and green on the full skirts. At least it is in one piece," Ning said, crossing to the wardrobe and opening the door. "It is to be hoped that the general remembers to send you some new dresses."

"Be quiet, Ning," Lan said, pressing his hands to his hot cheeks. No doubt the eunuch was right and he would not want to give the housekeeper any more to remark upon. "I still have many pretty dresses."

He went to the drawer and selected the pale pink corselet and panties embroidered with apple blossoms and a deeper blue inner robe to match the lining of the cerulean robe.

Ning wound the sash about Lan's slender waist and tied it, giggling madly.

"What's so funny, you imp?" Lan asked although he feared he might be making a mistake.

"I'm wondering how tightly to tie this. You may not be wearing it long enough to make the effort worthwhile."

"Jia is not alone in her taste for making fun at my expense," Lan said crossly. "You two are well matched. The silver and turquoise earrings, and the silver hair sticks with the phoenixes."

"I wish you had more jewelry," Ning said, opening the sparsely furnished case. "Our lord has already seen all you have, although I venture to guess he doesn't come to inventory your jewels."

"These were all I could save from my mother's trunk when she died," Lan said sadly. "They mean more to me than the most precious of jewels."

"But you have nothing new to show off when you meet with the other wives, and soon enough they will recognize the same earrings over and over," Ning complained. "How will they know you are the new favorite?"

Lan did not remark that Second Wife Ci'an had already done so as he put the earrings on and tilted his head to watch them sway. He felt happy and thought he looked rather pretty in this dress. "Compared to death, not having much jewelry isn't so much of a hardship. Come, Ning. Stop your sighing and do my hair."

Ning stood behind Lan, his quick hands straightening the unruly locks and using the sticks to pile her hair high. "You should adopt the phoenix for your good luck charm. You have arisen from the flames to a new life here. May it be a long one."

"Thank you, Ning. I wish the same for you."

Their eyes met in the mirror, and Lan said, "Please tidy up those things and then leave me, if you would be so kind."

"Yes, your Highness," Ning said, using the term of address that had been left unsaid between them since Lan's brother, Wu Min, had forbidden it. He hung up the cheongsam Lan had discarded and closed the drawers. Then he closed the door to the wardrobe and drew the curtains across the windows to ensure there were no cracks where anyone could spy in. He lit the lamps and the fire, bowed to Lan'xiu, and withdrew, tactfully keeping silent for once.

Lan'xiu seated himself on the bench at the end of his bed to await his lord and master. His feet were planted square on the floor, his legs and knees together. His back was straight and he placed his hands on his knees. After Hüi Wei's secret visit, Lan understood that for some reason, Hüi did not want to admit to his attraction. Otherwise, why conceal a visit to a concubine he owned and had every right to take his pleasure with?

That was the lot Lan had chosen when he made his choice to live as he did, and he did not expect Hüi to share the burdens of that choice. He would have been content to receive his lord's occasional discreet visit and keep it secret, bearing the taunts from some of the other wives when it became obvious he had not captured the general's interest.

But now his lantern had been lit. Hüi Wei had chosen *him*, knowing everything about him, and he was announcing his acceptance publicly to Lan'xiu's narrow little world. However painful it would be to see the lantern lit elsewhere on the morrow, tonight Hüi wanted him, Lan'xiu, to spend his time with.

With that thought, Lan'xiu felt his palms start to flutter. He never knew what to expect when Hüi showed up. Last time his clothing had been ripped from him and Hüi had taken him roughly, making him a prisoner by using his ruined dress as a restraint. Later he had made love as gently as if Lan had been untouched.

It was too soon for Lan to know the moods of this man; perhaps there were too many for him to ever be able to anticipate. So far he had enjoyed all Hüi had chosen to do to him, and it was his part to wait and to accept.

His inexperience made him anxious that he did not possess the arts to please Hüi, but asking one of the other wives was out of the question, especially after Ci'an's cruel jibe. He would have to rely upon Hüi to guide him to do what he enjoyed.

His cock was getting thicker, pushing against the silk of his panties. He could feel the fluid form at the tip and dampen the fabric.

He moved his shoulders to feel the heavy embroidery of his corselet rub over his nipples. Lan liked that feeling, too, it added to the anticipation of waiting for Hüi.

His breath was coming shorter and his heart pounding when he heard the click of the door as it opened. Lan looked up, not realizing his face wore an expression of joyful anticipation.

TO HÜI, Lan'xiu was the picture of beautiful submission as he sat waiting before the bed, as if suggesting his willingness to either sit and converse or to be thrown upon the mattress and fucked as hard as Hüi Wei wished.

Say what one would about the willingness of women, there was a strength to Lan'xiu that made his submission that much more pleasurable for Hüi. He was a strong man, and he was uneasily aware that his passions could make him lose control. With Lan'xiu he never worried about hurting him.

The roughness of their last encounter had been much on his mind. In fact, rather than visiting with another wife to take care of his need, he had preferred to be alone with his memories and imaginings until his yearning grew too strong to resist.

Speaking with Jiang and finding acceptance of this different choice had calmed Hüi. He had come to Lan'xiu not to ravage this time, but to ravish. All his plans flew from his head when he saw the beautiful young man awaiting him with every evidence of being as eager as he was.

"Lan'xiu!"

"My Lord," Lan replied and made as if to rise and bow.

Hüi raised a hand and motioned to Lan to remain seated. "When we are together in private, call me Hüi." He crossed the room and sat beside Lan'xiu upon the bench, who shifted slightly to make room upon the cushion. "I missed you," Hüi said as he had the last time they saw each other.

"And I you, Hüi," Lan said with a shy smile.

Speechlessly, they gazed at each other, as if the hunger was too great to move.

Slowly, Hüi put his arm around Lan, stroking his shoulder with his fingers. Lan'xiu responded by leaning in against him. Hüi could smell Lan's perfume and a clean, sweet scent mingled with it. Underneath it all was just a hint of male arousal.

Controlling himself, Hüi slid his other hand along Lan's thigh and was rewarded by a slight widening of Lan's legs. Hüi drew his hand up to Lan's chest, insinuating it between the silken layers of outer robe and inside the inner robe. He felt the softer silk of the corselet and felt the erect nub of a nipple poking against the satin. Hüi slid his thumb over it, enjoying the feeling of the firm, flat chest under the silky fabric and the hard tip of the nipple protruding from the silk as he pinched it gently.

Lan's chest rose and fell swiftly, his breaths gentle sighs near Hüi's ear, but he made no other sound. Hüi moved his hand to find the other nipple, tugging on it as he lowered his lips to kiss the base of Lan's throat, sucking hard enough to leave a mark. He could feel Lan drop his head back to give him better access.

He withdrew his hand from the robe to embrace Lan and hold him closer. He felt Lan's arms go around him, clutching at him. He kissed his way along the elegant jaw line to Lan'xiu's lips, inserting his tongue to explore the willing mouth open to him.

His hand crept lower, working between the edges of Lan's robes till he found the smooth skin of his inner thigh. His fingertips were gentle as he slid his hand under the silk, finding Lan's erection straining against the silken panties. He rubbed the hardness softly, hearing the catch in Lan'xiu's breathing.

Running his thumb over the dampened silk, Hüi moved his other hand to cup one rounded buttock, squeezing it rhythmically as they kissed. He disengaged from the kiss, breathing hard into Lan's scented hair. "Have you ever ridden a horse, my Lan'xiu?"

"Yes, my Lord," came the whispered response.

"I want you to ride me," Hüi said, his big hands trapping Lan when he felt a tremor as if the young man intended to rise. "No, don't disrobe."

He put both hands under Lan's cheeks and lifted him bodily, pleased when Lan lifted one leg as if mounting a horse and sat astride him with his knees supported on the bench, facing him, looking at him questioningly but with a little smile on his face.

Immediately, Hüi took his rosy lips in another kiss, his hands sliding under Lan's skirts and up his firm thighs. He could feel the hard shaft pressed against his belly when he slid his fingers inside the silk panties, finding the dark valley between the globes of Lan'xiu's ass, his fingertip teasing over the pulsing entrance.

Lan'xiu arched against him, wreathing both arms around his neck and moving gently as if riding a horse. The feeling of their groins rubbing together made Hüi groan in pleasurable frustration at the layers of clothing between them. It was frustrating but at the same time heightened the forbidden feeling of the act.

"I want to feel you inside me," Lan whispered, his breath hot on Hüi's ear.

"I want that too," Hüi replied.

"How can we do this?"

"A good general is always prepared," Hüi said. He withdrew one of his hands from under Lan's robes and retrieved the small vial of oil he had placed in readiness in his pocket.

Lan giggled as he opened the bottle, helping Hüi slick his fingers. "Most superior strategy, my Lord."

"You bring out the best in me," Hüi replied.

Lan's eyes closed, and he drew in a sharp breath when an oiled finger found his hole and pressed against it. "A good general knows… how to claim… what is his own."

Hüi didn't know which was more enjoyable, watching the expression of pleasure tinged with pain flit over Lan'xiu's face or the sensation of sliding his fingers into the tight, hot hole, past the guardian ring of muscle to feel the smooth inner channel clench about him.

With his teeth gripping his lower lip, Lan rode the fingers, his hips undulating with the thrusting movement.

Seeing the profound effect he was having reminded Hüi of his own aching cock, hard and in dire need of attention. "Take me out," he murmured in Lan's ear.

He sighed at the feeling of Lan's hands fumbling under his long vest, finding the opening to his trousers, undoing them and at last the slide of skin against the palm of Lan's hand.

Keeping his fingers within the narrow passage, Hüi urged Lan to kneel up and lifted the barriers of clothing between them out of the way. At last he moved the silk panties as far to the side as he could and withdrew his fingers. "And now, my beauty, mount me and I will take you for a gallop."

LAN'S thighs trembled with the effort as he held himself above Hüi's lap. Hüi positioned the tip of his cock against his pulsing hole, and Lan could feel the familiar protest of his tight muscles. He bore down just as Hüi thrust upward, and the head penetrated, sending a thrill of burning pain though Lan's body. He gasped at the sudden stab of pain but knew it would soon pass.

Hüi was patient, holding him up, his hands cupped around the cheeks of his ass, waiting until Lan began to breathe again. Lan felt his muscles relax with the passing of the pain and all at once felt as if his very being sucked Hüi's cock inside him. He was fully impaled as he slid down the thick shaft until his buttocks rested against Hüi's rough trousers.

If anyone had entered the room at this point, it might have seemed indecorous to witness the two lovers in such a close embrace, but their clothing covered them completely. No one would have known that Hüi was fully buried within Lan's body, if they could have overlooked the sensuous sighs that filled the air.

Hüi's hands tightened on his cheeks and lifted him. Lan rose and sank again upon the cock filling him completely. He felt completely and utterly possessed, taken and owned. When Hüi raised him again and he slid down upon the throbbing pole once more, he was filled with the exquisite sensation echoing throughout his body.

Then Hüi raised him up and held him motionless in the air, inches above his lap, thrusting hard up inside him. "You are mine," he growled, his hips moving faster and faster. Lan felt as if he might be sundered in two, but if his beloved desired to take him this way, he was willing. The feeling of submitting to Hüi's pleasure only increased his.

Finally, Hüi slammed up inside him three last times before the heat of his release flooded Lan's channel. The hands gripping his buttocks relaxed their grip, and he came to rest, panting against Hüi's neck although he had not come himself. But that didn't matter. All that mattered was Hüi and his pleasure.

They rested like that against each other for some minutes while Hüi's breathing calmed. Then Lan was startled to feel one of Hüi's hand leave his ass, traveling around his body under his clothing to grip his erection through his silk panties.

"Shall I give you pleasure now, my Lan'xiu?" Hüi whispered, stroking his fingers lightly over the firm hot flesh hidden within the folds of fabric.

"If it pleases you, my Lord."

"It does please me. It pleases me to make you await me and submit to my desires. I like seeing the pain I cause you on your face, knowing that you submit to it because I would have it so. I enjoy seeing that pain turn to pleasure, knowing you will bear it for me each time I enter your sweet body. I enjoy feeling the tight clench of your ass on my cock, knowing that you need this as much as I do."

Lan'xiu convulsed helplessly as he spurted within his panties as Hüi stroked him, cock still embedded within him, feeling used and yet valued and loved, though Hüi had spoken those words only once.

He rested his head against Hüi's shoulder and drifted in the dreamy afterglow, Hüi's arm supporting him while one hand still curled around his limp cock.

Finally, he felt Hüi start to shake. "What is it, my Lord?"

"You'll have to get off me. My leg is getting a cramp, and I'm going to fall out anyway."

Lan giggled and the tightening of his muscles made Hüi's cock slip out. Stiffly, he moved to get up, with Hüi's hand supporting him. "I should wash."

"No, don't," Hüi ordered, staring at him intently. "I like the idea of my seed wet against your silken panties, dripping out of you while we sit and converse."

"Very well, my Lord." Lan gave him a demure smile and sat beside him on the bench again while Hüi adjusted his clothing.

"Do you like that too?"

"Yes," Lan said softly. "Anything that makes me feel I am yours. When you leave marks upon my body, I touch them the next day and remember—"

Speechlessly, they stared at each other once again, until Lan'xiu sighed with regret. It surely must be time for Hüi Wei to leave him.

"Would you like tea before you go?" Lan made as if to rise to ring for Ning.

"Wait, my love." Looking embarrassed, Hüi handed Lan'xiu a small package wrapped in red silk.

It was surprisingly heavy in Lan's hand. When he unwrapped it, he gasped at the sight of glittering diamonds and rubies. "These are so beautiful! These are... for me?"

"I had them made for you," Hüi said almost shyly. "I noticed you don't have much jewelry, even though what you have is very nice—" He broke off in confusion but relaxed at the delighted smile on Lan's face. In a rush, he said, "You should have something as beautiful as you are, something that draws attention to your exquisite face."

"Thank you." Lan lifted the earrings to admire them in the light. "The rubies are like fire! And the diamonds sparkle like the stars at night."

"Put them on so I can see them on you," Hüi suggested.

Lan removed the turquoise earrings and ran to his dressing table to put them in their box. He put the new earrings in the holes in his ears and tilted his head to watch the graceful sway of the jewels in the mirror.

A diamond lily framed an oval ruby at the top, joined by a chain to a bell-shaped center medallion. A larger ruby held the center, surrounded by pear-shaped and round diamonds. The bell had two pearls dangling from the bottom, while at the center another chain led to a cup-shaped ornament studded with diamonds. This cup was turned upside down and from the bottom, ruby beads circled the circumference.

He turned to let Hüi see the effect.

Hüi smiled with pleasure. "The diamonds light up your face with happiness."

"It is not the diamonds that make me happy," Lan replied, casting his eyes downward, trembling at his forwardness.

"What is it, then?" Hüi got up and came to Lan'xiu and took him into his arms.

For minutes that seemed without end, Lan was content to simply remain within the embrace of the strong arms that circled him. He could feel the thump of Hüi's heart and realized that his was beating in time. His emotions threatened to overwhelm him, and he didn't know how to answer. That he was happy to be with Hüi? That Hüi had wanted to give him a present? Finally, he answered simply. "You. You make me happy."

"As you have made me happy, my Lan'xiu," Hüi answered.

Lan laid his head on Hüi's broad shoulder, all thoughts of the earrings forgotten. Hüi was happy with him, and all else had no meaning in time.

Hüi cupped his chin and made Lan look at him. "I don't really want to hurt you. What I said before about the pain on your face, I would never truly harm you. I don't know why I like it."

Slowly, Lan said, "I do, my Lord. It is a sign by which you may measure my desire for you. I know it will hurt and yet I cannot help myself; my need to be possessed by you outweighs the pain."

"Yes. That is it." Hüi sighed in satisfaction. "You understand me as no one ever has. And will you let me see that exquisite expression when I first cause you pain to give you pleasure?"

"Whenever you like, Hüi," Lan answered, love glowing in his eyes. "I love belonging to you."

"I believe you mean it." Hüi said. "You have not asked me for jewels, or power or money. I cannot give you children. You need nothing from me."

"Except your love."

"That you have, my Lan'xiu. All that is in me is yours." Hüi held Lan close. "The others want something from me. And I have done my best to give it to them, but with you, I feel that all that I am is enough for you."

"And I never expected to find anyone who would love me as I am," Lan'xiu whispered back, clinging to Hüi's broad shoulders. "I thought I would go to my grave and then to the afterworld scorned and despised as something unnatural—"

"Hush, my beautiful Lan," Hüi said. "We have found something to celebrate between us, and that is all that matters. I love making love to you as I have never done with any woman. I will love you until the day I die."

"I love you as I have never loved anyone," Lan said.

They sat within their safe embrace until Lan'xiu yawned.

"Boring you already?" Hüi laughed.

"No, you are… very vigorous, my Lord, in your lovemaking." Lan giggled and yawned again. "Will you stay with me?"

"Is that all you want from me?"

"I love to sleep within your embrace. When I am alone I wrap my arms around myself and pretend it is you, but that is small comfort compared to being held in your arms."

"Then I will stay," Hüi said.

Lan rubbed his cheek against Hüi's. "Let's go to bed."

Chapter Fourteen

WHEN Ning entered the bedchamber by the early light to rouse the general, he found that Hüi Wei had already gone. Anxiously, he examined the pile of Lan'xiu's clothing on the floor. They certainly needed to be washed, but other than that, they showed no signs of the usual destruction Hüi tended to leave in the wake of his visits.

Lan'xiu slept with a happy smile upon her face. Ning approached the bed to pull up the sheets to hide her exposed nipples and stopped dead in his tracks at the gleam of red in the tangle of her hair.

The most magnificent ruby and diamond earrings shone in her ears. He almost gave out a shout of triumph and settled for pumping his fist in the air silently, not wanting to wake her. Finally! That spiteful cat Ci'an would swallow her piddly jewels in a rage when she saw these earrings, and he hoped the stones would scratch her throat bloody on the way down.

Although, in his opinion, the general could easily have afforded to give Lan'xiu another set of earrings. Two was a measly number for the most beautiful concubine in all of China—nay! Not just China, all the world—

"What are you doing, Ning?" a sleepy voice asked.

Recalled to his setting and place, Ning composed his face. "Admiring your new earrings, Lan'xiu. It appears *someone* has found favor with the master."

"Go away." Lan'xiu rolled over and covered his ears with his hands, which likely enabled him to ignore Ning's squeals when he made the next discovery.

He had found a parcel upon the bench at the foot of the bed, neatly tied up in a length of printed cotton. When he opened it, he found a new set of silken underthings, exquisitely delicate and embroidered with ghostly cherry blossoms, and two new cheongsams. The first was a glorious crimson, the perfect color to set off the new ruby earrings, with white and purple dragons embroidered on the sleeves and hem. Gold cloth edged the neckline and hems, and golden waves were embroidered into the fields between the dragons, as if they were emerging from an ocean of gold.

The other dress showed all the colors of the peacock, in green, chartreuse and brilliant cobalt blues. Black and gold bands decorated the edges, and the buttons looked to be sapphires set in gold. A smaller package fell on Ning's foot with enough weight to make it smart. He opened it to find ornate enameled peacock earrings, with gracefully dangling tails set with emeralds and sapphires.

One last wrapped parcel lay on the bench and Ning examined it to find a slim, beautifully engraved dagger with a jeweled handle held within a scabbard that could be strapped to wrist or leg; a most suitable gift for a beautiful but warlike girl who faced envy within the household.

He stared at the array of gifts, stunned into unaccustomed silence. "Behold the new favorite," he whispered. He stared at the sleeping Lan'xiu, wondering what had transpired between the lovers the previous night.

TODAY, Lan'xiu took pleasure in putting on the new red dress Hüi had left for her. When she'd awakened, filled with the languorous afterglow of the night's lovemaking, she had touched her new earrings with a secret little smile.

She'd been shocked when Ning had shown her the two new cheongsams and the pretty corselet and panties Hüi had left behind. Lan couldn't imagine why he hadn't given them to her with the earrings but decided that perhaps it was his way. Then she was struck speechless by the emerald earrings and the dagger. She couldn't decide which she preferred.

When she donned the new crimson cheongsam, Lan'xiu knew a moment of quiet satisfaction at the thought of what Ci'an might think when she saw the new ruby earrings. After the spiteful comments from Second Wife about her single pair of earrings, Lan knew the woman was sure to notice, if she decided to honor Mei Ju with her presence. To Lan, Ci'an appeared to be in robust health, showing no sign of the weakness that demanded attendance from the physician. She speculated that boredom rather than ill health was the true reason Ci'an often chose to send her excuses.

Just to be on the safe side, Lan'xiu had Ning strap the dagger to her arm, knowing the sleeves would conceal the weapon. She felt just a bit safer with it on her person.

But today she felt she must show off the new earrings Hüi had given her. She had worn them, alternating between them every day since he gave her the gifts, but with only herself and Ning to admire them. Even though she knew they would excite the envy of the other wives, she couldn't help herself. She felt so beautiful and loved wearing them, and the brush of the ruby beads against her neck made her feel as if Hüi's fingers and lips caressed her in public.

The only regret Lan had was the pain it might cause First Wife Mei Ju to see that Hüi had given her so magnificent a jewel, especially when she remembered the jade bracelet. Although it was sweet, there could be no comparison.

But Lan'xiu had enough competitive spirit to enjoy the prospect of proving to Ci'an that their husband did hold her in some esteem after all.

Ning made sure to wrap her up well, as the snow lay deep upon the ground. Lan'xiu was borne around the square in a chair, but Ning had to trot along behind and Lan bethought herself that she might request a pair of boots for him. The slippers he wore would surely be soaked through.

Excited chatter met Lan'xiu's ears when she entered the sitting room at Mei Ju's home and she found that each of the other wives were eagerly showing off new pieces of jewelry to each other. Mei Ju's kind round face shone under an incongruous new headdress with many dangling gold charms, and Bai had a rope of pearls around her neck that reached past her waist. Alute wore a coral bracelet with an enameled silver clasp, while Fen and Huan each wore intricately carved matching jeweled combs in their hair, save that one was ivory and the other ebony.

Lan'xiu was amused by Hüi's crafty strategy. To camouflage his gift to her, he had also given something to each wife, so that their attention would be upon their own presents. Mei Ju kept touching her headdress and shaking her head to make the ornaments jingle to the extent that she did not even notice the magnificent earrings in Lan's ears.

Bai, however, noticed them immediately and nodded acknowledgement. Lan'xiu glanced at her pearls and smiled back, pleased to have won the friendship of this dainty, mad girl who winked and tapped one of her own earlobes without a hint of envy.

Holding her head high, Lan'xiu prepared to enjoy the quiet gathering with the confidence her new dress and earrings gave her. She liked her earrings best and surprisingly found that it made her feel safer to realize Hüi had guarded her by devising gifts for each wife. It didn't even make her jealous; after all, these women had been here long before she came. Hüi knew each one of them, but she could not doubt that she and Hüi shared something special after what he had said to her, and the tone of his voice when he said it.

Dreamily remembering their last night together, Lan'xiu startled and jumped to her feet upon hearing the sound of Ci'an's shrill voice. Having done so, she could think of nothing better than to go to the window, partially concealing herself behind the curtain, hoping the wintry chill of the glass would cool her heated face. All her newfound confidence drained away in the dread of knowing that Ci'an would find some way to call attention to her new earrings.

As Second Wife moved into the room, she could see Ci'an's person loaded down with so much jewelry it was difficult to tell the color of her gown. Lan'xiu knew intuitively that somehow news of Hüi's gifts had come to Ci'an's ears. Considering what Mei Ju had told her, Lan guessed that Ci'an had received nothing from Hüi, and this was her defiant attempt to exhibit her wealth and thumb her nose at the rest of the wives.

"Don't stand there hiding in the shadows, Lan'xiu. Come out and let us see you. You are so pretty to look at," Bai called at this inopportune moment.

"Yes, you might as well let us admire you," Ci'an agreed. "You never say anything worth listening to. Like our simple little Alute here, isn't that so?" She leaned forward to poke a finger at Alute, who shrank away from her, looking unhappy to be singled out. "Is that a new bracelet I spy?"

"Don't, Ci'an," Alute pleaded, batting at the other woman's hand.

Lan'xiu crossed the room to sit next to Alute, hoping to divert Second Wife's attention from her. "Greetings, Second Wife," she said, bowing low as a token of respect before she sat down.

Well satisfied with Alute's shrinking response, Ci'an turned her attention to Lan'xiu, the triumphant smile fading from her lips as she caught sight of the ruby earrings.

Ci'an's body stiffened and she almost shook with rage, but she controlled her reaction, forcing a smirk to her lips. "Ah, my sister wives, I see you have all earned your keep with your master, but judging by appearances, the Princess of Nothing has snared the top prize. Are those diamonds and rubies I spy dangling from your ears?"

Bravely, Lan'xiu tried to answer without rancor. "You said you didn't like my turquoise earrings. I didn't want to bore you."

"I never bored Hüi Wei when he came to me. There were times I scratched his back bloody, but he always left my bed well satisfied." Ci'an gave Lan'xiu a triumphant smile. "Early days for you, stupid girl. A novelty always pleases to begin with, but your insipidity will soon begin to pall. What province traded you for their safety? Who sold you for such a paltry bit of jewelry?" She reached forward to flick at the earrings, but Lan'xiu parried her grab.

"I did not say where these earrings came from. They are mine and I like them." Too late Lan'xiu realized Ci'an's sharp eyes had caught a glimpse of the dagger up her sleeve.

"What's this? She is armed! She is a spy, sent to kill our husband!" Ci'an sprang to her feet and tugged at Lan'xiu's sleeve to expose the scabbard.

"I am no spy!" Lan cried and jumped up, knocking the other woman's hand loose. She saw the other women staring at her, shocked, and realized they were unsure and stupefied by Ci'an's accusation. "If I had been sent to kill the general, then why haven't I already done so?"

"To divert suspicion!" Ci'an blared triumphantly.

"Suspicion of what?" Lan'xiu could not hold in her laughter. "What better opportunity could I have had than the general's first visit? And yet he lives on to give me these." Lan touched the earrings shivering in her ears. "And this dagger was a gift from him as well."

"Why would you conceal a dagger up your sleeve then?" Ci'an asked, eyes narrowed.

A sudden inspiration struck Lan'xiu. "First Wife advised me always to go armed to any meeting with you, Second Wife."

Ci'an cast about for some insult to maintain her ground. "And yet your belly remains flat even though our husband has been trying hard to get you with child! It has been months, and when he discovers you are barren, he will cease to light your lantern and then that pretty dagger will be cold comfort between your legs."

"I'm sure you would know, as your lantern has been cold and dark a very long time."

Bai gasped in surprise at Lan's sharp retort and then laughed out loud. Mei Ju looked astonished but hid her mouth behind her hand, giving a quiet cough that sounded suspiciously like a giggle. Alute drew a little behind Lan'xiu as if to render herself invisible.

"So, the little mouse has a tongue as sharp as a serpent," Ci'an said at last.

Lan'xiu thought she detected a note of reluctant admiration in Ci'an's voice. "I sting too." She wished she dared draw the dagger, for she was sure it would give her great pleasure to run Ci'an through, but it would never do to fight with an unarmed woman, particularly in Mei Ju's tidy sitting room. "I am no spy," Lan repeated, turning to Mei Ju.

"I know you are not. You are a very sweet, innocent girl," Mei Ju said, glaring at Ci'an. "Second Wife, I realize you have some inexplicable partiality to these dramas and histrionics, but you have finally lost your grasp upon reality. Look at the princess. She is slender and small. Hüi Wei could disarm her without any trouble at all if she threatened him. I am sure if he did not wish Lan'xiu to have a dagger, she would not have one."

"She could kill him in his sleep," Ci'an said sulkily, but the tautness left her body and she sat down.

The other wives tittered at the indelicate comment. Even though Ci'an was often crude, they appreciated a risqué joke. Hüi Wei did not *sleep* when he visited them.

"Oh, shut up, Ci'an. You've stirred up enough dust for one day," Bai said. "Why can't you ever behave?"

"That would be boring," Ci'an said provocatively, her lips curling, but she took good care not to look Lan'xiu's way.

Lan'xiu seated herself next to Alute and yawned delicately. Bai laughed at the subtle jibe at Ci'an. "Perhaps you should surprise us one time by acting pleasant. Your tantrums have grown rather commonplace."

Turning away abruptly, Ci'an demanded, "Is no one going to offer me anything to drink?"

"I have a fresh pot of jasmine tea here—" Mei Ju started, reaching for the new bronze and jade teapot that had been Hüi Wei's gift to her along with the headdress.

"I require something a bit stronger than that," Ci'an announced. "You! One of you soldiers at the door assigned to prevent me from killing any of these lovely ladies! Run to my house and fetch the bottle of *huáng jiǔ* on the sideboard. And mind you don't sneak a sip for yourself. I know the level of my bottle," she ended sharply.

The second soldier hesitated until Mei Ju nodded her acquiescence.

It seemed to Lan'xiu that the women in the room held their breaths for the short time until the soldier returned with the bottle.

"Now we can get drunk and gamble," Ci'an announced. "Mei Ju?"

"You know I never drink spirits, but I always enjoy a good game of chance," Mei Ju responded. She instructed her maid to fetch some glasses.

"Perhaps together we can win those new earrings away from the princess or snap up the bracelet Alute wears. Clearly, the two beautiful idiots have spread their legs to good purpose for our husband to purchase their favors so extravagantly. One might think their private parts were made of gold that he snatches at them so greedily."

"Ci'an! Mind your manners or you may as well return to your house! Remember you are a guest in my house!" Mei Ju rebuked her.

"Manners? Why, what is it other than good manners when I have offered to share my very best drink?" Ci'an said, a malicious smile curling her red lips. "Will you have some, Bai?"

"Oh no, I find I don't need intoxicants to elevate my spirits," Bai replied blithely. "I have an appointment to dance with the moon later and must be on my toes."

"Lord, what a moon-calf. Whatever does Hüi see in you? Fen and Huan? I'm sure you'll come to a decision *together* since you do *everything* together." Ci'an laughed at her sly dig. When neither woman replied, she said, "Still ignoring me, I see. It won't do you any good. You can't make me vanish by pretending I'm not here." She looked toward the large temple chair Alute and Lan'xiu shared. "That leaves the two lovely dummies. Oh, pardon, one lovely and one dummy. Perhaps some liquor will loosen your tongue, Alute, although I doubt you would ever find anything even slightly intelligent to say."

"Yes, thank you," Alute said desperately, as if hoping to quiet Ci'an. She accepted the glass of golden liquid and held it in her hand.

"And you, Princess of Nothing? You must wish to drown your sorrows. Not yet pregnant and you didn't get to use that knife on me." She raised her glass as if in a toast and tossed back the entire contents. "Yet."

"Thank you for your kind offer. I will take a glass," Lan'xiu said with quiet dignity, although the jibe cut her to the quick. She could feel the rage and jealousy emanating off this cold woman and wondered how she had ever managed to bear a child.

"You think I am very cruel, don't you? Poking fun at these *sweet* innocents." Ci'an refilled her glass and waved it at the other women.

"I think you are very unhappy," Lan'xiu said.

Ci'an's mouth dropped open in shock, and she stared at Lan'xiu, speechless for once.

"I am sorry. I should not have said anything so personal," Lan'xiu said.

"Girls, this is not how we should behave," Mei Ju said in distress. "Please, cannot we simply be polite and have a pleasant afternoon, just *once*?"

"I am sorry, First Wife." Lan'xiu bowed in her direction.

"I didn't mean *you!*" Mei Ju exclaimed in exasperation.

Ci'an swallowed hard. She seemed to make a great effort to pull herself together. In a quieter voice she said, "I apologize as well. Alute, Princess Lan'xiu, please join me in a toast to our kind hostess, and I will promise to behave for the rest of the afternoon."

"A red letter day!" Bai cheered, holding up her teacup and sloshing some of the contents onto the rug. "Ci'an apologizes! It should be carved in stone and set in the middle of our square, for surely this day will go down in history."

The room was silent again for a moment, awaiting Ci'an's reaction. She gritted her teeth but gave a dangerously glittering smile. "I was born to make history, one way or another." She tossed back her second drink, and Lan'xiu wondered at her apparent imperviousness to the strong drink. If she had downed her glass in a similar manner, she would have been flattened.

The rules of etiquette demanded she and Alute drink. Lan touched her glass to Alute's and lifted it to her lips, although she never drank. It would not be wise to lose control when one's very survival depended upon keeping vigilant guard over a dire secret, but she let the liquor touch the tip of her tongue.

It looked so pretty in the glass, golden like liquid honey, but the taste! Hastily, Lan'xiu allowed the tiny amount she had taken to slip back into the glass, hoping no one would notice if she did not finish it.

Alute did not seem similarly affected, and she held her glass toward Ci'an to have it refilled. Lan'xiu wondered at the sly triumph on Ci'an's face as she did so.

When she was able to do so unobserved, Lan'xiu spilled the remainder in her glass into a potted jade plant. She blushed when she realized Mei Ju had witnessed her action, but the older woman gave her a smile and an approving nod. Lan'xiu smiled back and went to Mei Ju for a cup of tea, hoping to wash the bitter taste out of her mouth.

CHAPTER FIFTEEN

SHU NING had been sparring enjoyably with Jia in the kitchen after carrying down a tray of food that Lan'xiu had barely touched, attributing her lack of appetite to the choice of dish. As he mounted the stairs he heard sounds of distress coming from within Lan'xiu's chambers.

Ning raced inside, finding the bedchamber empty, and ran into the bathing room to find Lan'xiu on the floor. He bent over her in alarm. "Lan'xiu, what is it? You are never ill." He pulled her loose hair back and started to braid it hastily into a single plait.

Lan'xiu panted over the basin where she had just emptied her guts. She was freezing, but strands of hair were stuck to her face with sweat, her innards twisted in agony, and she was trembling with weakness. "Poison," she managed to mutter. "Ning, you must get a message to Hüi Wei."

"You think he will come to you?"

"Not to me. He must go… to Alute! She drank two glasses! That evil—" Another cramp seized her, and she retched helplessly into the bowl.

"What? What happened? Who poisoned who?"

Exhausted, Lan'xiu slumped to the floor, resting her hot cheek against the polished stone. "Second Wife Ci'an. She brought poisoned wine to the party. Alute took far more than I… get a doctor—"

"You cannot see the physician here!" Ning exclaimed.

"I know! You must get him… to see to Alute! Tell Hüi Wei! Or Mei Ju! She will know—" Lan'xiu started to retch again.

Ning wrung his hands, not knowing what to do. It had always been one of his secret fears that one day Lan'xiu would need a doctor, which meant certain death either way. If whatever ailed her did not kill her, the revelation of her deception surely would lead to difficulties. So far, she had enjoyed excellent health but now—

Lan'xiu lifted her head. "Ning, why do you delay! Go! There is no time to lose! Alute must not—" She drooped limply to the floor again.

Ning emptied the basin and rinsed it out, placing it near her again. Then he bathed her heated face with a wet cloth. "Lan, I am going, do you hear me? I'm going and I'll be back as quick as I can."

Lan appeared to have lapsed into a faint, and he didn't like to leave her like this but it was necessary. Also necessary, although it pained him to do so, Ning decided he must lock her within the room. That way, no matter how much noise she made in her suffering, the household staff could not reach her to aid her—or discover her secret.

He ran down the stairs with no thought for his own dignity and tore out the front door, barreling into the broad frame of Hüi Wei and bouncing back off his solid form.

"Ning, what's amiss?" Hüi asked in alarm.

"My Lord Qiang," Ning said, giving a hasty bow. "Lan'xiu is ill but I dare not fetch a doctor to her. Moreover, she says that Sixth Wife Alute has been poisoned. She needs a doctor immediately! I will return to Lan'xiu, and you go to fetch aid for Alute! Be smart about it! Hurry!" Barely realizing that he, a lowly eunuch who served the lowliest of concubines had just hurled an order at their lord and master, Ning didn't wait to see what Hüi would do. He bolted back into the house and flew up the stairs to return to Lan'xiu.

When he unlocked the door, he could hear the sounds of her misery. She was being ill again, and the moans that tore from her throat made him cringe in sympathy. He went to her and held her up from the floor where she could still retch uselessly over the bowl. Placing a cool wet cloth on the back of her neck, he began to sing to her, the lullaby she'd loved as a little girl. It seemed to calm her for after a while she became quiet, a dead weight in his arms.

"Please don't die, Lan'xiu, please don't die. We've come so far; it's not your time. Your soul is here. The general came to you. Please don't die."

Ning never even noticed the footsteps behind him, but he started when a strange male voice said, "What's amiss with her?"

He jerked around to find Lord Jiang, looking down at them with concern. "It is noth-nothing. She-she must have eaten something that disagreed with her," he stammered.

"People usually do not die from a touch of indigestion," Jiang said sternly.

"She was poisoned," Ning said baldly, his tears starting to flow.

Jiang pushed Ning aside and took Lan'xiu's limp form from him. "Princess Lan'xiu, can you hear me?"

Ning saw Lan'xiu's eyes flutter, and she nodded her head almost imperceptibly.

"I know your secret, Lan'xiu. You have nothing to fear from me," Jiang said gently.

A shudder went through Lan'xiu's body before she went limp again, whispering hoarsely, "My Lord—"

"Hüi has confided in me," Jiang said. "The main thing now is to get you well. I'm no doctor, but I have some field experience. Ning said you were poisoned. How and when?"

"And who?" Ning muttered.

"Ci'an... brought... the wine... was bitter...," Lan'xiu struggled to say. "I had barely... a sip. Alute... she took much more...."

"Hüi Wei has gone to fetch the doctor to Alute. Don't worry about her now." Jiang turned to Ning. "Run to the kitchen. Get your housekeeper to mix up some mustard water. I will also need the whites of several raw eggs. Be quick about it!"

"Yes, sir!" Ning flew down the stairs and flurried Jia into fulfilling his demands.

"What is amiss with the mistress, Ning-xiānsheng. Is she losing the baby?" Jia cried.

"What baby?" Ning asked, too distracted to realize what he was saying.

"It is known that the princess is with child, but she is a delicate girl. I heard that she-devil Ci'an gave her a dangerous liquor to drink and now she is having a miscarriage!" Jia wept and flung her shawl over her head, rocking back and forth, wailing.

Later Ning would wonder how such a baseless rumor came to be accepted as common knowledge, but now he seized upon it, knowing he could not explain a poisoning he did not understand, and that news of a miscarriage would not only garner Lan'xiu much sympathy but would also serve to defend her secret even better. "Let us hope that the doctor arrives in time," he said. Then he ran back upstairs with the elixir. "Call for Captain Wen."

Jiang lifted Lan'xiu against his shoulder and ruthlessly tilted the emetic down her throat.

Instantly she became sick once again, this time bringing up blood. When her heaving had diminished, Jiang administered the raw egg whites. Ning made a face as he watched her swallow the slimy mess, but it appeared to help.

"I only pray to the gods that I have done right by her," Jiang muttered. "Heaven grant the gods let her live."

"She *must* live," Ning said intensely.

Jiang glanced at him shrewdly. "She is one who inspires love deeply. I want her to live, not just for her sake and yours. I fear for Hüi Wei if she were to die."

Ning wasn't as concerned with the general, but this was not the time to voice that opinion. "Do you think you were in time?"

"I don't know," Jiang said irritably. "How long was she ill? What poison was administered to her and how much did she take? At least I hope I did her no harm."

Ning settled on the floor, his back against the copper bath to wait with Jiang. Both of them fixed their gaze on the white, unconscious face, listening to Lan'xiu's labored breathing grow quieter. Shadows began to deepen, and Ning was thinking of lighting a lamp when the door opened. He sprang to his feet, ready to chase any of the servitors away if they intruded, but stopped when he saw it was Hüi Wei.

"Is she all right?"

"Resting now. I administered an emetic and a soothing agent," Jiang said. "What news of Alute?"

"She is dead."

Ning piped up. "Lan'xiu said something about Ci'an, Second Wife, also drinking the wine."

Hüi Wei's face was grim. "Ci'an laughed when I told her Alute died, but she didn't answer any questions. She gave me the bottle of wine, but I'm sure she switched it for an innocent one, she gave it so willingly. They all drank from the same bottle, and Ci'an had even more...."

"We should get the princess to bed," Jiang said practically.

"Let me bathe her first," Ning said.

Silently, the three of them removed Lan'xiu's clothing. Despite his concern, Ning noticed how staggered Jiang seemed by the beauty of Lan'xiu's form: every line scribed so elegantly, every plane of muscle, the delicacy of his bone structure.... Ning was so used to thinking of Lan'xiu in a particular way, seeing him through the other men's eyes jolted him into a renewed awareness of Lan's masculine form. Ning sponged the sheen of sweat from Lan's body and the blood from his lips, and hoped the general realized what a lucky man he was.

Ning wrapped a sleep robe about Lan'xiu, and Hüi himself lifted the insensate young man and carried him to the bed.

Lan'xiu seemed to be sleeping more easily now, his face pale on the pillows. With the quilt drawn up, his slight body made barely a mound under the cover. Ning set a lantern on the chest by the bed and sat down.

"I will watch over her," Hüi said. "Get your dinner, Ning. You will be needed to remain alert by her side all night."

Reluctantly, Ning walked to the door, and then an idea struck him. He turned back. "My Lord!"

"Yes."

"The women below stairs believe that Lan'xiu has lost your child."

Hüi and Jiang stared at each other. Jiang nodded.

Hüi said, "You may tell them that is the truth."

"Thank you, my Lord." Ning withdrew, well satisfied. No need to spell things out for either man; they were both clever enough to recognize the opportunity and seize it, using it to the advantage of all concerned.

He arranged his face suitably for mourning and descended to confirm the bad news to Jia, knowing that every soul within the palace walls would know before dawn that Lan'xiu had been pregnant with Hüi's child and lost it. He resolved to subtly imply that somehow Ci'an was at the bottom of the tragedy. After all, every lie was the better with a little truth sprinkled in for seasoning.

HÜI WEI groaned as he watched Lan'xiu sleep. "Poor Alute," Naturally he was disturbed at her tragic passing, but he knew it was nothing compared to what he would be feeling had Lan'xiu been the victim.

"Do you think Ci'an truly did this?" Jiang asked.

"Yes. I don't know how, but she managed it somehow. She has always hated Alute, because she was pretty and restful," Hüi said.

"And she gave you a son," Jiang said shrewdly.

"I thought Ci'an was resolved to take Mei Ju's place. I never suspected that she would turn her sights to the concubines below her," Hüi Wei said, holding tightly to Lan'xiu's hand. "I should have foreseen—"

"One cannot foresee everything. And you have enough to look after without having a war raging within your household. It seems Ci'an has changed her strategy," Jiang said, "Which raises the question—"

"How did she drink of the same bottle and suffer no ill effects," Hüi interjected.

"I suspect Ci'an may be an arsenic eater," Jiang said. "Tell me, is her hair glossy and her eyes bright?"

"Like a panther in a forest," Hüi said. "She is most unfortunately very beautiful. However, I have taken care not to supply her household with arsenic for their cooking."

"She must have bribed a servant to bring it to her," Jiang suggested.

"You yourself insisted that we change her servants weekly. Soldiers are routinely reassigned before she has a chance to charm them. Besides," Hüi said dryly, "Ci'an does not possess the gift of making friends easily. Who would want to serve her?"

"It must be bribery, then. She is getting the arsenic from somewhere."

"And you will find out where," Hüi said. "This must not be allowed to continue." He returned his gaze to the sleeping Lan'xiu, clasping his hand as if his touch could keep him from the grave.

Jiang stood up and touched Lan's forehead. "She seems to be doing better. I think we were in time."

"You were in time, my friend. I shall always be grateful to you." Hüi Wei reluctantly stood up. "I have things to arrange, and I must speak with Mei Ju. She is very upset. And the other wives must be kept safe."

"Perhaps it is time that Ci'an was removed from the household," Jiang said.

"Perhaps," Hüi said in distraction. "I will return to Lan'xiu's side as soon as I can. Let her know if she wakes. When Ning returns, do you think it safe to leave Lan'xiu here within his sole care? I must make some arrangements for Alute and my son."

"As long as you ensure that Ci'an's door is bolted and the soldiers alerted to prevent her escape, I would judge it to be safe," Jiang said, pulling his lip. "Ning seems to me willing to throw himself between Lan'xiu and anything that endangers her."

Hüi nodded, staring at Lan'xiu's face. It was funny how when he first met Lan'xiu he could see only the beautiful woman. Now that he knew Lan's secret, he marveled that no one else's gaze had pierced his disguise. For all the sculpted delicacy of his face, Hüi saw the beautiful young man he loved. It was a shock to realize he had come to accept Lan's preference in dress and manner so completely that he never wondered over it anymore. The thought of that taut perfect body, hidden like an unsuspected jewel beneath the soft silks and embroidery—he shivered with pain at the thought of never reaching for Lan again, seeking under the womanly raiment for the real treasure of Lan's silky smooth skin and hard cock—

Hüi dashed a hand over his eyes to clear his vision. "A tragedy."

Jiang answered, "A tragic day indeed, and yet we have cause to rejoice that Lan'xiu did not fall to Ci'an's plot."

"We must discover how Ci'an caused the poison to be smuggled in," Hüi repeated, still lingering as if he could not find it in himself to leave Lan's side.

"Why not simply discover how yielding her flesh is to the steel of your sword? You should have had her put to death years before this," Jiang said harshly.

It surprised Hüi; he had not known how bitterly Jiang felt toward Second Wife. "I need to know. I can't explain…. I need to know…. Watch over her." With that he finally hurried from the room.

JIANG'S stomach growled. He glared down at it. It was an inopportune moment of comedy amidst tragedy as so often happened in life, but to be hungry after witnessing Lan'xiu casting up the contents of her stomach was incredibly unruly of his body, in his opinion. He sighed, not knowing how long Ning would linger below stairs. Then he entertained a few ungenerous thoughts about eunuchs, which he repented of the moment the door opened and Ning came in bearing a tray.

"How is she?" Ning asked anxiously, looking at Lan'xiu's face.

"Sleeping," Jiang answered. "Is that for me? For I could surely use a bit of food."

"Yes, I had my supper downstairs." Ning pulled a small table within Jiang's reach with his foot and set the tray down. "Excuse me. I thought of another task that must be seen to."

He went to a chest against a wall and withdrew a white sheet. He disappeared within the bathroom and returned with the sheet now red with blood.

Jiang wondered until he remembered Lan'xiu throwing up blood. "What are you doing?"

"Below, the servants all believe that Lan'xiu has miscarried. I am simply providing evidence that will speak for her. I will not say a word when I dispose of these."

Nodding, Jiang continued to eat as Ning left the room with the bloody sheet. Jiang had finished his supper and set the tray on the floor outside the door before Ning returned.

Ning sank down upon the chair where Hüi had been sitting and took Lan'xiu's hand. Jiang thought he meant to hold it but instead, Ning felt for her pulse. He nodded as if satisfied and laid her hand down gently.

"She will do," Ning said in a relieved tone.

Jiang realized for the first time how drawn and worried the eunuch looked, and wished he might do something for him as well as for Lan'xiu. He noticed the boy in the bed licking his lips and went to him, raising him up against his shoulder. Divining his intent, Ning was there immediately, carefully spooning a little water between the parched lips.

"He doesn't look very well," Jiang said softly.

"*She* is resilient. She heals quickly. Lan'xiu will surprise you. Tomorrow she will be out of bed, demanding to stand on her own two feet," Ning said defiantly.

Jiang hid a smile. "If she is well enough to get out of bed tomorrow, I will give you five hundred tael of silver."

Ning's eyes gleamed. "I hope you have it by you, for tomorrow I shall be hounding you to pay what you owe me."

"How can you be so sure?" Jiang laid Lan'xiu down on the pillows, noting the small wrinkle between her brows had smoothed out. "Has she ever been injured before?"

Ning gave him a sidelong glance, apparently deciding if he could be trusted. "She fell off her horse once as a child and broke her leg."

"Her leg? I thought I saw a scar on her back."

With a secretive face, Ning said, "That was another occasion when her strength saved her life—and mine."

"What happened? Who did this evil act?" Jiang recollected what he had learned about Wu Min's court. "Did the murderer who slew her mother attempt to assassinate Lan'xiu too?"

"It was her brother. He tried to rape her. It was then he discovered that she is—not all she seems. He stabbed her and nearly killed me, but Lan'xiu managed to get us both away. She was not able to save her mother in time, however."

Jiang gasped at the horror of the story. It was not that such things were unheard of, but Lan'xiu seemed so beautiful and gentle. A pity that something so heinous should happen to her, but the gods sometimes laid out a difficult path even for those most deserving of kindness. "I am glad you both survived."

"Only to fall into this fix," Ning said with a sigh. "Lan'xiu used to run and ride through the mountains around her home. First her brother jails her, and now she is kept trapped within a gilded cage, with no sight of the mountains or lakes she loves."

Jiang hesitated. "Hüi Wei thinks she loves him."

"She does, truly. I have never seen her like this before," Ning said. "And for love of him, I am sure she will stay here, waiting for her lantern to be lit, taking what few crumbs he offers."

"I am sorry," Jiang repeated, but he had much to think about.

When Hüi Wei did not return, Jiang grew worried about what could be keeping him. It could be nothing dire, but then perhaps another calamity might have claimed his attention. When the sky grew light, Jiang deemed it safe to leave Lan'xiu in the care of the faithful Ning and took his leave. To his relief, Lan'xiu's color was better, and she seemed to have fallen into a natural sleep.

NING was grateful to see Jiang go. To have these men pushing in where it had always been only him and Lan'xiu was unsettling for him. He could not deny that they had been helpful, and it had even made him feel safer while guarding her, but he could relax now. The secret he had held for Lan'xiu for so long had become sacred to him, and he wasn't sure he liked that now these two men were privy to it. No telling if or when they might make a slip, and he had no power to constrain their tongues.

After Jiang left, Ning locked the bedroom door and made sure the door to his adjoining room was locked to the hallway as well.

Lan'xiu looked perfectly beautiful and relaxed, asleep on the bed with her hair in one thick plait. She had turned onto her side, lying with her cheek pillowed on one hand, her mouth slightly open.

Ning yawned. He had been awake more than twenty-four hours at this point and felt exhausted himself. Secure in the knowledge that no one could get in, he settled himself on the window seat and nodded off.

CHAPTER SIXTEEN

LAN'XIU stretched with her eyes squeezed shut. She knew she was in her bed and alone, but something did not feel right. She placed her hand on her stomach. She was feeling very empty, but she did not wish to eat. Her ribs and stomach muscles were sore, her throat ached, and her mouth was dry. She felt weak and, even worse, uneasy without quite knowing why.

She also needed to relieve herself badly.

A sixth sense for danger made her squint around the room first rather than opening her eyes. A snore made her giggle silently, but she stopped because it hurt her ribs too much. She recognized that snore; it was Ning. She opened her eyes and smiled at the sight of him curled up on the window seat. No doubt he would berate her later for not waking him to help her to the bathing room, but she refused to admit she might need help.

A vague memory of being violently ill and Ning singing to her made her suspect he had been up with her all night. He did enough to serve her; she did not need his help for this.

After relieving herself, Lan'xiu looked into the mirror and gasped at her beastly appearance. Dark circles under eyes like burning coal stood out in her white face. In addition, she had a deep crease across one cheek from the pillowslip. After washing her face and drying it, she pushed back the strands of hair surrounding her face that had loosened from her braid while she was sleeping.

But her bare feet were getting cold on the stone floor, and she didn't want to linger in the bathing room. She had some confused recollection of being miserable there last night, but she pushed the memories away. She wasn't ready to deal with them, and there seemed to be no obvious injury other than general soreness. She decided to go back to bed.

She was barely settled when a tap sounded on the door. Instantly, she sat bolt upright in the bed, her heart pounding in alarm. Ning was also jerked out of a sound sleep and on his feet in an instant. They both remained silent, waiting.

As they watched, the doorknob twisted and rattled slightly, but no one entered. Ning made the motion with his hand of locking the door and held up the key. Lan'xiu nodded.

A faint rustling and some whispers sounded outside, and they waited for the intruder, whoever it was, to go away. Then a second, louder knock sounded.

"Is that you, Jia?" Ning called out.

"It is I, Dr. Mu, the court physician," a male voice answered. "The Governor Qiang Hüi Wei sent me to give Princess Lan'xiu some medicine."

Two pairs of frightened eyes met. Ning shrugged and Lan'xiu sat tense, the quilt clutched to her bosom.

"Hüi Wei is concerned and ordered me to see the princess with my own eyes and report back to him that she is well."

"Open the door," Lan'xiu told Ning.

"I do not have a good feeling about this," Ning said. "I told—"

"Open it. If it is a trick, we will be ready."

NING paused and then went to the door. When he opened it, a short man with a doctor's hat entered the room, bowing low. He remained just inside the door, looking at Lan'xiu curiously. He held out a small glass bottle to Ning. "Medicine for the princess. I will not touch you without your permission, Princess. My only mission is to assure myself that you are well."

"Thank you for your concern, Dr. Mu. As you can see, I am quite well," Lan'xiu said.

"But your throat pains you, doesn't it?" Second Wife Ci'an said, pushing her way into the room past the doctor. Her hair was pulled back into a single queue, and she wore a plain jacket with men's trousers and a hat like the doctor's. In her right hand she held a short sword, and she was grinning wickedly. "Did you get sick from the wine? Pity you didn't come down with the same permanent hangover as stupid little Alute."

"You must be mad," Lan'xiu breathed. "You cannot hope to come here to murder me and get away with it."

Dr. Mu was looking at Ci'an with a little nervousness, but he hovered behind her, still clutching the glass bottle Ning had not taken.

"Your servants will say two male doctors came to your house. They will find you dead with your tame eunuch. No doubt people's lurid minds will imagine some lover's quarrel where you killed each other. Perhaps we'll pose you. Naked, with your legs spread apart and running with blood." Ci'an licked her lips and laughed.

"Ci'an-xiānsheng, you cannot be serious. You cannot do this!" the doctor said nervously.

"Shut up, you stupid little worm. Address me as Second Wife! At least for now until I am First Wife," Ci'an snapped. She approached the bed and raised her short sword. "I shall enjoy this. Let Hüi Wei suffer when he loses your precious little cunt. Your death is a paltry price for that satisfaction."

"Ning!" Lan'xiu cried out. "My sword!"

Ci'an raised her own sword above her head and brought it down, swinging wildly.

While Lan'xiu sprang from the bed and raised her right arm to block the blow, knowing the blade would bite deep into her flesh, Ning raced into his room where the weapons were hidden.

Ning ran back clutching two swords and tossed one to Lan'xiu, who caught it in her left hand. She whirled to face Ci'an, her plait flying, her face set in a fierce smile. "And now we fight, Ci'an."

"To the death!" Ci'an snarled. She raised her sword and charged in again.

NING yanked the doctor back against the wall, holding his sword against the man's throat. He dragged him out of the room, shrieking at the top of his lungs, "Jia! Jia, you useless sow! Jia, come to me!"

He wanted nothing more than to slay Ci'an and place her lifeless body at Lan'xiu's feet as an offering, but he knew the princess would never forgive him if he did not allow her to fight. He would have to leave it to her to defend herself.

The noises within the room did nothing to comfort him, but at least the doctor seemed shocked into compliance, for he did not struggle.

When Jia at last appeared in the hall downstairs, Ning flung a few orders and choice words at her and edged back into the room, dragging the doctor with him.

Lan'xiu's sleeve was crimson with blood, but her intense eyes glowed with the joy of battle and the concentration Ning had taught her. He knew that she was aware that he was there, but she never made the mistake of taking her gaze off Ci'an.

It was clear that Ci'an was buoyed along by hatred and not training, for her form was bad and she lacked discipline. She hacked away wildly with her short sword, as if sensing weakness within the princess, relying on brute strength rather than finesse.

However, Lan'xiu fought her off cleverly, using techniques that Ci'an did not have the knowledge to recognize or combat. Aware that her recent illness and the blood dripping from the wound in her arm would curtail her endurance, Lan did not attack. She would first allow Ci'an to commit to one of her wild swings and then parry it, letting the blade slip harmlessly over her own. She ducked past Ci'an and whirled to face her again.

"I hate you!" Ci'an said through clenched teeth. She lunged, aiming for the wounded arm.

"I rather gathered you did." Lan'xiu slid away from the attack again, and Ci'an staggered forward off balance when her sword connected only with empty air. Lan'xiu raised her longer blade and sliced Ci'an's cheek and earlobe before she danced away out of reach.

"You bitch! You scarred me!" Ci'an dropped her sword and raised her hand to her face, staring at the blood in disbelief.

"That is not the only scar you will carry as a keepsake to remember me by," Lan'xiu said contemptuously. She kicked Ci'an's sword closer. "Pick it up! You promised to kill me, remember?"

Ci'an dove for the sword and circled Lan'xiu, a little more cautiously now, looking for an easy opening, still without any understanding of her own difficulty in battling a well-trained, left-handed swordswoman.

Ning circled his arm about the doctor's throat, keeping his body pressed against his own, ready to strangle him if he felt the doctor move. It was thrilling to witness Lan'xiu in action in her first real fight, and he didn't want to miss anything, even though he feared for her. If the doctor turned rabbit and scampered off, he would be forced to catch him, so Ning maintained a firm, choking grip on him.

LAN'XIU could feel her breath coming more quickly but, despite that, kept a contemptuous smile upon her lips, knowing it would irritate Ci'an into making a mistake. It was her only advantage now, when she was weak from being ill. The dull throb in her arm made her aware that she was still losing blood. She would have to take control and end this fight, for she could not afford a long one.

Ci'an shrieked in frustration and raised her sword, charging at Lan'xiu. "You will have a scar like mine to remind him of me when he looks at your dead body!"

Lan'xiu darted away from Ci'an's blade and feinted as if too weak to ward off the blow. Ci'an cried out in triumph and tried to lever the sword from Lan'xiu's hand. It was the move Lan'xiu was waiting for. She employed the same trick Hüi Wei had successfully employed upon her during their first meeting and used Ci'an's force against her to flick the blade out of her hand.

Thwarted and frustrated, Ci'an charged at Lan'xiu with her hands outstretched, as if to strangle her. Lan'xiu launched herself into a somersault through the air, avoiding Ci'an's grasp and landing behind her. As Second Wife turned to face her, Lan'xiu drew her blade down Ci'an's other cheek and away from her, slicing off her earlobe and the earring in it.

"So much for your taste in earrings."

Ci'an screamed in pain and clutched her bleeding ear. "I shall kill you for this!"

"You said that already, but you don't seem to be making much headway," Lan'xiu said. It was costing her more to hide her pain now, but the chance to best Ci'an was too heady for her to resist. "If you care to try again, your sword landed there."

Without bothering with the sword, Ci'an aimed a high, roundhouse kick at Lan'xiu, who leaned away to let the foot sail by her head. When Ci'an was forced by her momentum to turn away, Lan kicked her in the ass, knocking her to the floor on her hands and knees.

"There, you are much closer to your weapon now. Pick it up," Lan commanded, sounding every inch a princess.

Ci'an moaned as if in too much pain but then suddenly lunged for her sword and came up slashing wildly. Lan'xiu blocked her amateurish attempts and waited for another mistake. Sensing that Ci'an was sucking desperately for air, Lan'xiu used a series of short stabbing motions to repeatedly prick Ci'an in the face, neck, and hands, inflicting long, bloody scratches to enrage her. Ci'an dropped her sword and started to scream, batting ineffectively at the unrelenting blade with her bare hands.

Lan'xiu drove her back into the bathing room and said, "Wait in there. I would prefer you not to bleed on my rug."

The thunder of footsteps sounded on the stairs, and at long last Dr. Mu tried to escape Ning's grasp. "I think you will wait here with me," Ning told him in a silky voice, tightening his grip.

Ci'an was sobbing now, examining her wounds in the mirror with horror and trying to staunch the bleeding.

Lan'xiu still held her sword at the ready, but her arm was trembling and she hoped that Ci'an would not attempt another attack.

"Lan'xiu, my love!"

And then Hüi was behind her, sliding an arm around her waist to hold her upright, as if he sensed her pride would be wounded if Ci'an witnessed her collapse.

Ci'an turned when she heard Hüi Wei's voice, holding up her hands to cover her face. "I need the doctor! Don't look at me, Hüi. Your stupid little princess has *ruined* my beauty!"

"I will never look upon your face again," Hüi Wei said harshly. "Take her away, Jiang."

"And take away this piece of trash too," Ning said, shoving the doctor forward.

The doctor fell to his knees, his hands clasped, begging, "Do not kill me, oh gracious Governor. Second Wife bewitched me into helping her. It was her wicked terrible beauty that put me under a spell—"

"And that," Jiang said, "is likely how the poison got into the wine."

The clatter of booted feet sounded on the stairs, and Captain Wen entered the room, ordering the accompanying soldiers to remain on guard outside.

"Shu Ning, you are well?" Captain Wen asked urgently.

"I am quite well, thank you." Ning nodded, not taking his eyes off the doctor.

"Take them to the dungeon. Put them in chains," Hüi ordered Captain Wen. "Please go with them and see to it," he added to his friend.

"I cannot just now," Jiang said. "Perhaps Ning could take my place? He might enjoy being in command for a change. Captain Wen, will you take charge of the prisoners?"

"Yes, sir." Captain Wen bowed and cocked his head at Ning. "Will you accompany us, Ning-xiānsheng?"

"That I shall," Ning said, his eyes gleaming. "I should like to ensure that Ci'an is securely imprisoned where she will not come near the princess again."

Impatiently, Hüi waited till Captain Wen and Ning had delivered the prisoners to the soldiers outside the room before telling a curious Jia, hovering by the door, "That will be all, thank you. You may return to the kitchen."

Reluctantly, Jia withdrew, and Jiang shut the door. "Lan'xiu's arm needs stitches, and there is no physician we can call to her."

"I am all right," Lan'xiu said faintly. As soon as Ci'an was out of sight, her arm fell to her side, and she dropped her sword at her feet. She sagged gratefully against Hüi Wei's body.

HÜI WEI picked him up and held the slight body in his arms, staring at the weary face of his love. "How did she gain entry? What happened?"

"Later, Hüi," Jiang said. "I shall fetch some wine. She may be more comfortable if she's drunk when I stitch her up. And then we shall not leave her alone again until she recovers."

Lan'xiu moaned slightly when Hüi Wei set him down on the bed, piling pillows behind him. Then Hüi ripped the sleeve open to view the wound. "How did she manage to cut you so badly?"

"That's another robe you owe me, my Lord," Lan'xiu said faintly.

Hüi chuckled. "And I am glad to pay the price, but tell me what happened. How did Ning come to let Ci'an in?"

"The doctor spoke through the door and said you had sent him, insisting he see me. Ci'an came in behind him, disguised as a male doctor. She attacked and I blocked with my arm while Ning went to fetch my sword," Lan'xiu said. He closed his eyes. "I'm tired."

Hüi Wei realized he was smiling. It was not simply relief in finding Lan'xiu was not severely wounded; it was pride in his unexpected lover. "My warrior princess," he murmured.

Lan'xiu's eyes flew open and he demanded, "What did you call me?"

"My warrior princess," Hüi repeated. "What have I said?"

"Those are the very words of my destiny," Lan'xiu whispered. "The seers told my mother at my birth. That is why she named me as she did and dressed me in skirts. And I never thought it would come to pass."

"And now here you are," Hüi Wei said.

"A prisoner," Lan'xiu said with a sad smile. "But at least I have found you."

"You truly feel like a prisoner?" Hüi asked, hurt. "You have my heart. Is that not enough?"

"I am trying," Lan'xiu said brokenly. "It's not that I don't love you, I do. But I long to see the sky, to breathe the free air. Oh, for a gallop on my horse! I miss it so, being free to come and go as I please."

"It is for your own protection that you are kept here," Hüi tried to explain. "It is the custom—"

"Even for a warrior princess?" Lan'xiu sat up, pushing his hands away. "Try me in battle. I could come with you. I could—"

"Lan'xiu, it would mean my death if I lost you in battle," Hüi said. "And even I do not fight on the front line any longer. I prefer to achieve peace by other means, and if that is not possible, it is my role to direct the mighty force of the soldiers rather than engage personally in combat. But I see that you are different from my other wives...." He paused awkwardly.

Their eyes met and both began to laugh.

"Moderately so," Lan'xiu managed to say between giggles.

"I didn't expect merriment in my absence. What did you find to get her drunk already?" Jiang said, coming back into the room.

"Nothing," Hüi said, not taking his gaze away from Lan'xiu's. "I am getting to know her better."

Since Hüi had first seen Lan'xiu, he had intuitively felt that the household was no place for her, although he was loath to admit it to himself. It wasn't simply his beauty; he had a rare fire that gave him spirit but also allowed him to melt to Hüi's needs. They fit, and whenever Hüi had to be away from him, he suffered.

Jiang was smiling as if indulgent of their mirth as he poured a glass and held it out to Lan. "Drink this and be as merry as you like. It will help you bear the pain."

Lan hesitated, perhaps from the habits of a lifetime of caution, but Hüi reassured him. "We will not leave you. Have no fear."

"I fear this will loosen my tongue," Lan'xiu confessed. "I've never drunk much wine before." He made a face as he sipped at the liquor and began to giggle before the glass was half-empty. "How did you make the room spin like that?"

"I think she's had enough," Jiang said.

Hüi took the glass from Lan's trembling fingers. "Lie down, my love. I will hold your hand while Jiang repairs the damage."

To distract Lan, Jiang asked, "Princess, why didn't you simply slay Ci'an when you could? You had her disarmed and trapped."

"If you can forget what I am, I never can," Lan said, slurring his words. "It would not have been an honorable act to kill a woman."

"Hush now, do not distress yourself," Hüi said. "Keep still, and then you may sleep."

Obediently Lan'xiu slid down against his pillows. The alcohol did allow him to withstand the pain without a sound, even though he bit his lip as Jiang stitched the gash in his arm. Then Jiang bandaged the wound and patted his shoulder. "Sleep well, Warrior Princess," he said before he left the room.

HÜI slipped behind Lan'xiu, leaning against the pillows so he could hold his lover in his arms.

Groggily, Lan'xiu said, "Did you hear? He called me Warrior Princess."

"And so you shall be, Lan'xiu, *my* warrior princess." Hüi felt Lan's head snuggle against his chest and lowered his cheek to touch his hair.

Even disheveled and bloody from the fight, Lan'xiu never looked more beautiful to him. Maybe that's what he needed, a warrior princess who was the prince of his heart in disguise. It all made a strange sort of sense.

Hüi's eyes grew heavy. It had been a long night sorting out the shocking damage Ci'an had wrought, and there was still her fate to be dealt with. Because he didn't want to endanger Lan'xiu by falling asleep with the door unlocked, although it went against the grain to cower behind a locked door, he forced himself to remain awake until Ning came back. But even a general needed to sleep at times.

When Ning returned, strutting a bit with pride, Hüi ordered, "Lock the door, Ning. I need to rest." He had no energy left to explain, but Ning did not seem to mind.

Ning went and locked the door. It was all Hüi could do to remain awake long enough to hear the click of the lock. Through the mists of sleep closing around him, he thought he heard Ning mutter proudly to himself. "Ning, Guardian to the Governor General of Yan and Qui, and his consort, the Princess Zhen Lan'xiu. That's me. That reminds me, Lord Jiang owes me five hundred tael. I shall have to make sure to collect on that bet."

DROWSILY Lan'xiu became aware of Hüi Wei bending over him and felt the gentle stroke of his fingers on his cheek. Hüi bent to kiss him. "Keep her safe, Ning," he heard him say, and then he was gone.

Lan'xiu slumbered peacefully through the day, waking several times to drink some water, but he didn't say much. Ning told him what Hüi had said and he smiled.

He awoke when the sky was growing dark and Ning was lighting the lanterns, feeling a bit drained, his arm throbbing but not actually painful.

"Do you think you could eat some soup, Lan'xiu?" Ning asked when he noticed he was awake.

Lan pushed himself up against the pillows, and he hurried to help, piling them helpfully around him.

"Stop, Ning," Lan'xiu laughed. "I don't need twenty pillows to sit up."

"The general bade me to take care of you," Ning said.

"As if you wouldn't even if he said nothing." Lan looked at Ning affectionately. "Get my soup and stop fussing. I shall be quite well."

"Very well. Don't try to cross the room on your own while I am away," Ning admonished her. He rushed to the kitchen, returning quickly with a covered bowl on a tray. "Mind you drink it all!"

"Don't bully me," Lan'xiu said crossly. But in fact, he ate almost the entire bowl. He hadn't felt hungry when Ning suggested he eat, but the soup tasted good and it was warm, and he enjoyed it.

Ning picked up the tray to return it to the kitchen when a tap sounded on the door.

Lan'xiu sat straight up in bed, a look of alarm on his face. "My sword!" he hissed.

"Not this time," Ning said grimly. "You couldn't stay on your feet for five minutes." He set down the tray hastily and drew his own sword, creeping quietly to the door, and yanked it open suddenly.

LAN'XIU laughed in relief. "Fifth Wife Bai. How kind of you to come to see me."

Ning eyed the young woman suspiciously as she entered the room.

Bai held out her arms as if dancing. "Would you like to search me for weapons?"

Blushing, Ning stammered, "I would, but it would not be proper."

"I could strip for you," Bai offered.

Lan covered her mouth and giggled. "I don't think that will be necessary. Don't tempt her, Ning. She might do it."

"I like it when people dare me," Bai said, grinning impudently at Ning.

"I will keep you both company," Ning announced and sat upon the chair beside Lan's bed, his eyes fixed upon Bai's face.

"After what Ci'an did, I can't say I blame you." Bai drew up a chair for herself and sat beside Ning. "I was worried about you, Lan'xiu, but you look well. Just a little tired."

"I will soon be well again, but it was kind of you to concern yourself with me."

"The household is roiling with rumors," Bai said, her face growing serious for once. "First we heard of poor Alute's death, and Mei Ju made herself sick from weeping. Huan went to Fen's house and threw all the servants out, bolting them both inside. Then came the news that you had been taken ill as well." Bai stopped and looked down discreetly for she could not address the miscarriage directly. "Mei Ju told me that our husband was nearly mad with fear for you."

Lan'xiu's eyes stung with tears, and she blinked quickly to clear them. It would never do to let Bai see this uncommon display of emotion. "I was so sad to hear of Alute's death. She did nothing to deserve this." Lan pulled her sleeve down to cover the bandage but too late to prevent Bai from noticing.

Bai, however, uncharacteristically, did not comment upon it. "I came to see that you were on the mend, but also I bring other sad news." She glanced at Ning, as if asking his permission in case it would upset the princess.

Ning gave her a nod.

"Please, tell me," Lan'xiu begged. "First Wife Mei Ju is well, I hope, and her children!"

"They are all fine," Bai said soothingly. "This is tragic news but perhaps also in the nature of the gods taking justice into their own hands. Ci'an has killed herself."

"Good!" Ning burst out. "Save the soldiers the trouble!"

"Hush, Ning. Who knows what demons tormented her soul and caused her to act as she did," Lan said. "How did she do this dreadful deed?"

"She climbed to the watch tower and threw herself onto the cobbles below," Bai said. She put her hands over her face.

Lan'xiu could see how affected Bai had been and leaned forward to touch her hand. "Poor Bai. I hope you didn't see it."

"I heard her scream as she fell," Bai said in a haunted voice. "And the street was shining red until the soldiers washed her blood away." She took her hands away from her face and looked at Lan'xiu with agonized eyes. "It was horrible."

"I'm sorry you had to witness that," Lan'xiu said, holding Bai's hand.

"That is not the worst thing. When the soldiers searched her house, they found a little boy, a son who said Ci'an was his mother. She had kept him in a darkened room, and no one even knew he existed!" Bai exclaimed. She said pityingly, "He is so small and pale. Mei Ju has taken him into her home and is caring for him."

"That is evil! How dared she treat a child so!" Lan'xiu cried out. "But why? *Why* would she hide a son from Hüi Wei?"

"This boy was certainly born after Hüi no longer came to Ci'an. He would have known the boy was not his. Some think she meant to kill us all and Hüi Wei too, and put her son upon his throne," Bai said.

"Ci'an did not hide her hostility toward Mei Ju, but she cannot have been demented enough to kill the children too!" Lan cried in distress.

"Do not be so sure. She was a monster." Bai gulped and her face twisted in horror. "They found also skeletons of three infant girl babies, packed in the trunks in her attic."

After a horrified silence, Lan said, "I can't imagine what drove her to such madness."

"She was always hungry for power," Bai said. "Before you came, and before Alute gave birth to her son, Ci'an wanted only to supplant Mei Ju. One can move up in rank in the household through other means than death. You have."

"I?" Lan asked in astonishment. "How can that be?"

"You are now concubine of the first rank, right after First Wife Mei Ju," Bai said. "Did no one tell you?"

"I have been asleep," Lan said, as if in a dream. "Ning?"

"I've been here with you. I heard nothing of this," Ning answered.

"For our husband to do this, he has great feeling for you," Bai said. "He has never changed a wife's rank before."

"I—don't know what to say," Lan said in a dazed voice. "But you! I thought you were one of his favorites."

Bai blushed hotly. "You must promise never to divulge this."

Lan'xiu nodded and Bai turned to Ning. "And you."

"I will not speak of it. I could put my fingers in my ears," Ning offered.

"If you were not a eunuch, I should probably ask you to, but I understand your need to protect Lan'xiu lest I suddenly go mad and attack her."

"You would not get close enough to her to try," Ning said fiercely, his hand on his sword.

"You needn't tell us if you don't truly wish to," Lan said.

Teasing Ning seemed to have given Bai a chance to compose herself. "All is not as it appears in the household. Hüi Wei has not lain with any of us since you came. In fact, Alute was already with child when she came within these walls. Her son is not his. She cried for days before she mustered the courage to tell Hüi Wei, but he was very kind to her. She was allowed to live and bear her child in peace, although her child is not mentioned in the succession. Hüi Wei is a kind man."

Lan'xiu's head was spinning. "But… when your lanterns are lit… what do you—" She stopped, realizing that her inquisitiveness was rude.

"After you came, Hüi Wei never went upstairs with me again. We would play checkers," Bai admitted. "He never did… what I said at the party when we first met. He is a kind man. Sometimes he would read to me. He is… very nice."

"You do not love him?" Lan'xiu burst out.

"I do not. It is not to my credit to admit this when he is such a good man," Bai said, hanging her head. "He is too old for me."

"He is not old!" Lan'xiu exclaimed hotly and then stopped herself.

"You *do* love him," Bai said with a pleased little nod. "I thought you did." She held up a hand when Lan'xiu started to speak. "You hide it well, do not fear. I doubt that is what spurred Ci'an to her rash acts."

"How did you know it then?"

"Your eyes glow like stars whenever someone speaks his name. One time, you did not lower your eyes quickly enough and I saw." Bai leaned forward to touch Lan'xiu's hand in her turn. "I am happy for you."

"But you. How can you stay here unloved and... not fulfilling the role you came to—"

"I loved another before I came here," Bai said softly. "I dream of being free to go back to him, although I know this cannot be."

"Have you told this to Hüi Wei?"

"I could not! I could not offend him so," Bai said. "My father is a highly placed official in my province. There are reasons I was chosen to come to here to be a concubine. I could not offend Hüi Wei or my father with my own personal desires."

Briefly, Lan'xiu met Ning's gaze. "Perhaps your dream will yet come true."

"Perhaps," Bai said sadly. "But whether it does or not, I had to come to see that you were still alive and well with my own eyes. Since we met, I felt that we were friends."

"We are," Lan'xiu said, her eyes filling with tears that she did not hide this time. She reached out to grasp Bai's hand and squeeze it. "We are friends."

"I am glad. I liked you the first time I met you," Bai said and gave her usual infectious laugh. "Friends forever!"

LAN'XIU needed another nap after Bai left. Everything Bai had said had taken the newly built foundations of his world and wrenched them away.

When he awoke, it was to feel strong arms holding him safe. He snuggled his cheek against Hüi's shoulder and gave a soft sigh.

"My Lan'xiu," Hüi said in response.

Something in his voice made him open his eyes. "What is it, Hüi?"

"It is nothing. When I am away from you, I worry that something—" Hüi bit his lip. "I came to see that you were safe. I thank the gods that I can still hold you in my arms."

"I, too," Lan said, resting his head upon Hüi's broad shoulder again.

CHAPTER SEVENTEEN

WHEN Lan'xiu woke again, Hüi was gone and Ning was in the room. He stretched languorously in the bed and asked Ning, "What are you looking so ferociously pleased about?"

"When my lord came to see you, I went out and investigated. It is as I thought. Ci'an did not commit suicide."

Lan'xiu sat up, holding his arms around his stomach, feeling suddenly nauseated as if the poison had come back. "What really happened?"

"The soldiers took her up to the tower and offered her the right due her rank to kill herself. She laughed and refused. Then they flung her from the tower onto the stones below," Ning said with satisfaction.

Lan'xiu moaned. Ning came to him and put his arms around him.

"Don't mourn her passing, Lan'xiu. The woman was evil. Ci'an preferred to force the soldiers to execute her, to cause them the guilt of her death." Ning hugged Lan'xiu tightly. "She would have killed you if she could. She did kill Alute and perhaps the three girl infants in her house. If I had been there, I would have cracked her skull and hurled her into the gates of the underworld myself."

"Oh, Ning. It seems tragedy and bad luck follow wherever I go. Perhaps I should leave here and Hüi's life would return to balance."

Ning gave him a shake. "Don't be silly. You are not to blame for this. Your beauty may have excited her jealousy and hatred, but Ci'an would have done murder whether you came here or no. Besides, you did not come here of your own volition, nor did you set out to inspire envy." He released Lan'xiu and laid him back against the pillows. "If you were to leave now, Hüi would follow you and bring you back, so it's too late for you to do anything silly like that. He wants you well so he can hear the squeak of your bed frame once again."

"Have you been listening at the door?" Lan demanded, frowning.

"Not at all, it was a figure of speech," Ning said, looking out the window. "That stupid Dr. Mu is also dead."

"Don't tell me he fell from the tower as well," Lan said with a hint of dread in his voice.

"No, he was beheaded. His crimes were too great for the general to overlook. He not only supplied Ci'an with the poison she used, they were having an affair," Ning announced. "The rumor is that Ci'an's son is his. The boy is certainly a weakling that a strong man like the general could not have bred."

"Ci'an? With that funny little man?" Lan'xiu shook his head. "How did you find all this out?"

Ning blushed a tiny bit and got up to fiddle with the drapes. "I asked Captain Wen. He commands the household guard."

"You have been hiding a romance from me?" Lan teased.

"He has been very useful," Ning said haughtily. "He was the one who came to our aid when Ci'an attacked you." Then he grinned and climbed off his high horse. "Perhaps it is a romance at that."

Lan'xiu laughed and laughed. "Who would have thought? My brother betrays me and sends me to a certain death, and we both find love. It is a funny world."

"It is fate," Ning said solemnly. "Now you must sleep. And try not to worry. The general is worried enough for all three of us."

"He worries over me?" Lan asked, his eyes veiled by his lashes but his face delicately pink.

"No, he's addicted to playing checkers and he needs a new partner," Ning growled. "Go to sleep."

He pulled the quilts up and tucked them about Lan'xiu's shoulders and put out the lantern.

THE next day Lan'xiu left his bed. Shakily, but he made it to the bathing room without aid, where he looked in the mirror and yelped in dismay.

"Ning, I do believe Hüi must love me a little bit if he has been looking upon *this* face with affection! Why didn't you let me bathe?"

"You will not bathe now. I will help you wash. You mustn't get the stitches wet," Ning scolded.

"I beg you to wash my hair. And comb it dry. I think it has blood in it," Lan said distastefully, feeling the stiff braid where his curls were escaping.

"We'll see," Ning said grimly.

The fires under the bath had been lit earlier, and embers glowed nicely there. A delicate curl of steam arose over the waters as he supported Lan'xiu to get into the tub, which was only half-full.

Lan gave a sigh of relief as he sank into the shallow waters.

An hour later, dressed in a becoming dressing gown of deep blue, his hair braided and put up with hair sticks, his eyes ringed with black liner and his lips reddened, Lan'xiu sat in a chair by the window, looking out at the blue sky. A bird in flight made him sigh with gladness and regret that he could only see bare branches and the tiled roofs of the household.

He looked up and smiled when Hüi Wei came into the room, accompanied by Jiang.

"Princess," Jiang said. "I came to look at your wound and change the dressings. You haven't been getting it wet, have you?"

"Ning was very careful," Lan'xiu answered. His eyes were on Hüi's face, and his heart soared when he read the love and concern written there, but he only said, "You look tired, my Lord."

Hüi smiled reassuringly and sat beside him, taking Lan's hand as if he could not bear to be near him and not touch him. "I have had much to do."

Lan'xiu winced slightly when Jiang eased the bandages off the wound.

"You are healing nicely," Jiang said. "I shall just dress this again with some healing herbs." He busied himself with his task, pretending not to notice the soulful glances and gentle touches between the two.

"WHY can't you settle down?" Ning demanded. "Read a book. You should not be tramping about in your room."

"I am completely well," Lan exclaimed, continuing to stalk around the room restlessly. "You treat me as if I were some delicate porcelain vase, and you have not let me set foot out of this room in a week!"

Ning came closer and grabbed the edges of her gown, bringing her closer so he could speak quietly. "You are not completely well, I know your arm still pains you, and you don't eat enough to keep a bird alive."

"I am well enough to walk about the square," Lan said.

"And you would have if I hadn't hidden all your shoes."

"Stolen, you mean. I want them back," Lan threatened.

"Everyone believes you to be too weak to even be out of bed. Moreover, perhaps you might recall you are recovering from a miscarriage, hmm? In mourning. Now act the part, and you shall have a reward."

"My shoes?"

"Better than that. Sit." Ning pointed at the chair by the window. "Or I shall make you go back to bed."

"All right, you tyrant!" Lan wrenched free and sulkily asked, "What are you keeping from me now?"

"The general plans to take you to consult with a doctor." Observing the look of panic on the princess's face, Ning hastened to soothe her. "He will take you to a specialist, outside the city walls, because your health is so uncertain. We will be away for three days."

Lan realized what Ning was trying to discreetly convey, and her face glowed with excitement. "Why didn't you tell me?"

"It has only just been decided." Ning fell silent and looked at her speculatively. "We must be accompanied by a special guard. Lord Jiang will stay behind to govern in Hüi Wei's place."

"And you wish me to request a certain captain to accompany us?"

Ning nodded.

"Naturally, you can put any such nonsense right out of your head—"

"Lan'xiu!" Ning protested.

"Hush, Ning, you silly goblin." Lan smiled at him. "I'm only teasing. I'm sure your Captain Wen will be pleased to come along with us."

"Hüi Wei comes to inform you of our journey tonight, so act surprised," Ning instructed. "Then ask for Captain Wen."

"Who is servant and who is mistress here?" Lan demanded.

"If you need to ask…." Ning grinned at her and went to fetch a traveling trunk.

ONCE outside the city walls, Hüi Wei smiled to see Lan'xiu's delight. He seemed to sit up straighter in the carriage and leaned out the window as if the very air smelled different to him.

Since the day Lan'xiu had startled him by revealing how trapped he felt, Hüi had thought deeply about what it would be like to have one's every movement scrutinized and governed by the whims of another. Lan had opened his eyes to the sort of life his wives led, and he had to admit that in Lan's place, he would also have felt as if he were in some sort of jail.

It was Jiang who had engineered this outing for Lan'xiu. At first, Hüi Wei had thought his friend crazy when he suggested taking Lan to a doctor, but when the entire plan was explained to him, it seemed genius. Hüi would not have admitted it even to Jiang, but where

Lan'xiu was concerned, he couldn't seem to think straight, so he would never have plotted this out for himself.

And yet now he was the one reaping the benefits. Jiang had stayed behind in Hüi's place and was not here to witness the joy on Lan's face as he looked out upon the open fields and houses of the villages that surrounded the city.

To Hüi, Lan was the most exquisite sight he had ever beheld. A fur hat framed his beautiful face, and Ning, given free rein with the tailors, had ordered a fitted leather jacket for him, new riding boots and a sturdy woolen skirt with a split that was concealed by an embroidered panel that hung from the waistband at front and back. The brown and caramel tones suited Lan'xiu's coloring, especially the wine colored scarf wrapped around his neck since he insisted on keeping the window of the carriage down.

Ning kept looking down at his own new boots with pride. When Lan had been given his new clothing, he had insisted that Ning procure some boots for himself, and wearing them made the eunuch feel like a swordmaster once more.

The cottages grew sparser, and eventually all that could be seen was miles of empty grasslands and the mountains purple in the distance. Captain Wen had deployed his men to ride at a distance, keeping watch in all directions, so Hüi felt safe in calling the caravan to a halt.

Lan'xiu looked at him questioningly as he rode to the carriage upon his magnificent black stallion. "Why are we stopping here, my Lord?"

"I thought you might like to ride the rest of the way—" Hüi stopped speaking as Lan's face lit up with incredulous joy.

Lan'xiu almost fell out of the carriage in his haste to open the door. Ning descended after him more sedately, but with no less excitement as he observed Captain Wen approaching, leading two saddled horses, one rather smaller than the other.

Hüi Wei was smiling broadly at Lan'xiu's eagerness as he dismounted and handed his reins to Ning. "Let me put you up in the saddle."

He bent and Lan put his knee in his offered hands, springing lightly up into the saddle, understanding for the first time why Ning had made him don the split skirt. The chestnut mare was fresh, having been led riderless on the journey, and sidestepped restlessly, prancing playfully as if trying to unseat her. Lan'xiu controlled the horse easily, staying with her every move.

"Thank you, my Lord! She is beautiful." Lan reached forward to pat the glossy neck. "Is that pony for Ning?"

Hüi had recovered his reins and mounted his stallion. "I thought Ning might prefer to remain at your side rather than ride inside the carriage."

"That I would." Ning took the reins from Captain Wen and swung himself into the saddle.

Lan'xiu nudged the mare's ribs lightly, and they started to canter. Without a moment's hesitation, Ning chased after him. The mare broke into a gallop and the princess leaned forward in the saddle, moving as if one with the animal.

"What a splendid rider the princess is!" Wen declared.

"She is, isn't she?" Hüi said proudly. Then he realized that he was galloping away from him and slapped the reins on his own horse's rump. With a startled leap, the stallion took off with his long stride, easily closing the distance between him and the princess.

Recalled to the consciousness of his duties, Captain Wen raced after them, his men falling in behind him.

Hüi allowed Lan'xiu to run her mare for almost a mile before he came up beside her and put a hand on her reins. "Gently, my love. You've been ill, remember?"

Her cheeks rosy and eyes sparkling, Lan'xiu laughed at her lover. "I have never felt more alive, my Lord. That was glorious!"

Ning rode up behind them, kicking at his stubborn mount that was content to amble along at a trot. "What a foul beast! Lan'xiu! You should not gallop like a hoyden! Remember you are a princess!"

Lan'xiu's smile faded. "I forgot about the soldiers and Captain Wen. Perhaps I should not have ridden off that way in front of them?"

"I think it's time for you to acquire your own guard," Hüi Wei said with a smile. "Captain Wen has chosen these men carefully, and they accompanied us knowing that they would take the oath to serve you."

"To serve *me*?" Lan'xiu seemed both pleased and perplexed. "But why?"

Ning rolled his eyes in exasperation, but Hüi did not permit him to interject.

"I will not chance losing you again. If you had your own guard, Ci'an would never have schemed her way into your room and raised her sword against you."

"She wasn't that much of a fighter," Lan said.

"You were ill! In no condition for a fight," Ning said sharply.

Captain Wen and his men rode up to the group in time to silence what promised to be a long tirade from Ning and sat at attention upon their mounts.

"It is time," Hüi Wei said to Wen.

Captain Wen kept his eyes on Lan'xiu. "Princess Lan'xiu, it is my honor, and the honor of my battalion, to swear eternal loyalty to you and your dependents. We are willing to fight for you and to die to keep you safe. Please accept this vow and oath of our service."

Touched, Lan'xiu looked to Hüi, who nodded acquiescence. "Captain Wen, it is my honor to accept your oath. I shall repay your loyalty with my own, as my life is now in your hands."

"Mind!" Ning cried out, "That means if Captain Wen orders you to get out of the way, you will jump! And don't get yourself into a fix that puts your men at risk to get you out. And—"

"That will do, Ning," Lan said in a dignified way, although she was glaring at him. "Thank you, Captain Wen. Please tell me your men's names."

Riding beside Wen, Lan'xiu was introduced to her new escort and nodded to each one, enslaving them instantly with her smile, if her riding had not already done so, although she was completely unaware of it.

Then she rode back to take up her position beside Hüi Wei, who thanked Wen and asked her, "Shall we ride on?"

"Hüi," Lan said when they were out of earshot of the guard. "Where are we going and why do I need a guard?"

"We are going to my summer palace," Hüi said. "Jiang has allowed the rumor to get about that I am taking you to a specialist to see to the injuries Ci'an inflicted upon you."

"A specialist for my arm?"

"The specialist will inform us that you will never be able to bear children."

"I could have told you that," Lan said in a quiet voice. "I won't have a doctor maul me about."

"There is no doctor, Lan," Hüi said. "I want you entirely to myself. We will be here for three days, although it is not summer and will likely be rather cold."

She rode in silence for a time. "Thank you, Hüi. But what of Captain Wen and his men? Surely they will know—they will realize that no doctor has come."

"The mark of a canny ruler lies in gauging the loyalty of his followers," Hüi said. "Even in my court, there are those who wish to do me harm, but sometimes it is better to keep them close rather than push them away. I underestimated Ci'an, and I do not intend to risk your safety again. These men have taken an oath of fealty to *you*. They will protect you no matter who comes to harm you."

Lan'xiu blinked rapidly and stared at the purple mountains in the distance. "How can you be sure?"

"I didn't have to rely entirely upon my own judgment." Hüi laughed and jerked his head at Ning, struggling to encourage his sluggish horse to put on some speed. "Ning chose the men with Captain Wen. If any of them betray you, Ning will make certain they end up on a spike."

Lan'xiu still looked troubled but didn't speak.

"Lan, my love, all men of power hold secrets. Men who take the oath are sworn not just to preserve your life but to hold your secrets sacred. You are safe now."

"Thank you, Hüi," Lan'xiu said. Then she laughed. "I hope we may find another horse for Ning. He will not thank you for mounting him upon that snail."

Hüi laughed with her. "I didn't know if he could ride so I bespoke a quiet mount for him. However, he shall have another for the ride home." His grin became teasing. "I remembered how well you rode me, so I had no hesitation in selecting a spirited horse for you."

Lan's cheeks grew rosy with remembrance and embarrassment.

THE three days they spent at the summer palace were like heaven to both Lan'xiu and Hüi Wei. They spent almost every moment together, allowing Ning to slip away without query, as they had no wish for his constant companionship.

They went for rides in the mountains and came back to warm themselves before the fire, caring little what or when they ate. They spent each night in the same bed, wrapped in each other's arms. Hüi made love to Lan'xiu whenever desire sparked between them. He loved waking beside him, stroking his long hair, kissing him breathless and then taking him, hard or gentle as the mood struck him.

If Lan'xiu noticed a certain starriness in the eyes of his friend, he did not tease Ning by inquiring too closely if Captain Wen was the cause. By this leniency, he hoped to gain leverage to stop Ning's inquisitive attention into his own doings.

It was so lovely to have Hüi all to himself that Lan'xiu fell into a melancholy the day they were to start back. After the freedom of wild rides in the mountains and the intimacy of dining and laughing with him, sleeping naked his arms, making love whenever they chose, Lan could not look forward to returning to his old life trapped within the harem.

To steel himself for that eventuality, Lan withdrew a little from Hüi. When the luggage was packed and loaded onto the roof of the carriage, Lan took to the saddle one last time, knowing that before they came to the nearest village, he would need to dismount and take his place within the carriage, like a proper well-bred lady of the general's household.

Hüi rode in silence beside him and with each mile they put behind them, Lan could feel the distance between them grow greater. *I chose my life and now I must embrace the consequences of my choice. Never again will we have this intimacy, but at least I will have these three days.* Lan remembered Mei Ju saying Hüi had taken her on certain trips and that had the effect of robbing this respite of the special magic with which he had imbued it.

When he turned to glance at Hüi, his lover's face was set in grim lines, and Lan couldn't fathom what emotions lay beneath that expression.

Finally, Captain Wen raised his hand and the column halted. Ning dismounted from his second, much livelier horse and opened the carriage door for the princess.

Feeling like a prisoner being led back to his jail cell after a brief escape, Lan'xiu dismounted. He patted the mare's neck, whispering farewell endearments to her, wondering if he would ever see her again. Then he turned and squared his shoulders, preparing to ascend into the carriage.

A whirl of a cloak surrounded him and he was swept into Hüi's tight embrace, hearing his lover's husky voice, broken with emotion in his ear. "I cannot live without the sight of your lovely face every day, my Lan'xiu. It is madness to be so near and yet not to see you. If I must, I will have your lantern lit every day."

Instead of crying in front of his soldiers, Lan laughed with joy and heartbreak, wanting to comfort his lover. "You must not, Hüi, you have other wives—"

"I care not. I must see you, I must have you—" Hüi clasped him so tightly, Lan was breathless and panting.

Crazy thoughts raced through his head, and Lan wanted to remind Hüi of Mei Ju's devotion, but he was too happy at this reassuring demonstration. "You will always be welcome in my bedchamber, whether you light the lantern or not. Oh Hüi! I miss you already! I can't bear for you to let me go."

"I want to hold you always next to my heart," Hüi declared. He tilted Lan's face up and kissed him full upon the lips, uncaring of the men who were watching. "I shall find a way, my love. We must not be parted after this. I couldn't bear it." Reluctantly, he released Lan and stepped away.

Lan'xiu glanced around to find Ning and Captain Wen staring at each other, while most of the men properly faced outward, on guard against the sudden appearance of any enemies, although a few seemed to be blinking rather fast. He put his hand on Hüi's cheek and laughed shakily. "Anyone would think we were parting for a year's separation when we will be living only yards apart when we return."

Hüi picked up his hand and kissed the palm. "You are right. We are being ridiculous. Into the carriage with you. I shall see you safely bestowed in your house before I—" He broke off and helped Lan'xiu into the carriage.

Lan permitted it, though he didn't need the assistance, only in order to feel Hüi's last lingering caress as he climbed the steps. Ning climbed in behind him and shut the door. Lan let down the window even though he could see his breath in the frigid air, and it started to snow, white flakes swirling in the interior of carriage. But even Ning did not voice a complaint about the cold as Lan kept his eyes fixed upon the straight figure of the general as he rode a little ahead.

AFTER the emotion Hüi displayed when they parted at the carriage, Lan had hoped her lantern would be lit that very night, but it remained dark for a week, and she heard nothing from him. It was only cold comfort that all the lanterns remained dark within the household square the entire time.

Ning had permitted Lan'xiu to resume her walks outside after they returned from consulting with the fictitious doctor, but they were alone in the park at the center of the square, despite the fact winter had retreated and the signs of spring were upon them.

The sound of birdsong and the tiny buds upon the fruit trees in the square could not bring a smile to Lan'xiu's lips. It seemed to her that despite what he'd said, Hüi had forgotten all about her.

The other wives apparently had as well. Ning had gathered the gossip they missed while they were gone and brought her the news.

"Fen and Huan now live together within the third house," he began.

"Did Huan allow the servants back in or are they doing the housework themselves?" Lan asked, although she really didn't care.

"The servants are back," Ning said. "And Bai has taken Alute's and Ci'an's sons into her house, because she said Mei Ju is too busy caring for her own children."

"I am sure the boys must love her," Lan said in a lifeless voice. She knew that she should pay a courtesy call upon Bai at least, considering Bai had come when she was ill, but she didn't wish to inflict her sadness upon Fifth Wife.

"Apparently. And Mei Ju has been indisposed," Ning continued. "There have been no parties for the wives since before we left."

"I should send her a note," Lan said absently. "I hope she is well."

"I have had a basket of oranges sent to her in your name," Ning said.

"Thank you, Ning. That was thoughtful of you," Lan said guiltily. "And what of your Captain Wen?"

"He is watching us even now, to ensure your safety. Remember his oath?" Ning said. "Honestly, Lan'xiu, you have been walking about as if you were asleep since we returned. What is wrong with you?"

Lan'xiu hesitated. Could she confide even in Ning when her heart was so wounded by Hüi's absence? After he had told her he couldn't bear not to see her face, he had simply vanished. "I have been… thinking," Lan said finally.

"Thinking!" Ning scoffed. He led her back to the seventh house and opened the door, putting his hand on her back and propelling her up the stairs to her bedchamber without stopping to let her remove her cloak. He shut the door behind them. "I suppose while you were *thinking*, it didn't occur to you that perhaps the general might be occupied with other things?"

It was on the tip of her tongue to say 'like another concubine?', but something about the suppressed excitement evident in Ning's face stopped her. "What do you know? You little troll, spit it out!" Her heart was pounding as her mind raced with all sorts of dangers threatening her beloved.

"Ah, so you *are* still alive," Ning said, smiling with satisfaction.

"Was that a trick to get a rise out of me?"

"No, it was not. However, I don't know what's going on. I only know that something is."

Clenching her fists, Lan'xiu strode back and forth in her room. "Something is wrong. I can feel it."

CHAPTER EIGHTEEN

SHE had been unable to eat. Her lantern remained dark, as had all the others within the square, but a feeling of hushed anticipation kept her from reading a book or occupying herself in some other way.

When she heard Ning's footsteps echo upon the stairs, she turned her head toward the door.

"My Lord General and Lord Jiang wish to speak with you," Ning said. "Downstairs in the sitting room."

Lan'xiu grew pale, wondering what matter was so serious as to demand the formality of a meeting in the sitting room. She never sat there herself, finding it too dark and gloomy. Her pretty yellow bedroom was much more comfortable to her, but Hüi Wei might feel now that she was well that it was not proper to admit Jiang there.

She checked her makeup and picked up a fan before going downstairs, Ning at her heels. When she entered the sitting room, Lan'xiu sank to her knees and made the proper prostration in front of Hüi Wei and then rose to her knees to bow deeply to Jiang. "Greetings, my Lords. May I offer you tea?"

"You may get up and sit—with us," Hüi said, as if barely stopping himself from telling Lan'xiu to sit next to him. He seemed mesmerized to see her again. "I always forget how beautiful—" Hüi stopped short and glanced at Jiang, who seemed to be very preoccupied with a thorough examination of the embroidery on his sleeve.

Modestly, Lan kept her eyes cast down and seated herself on the very edge of a chair, holding her fan to shield her face from Jiang's gaze. She had never entertained a man other than Hüi Wei in her house and was unsure what this visit portended and how she should act, despite the fact Jiang had seen her at her worst. The oracles had seemed to desert her ever since she had been forced to come to this strange land, but now she felt the familiar internal tugging. She knew not what it meant, but the excitement of her inner vision clearing was difficult to hide as she waited, trembling, to hear what the men had to say to her.

Jiang began, choosing his words carefully. "You must have heard that Second Wife Ci'an has begun her journey to the afterworld where the gods will no doubt help her find her reward for her deeds and misdeeds in this life."

Lan nodded without speaking.

"Her father, Daji, who lives at Henan, was not pleased when the messenger brought him the news of her death. He does not believe that Ci'an killed herself. It was he who made this a political marriage, and by her death he now holds himself released from the terms of the treaty."

Startled, Lan'xiu exclaimed, "Henan?"

"Precisely," Jiang said, seeming pleased with her quick comprehension. "The province that borders upon your brother's."

"Lan'xiu, what do you think your brother, Wu Min, will do?" Hüi leaned forward, looking intently at the princess.

She dropped her fan to her lap. "Wu Min will try to convince Daji his grudge against you is a valid reason to go to war. My brother will promise Daji that he will support him, and once Daji has committed his forces, Wu Min will wait until it is too late for Daji to draw back. He may or may not help Daji as he promised, as the winds blow."

"Then you agree with our assessment," Hüi Wei said, sitting back. It was clear he was thinking more about the eventualities of this encroaching danger than of her.

"Henan province has gently rolling hills and plains," Jiang said.

"My province Liaopeh is mountainous, with dangerous rocks and cliffs," Lan'xiu said. "It would benefit Wu Min if he were able to choose the terrain for the battle. He will place Daji in a plain that backs up against our highest peaks; there is a place perfect for a surprise attack. When your forces are occupied with fighting Daji, Wu Min could march his men in behind you to surprise you."

For some reason Jiang did not appear surprised at the princess's grasp of military strategy. "Then we must choose the place we stand and fight."

"Or perhaps choose to attack Daji rather than waiting for his pleasure," Hüi Wei said.

"Or walk into their trap, only to spring it upon them," Lan'xiu said.

Hüi's eyes gleamed with excitement that Lan'xiu thought like him. "My spies will bring information about their movements. If we think like the fox, perhaps we can split our forces to attack in two directions."

"That would depend upon what the two venal rats come up with," Jiang said cautiously.

"Thank you, Lan'xiu," Hüi Wei said, getting up and taking her hand to press a kiss to it. "We are grateful for this information. We must take our leave for we have much to plan."

"You march to war, my Lord?" Lan'xiu asked.

"As we have consulted you and told you this much, yes, we will go to protect our borders," Hüi said. "It was inevitable that matters should come to a head with both these men. We might as well take the initiative."

"Then I shall go with you," Lan'xiu announced, folding her hands in her lap.

Hüi was at her side in two steps, grasping her upper arms to lift her from her chair and shaking her. "You will *not* go with us! You cannot ride to war! You cannot fight!"

"Yes, she can," Ning said. "And besides, Captain Wen and his men are bound to her through their oaths of honor. They will protect her."

Both men had forgotten he was there, and Jiang stifled a laugh. So much for secrecy, but at least Ning had proven more discreet than most eunuchs.

Hüi growled inarticulately, glaring first at Ning and then his friend who was trying to keep a serious face. Finally he turned back to

Lan'xiu and muttered grimly, "I cannot lose you in battle. Not after I so nearly lost you to that devil Ci'an."

"You will not lose me, my Lord," Lan'xiu said. She smiled, secure in her foresight, at least of this. "I am going to help you to victory. I will be in no danger with you to protect me."

"I will not be able to pay attention to you," Hüi explained. "What if—"

"What if your spies bring you bad information? I know those mountains. I know the secret ways through them. Besides, didn't you say that you will not lead the charge? You will stay back and direct the troops," Lan said. "I shall be quite safe in the rear with you."

Hüi relaxed his grip enough that Lan's feet touched the floor again. He looked first at Ning, and then at Jiang. "I won't even ask Ning's opinion. He is so besotted with his princess, he would say anything to procure her whatever she wants, but you, Jiang, must see this is madness."

"I see nothing of the sort," Jiang said. "The princess is quite correct. She would be of immense help in the field. And she didn't do so badly against Ci'an even though wounded."

"You are all mad," Hüi said in disgust. With clenched teeth he said in a low voice, "Lan'xiu, I cannot see you hurt again. What if you should be taken prisoner?"

Her face paled, but Lan'xiu did not yield. "That is not in your destiny, my Lord. I see my way clear and it is imperative that I accompany you."

"You can cast oracles?" Jiang asked.

"Not for myself," Lan'xiu said. "For others, perhaps. My goddess deserted me when first I came here, but now I feel her presence again. Victory is by no means assured, but it can be achieved."

"I will have wine brought here that you may make the necessary sacrifices," Hüi Wei said. "Only then I will make the decision whether you are going, not you." He strode from the room without another word, and Jiang hurried after him after taking his leave of the princess.

"He seemed upset," Ning commented.

"You'd better find me some armor that fits," Lan'xiu said.

"We're going?" Ning rubbed his hands together eagerly.

"You bloodthirsty imp. Yes, we are going," Lan laughed.

"You haven't even asked for signs yet."

"I don't need to cast the bones, I can feel it in my own," Lan'xiu said. "I have a role to play in this conflict. One thing I do know: if I don't accompany him, Hüi Wei will not return."

"You don't mean to sacrifice yourself for him, do you?" Ning asked in alarm.

"I will cast the oracles tonight, and then we shall see, but tell me, Ning, loving him as I do, what good would life be to me without him?"

LAN was waiting for Hüi when he returned that night, without having his lantern lit.

"You knew I could not stay away," Hüi said, when he saw he was still awake.

"I hoped you could not," Lan said, holding his hands out to his lover.

Hüi took him into his arms, holding him and inhaling his scent. "This week has been hell, staying away from you, knowing you were waiting for me," Hüi whispered into Lan's skin. "I could not risk your safety with Daji's emissaries here within the city, watching with their sly eyes. I wanted you so much."

"I missed you."

"I cannot live without you near to me. I am going to take you into the palace so we are always near," Hüi said.

"What of Mei Ju and the others?" Lan asked, his heart pounding. He wanted desperately to live with Hüi, but the others were here first.

"I never knew what love was until I met you," Hüi muttered. "Now I understand—but no matter what pain I cause them, I can't help myself. I must have you near me always."

"Then you will take me with you to fight?"

"You understand, like Ning I hate to deny you anything you desire, but the thought of your precious body, hurt, bloodied, broken on the field of battle—I cannot even imagine living through such horror. It was bad enough seeing you standing there, your life blood dripping on the floor, shaking like a leaf in front of that devil Ci'an—" Hüi broke off and buried his face in Lan's neck again.

Raising his hand, Lan stroked Hüi's rough locks. "Believe me, my Lord, I do not want to die and leave you. I wish we never had to be parted. But I have received the omens tonight, and I will suffer no harm if I go with you. It was not made clear to me, but I have some part to play in this conflict on your behalf."

"Daji and Wu Min have their own spies. They must know the turmoil that has ensued in this household," Hüi said. "If they know that, they may also know that I hold you dearer than any other of my wives. You will be a target."

"Not if I am disguised as a man," Lan said.

Hüi released him, and they stared at each other for a moment before bursting into laughter at the irony. "News has been brought to me that Ning is busy trying to scrounge a suit of armor for you. Tell him to stop. I shall see to it myself. I shall send for you on the morrow, and you will have a suit made to measure. I shall not see my warrior princess go to war in a shabby, borrowed outfit."

"How exciting! I have always wanted armor," Lan said. He put his hands up to touch Hüi's face, caressing each cheek. "But not as much as I have wanted you."

"I have missed you, Lan'xiu," Hüi said in a throaty growl. He picked up the slight young man and, holding him, went to the bed where they fell upon the mattress together. The bed frame gave out a loud groan and Lan'xiu giggled.

"There goes my reputation," he said.

"The only reputation you need is that everyone knows how much I love you and want you," Hüi said.

He bent his head to take Lan's mouth in a deep, probing kiss.

HER heart was pounding when she rapped upon First Wife's door. Ning had argued that it could only cause both her and First Wife pain should Lan'xiu make this duty call, but she could not go without first thanking Mei Ju for her kindness.

Much had changed within the household. Mei Ju must have heard by now that Princess Lan'xiu, concubine of the first order, was being taken to live within the palace. Most likely Hüi Wei had done First Wife the courtesy of telling her himself. Lan'xiu steeled herself to face anger and hatred, knowing how she would feel in Mei Ju's place.

When the servant came to the door, she opened her eyes wide in surprise at Lan'xiu standing alone and uninvited upon the step. However, she permitted the princess to come inside while she went to announce her to Mei Ju.

To Lan's surprise, the servant came back and said, "Please follow me, Princess."

She was ushered into a small room on the second floor, where Mei Ju was sitting, staring out the window, dressed in a white gown of mourning, her empty hands resting on the arms of her chair.

Lan'xiu bowed low in respect. "First Wife, I have come to thank you for your kindness to me."

Mei Ju turned an implacable face to Lan'xiu, her eyes hard and dry. "And this is how you repay my kindness? You steal my husband's heart from me?"

Miserably, Lan'xiu stood silent. There was nothing she could say in answer to this ravaged agony; no defense she could make. She knew how she would feel if someone took Hüi from her now.

Mei Ju merely sat waiting for a response that never came, her hands clenching the carved arms of her chair. "I knew, when first I saw you, that you were too beautiful for a mere man to resist, but I did not think Hüi would raise you to supplant me. You played your cards very well, pretending to be so modest and sweet."

Lan flinched and her face worked with emotion. "I am so sorry, First Wife. I did not—"

"Be silent!" Mei Ju's voice was harsh, like shattering glass. "I don't care to listen to your excuses and apologies."

"Perhaps I should not have come." Lan'xiu waited a moment, but Mei Ju's face did not soften. She turned to go. "Please believe me, First Wife, I did not come here with any intention of causing you pain." She went to the door and opened it.

"Princess Lan'xiu! Wait!"

Lan'xiu froze and then turned to face Mei Ju, unable to conceal the torment on her face.

"I—I must apologize to you," Mei Ju said stiffly. "The gods have dealt me a cruel blow, but that is no excuse for me to visit my bitterness upon you. You have done nothing wrong."

Lan stood with her head bowed, not knowing what to do. "You are most gracious, First Wife."

"My—Hüi Wei has informed me that you had no choice when you were sent here, that your brother expected him to reject or kill you." Mei Ju shook her head, as if she still couldn't fathom why this would be so, but it was of little importance. "I knew when we met that you were in the grip of dread. I could tell you were innocent, that you possessed no arts to enslave Hüi's mind and heart."

"Lady First Wife, if there was anything I could have done—"

"I know." Mei Ju held up a hand. "Come, Lan'xiu, sit down by me. And call me Mei Ju."

Uncomfortably, Lan'xiu crossed the room and sat cautiously on the edge of the chair. There was nothing she could think of to say to assuage the pain of a woman whose heart had been direly injured, through no fault of her own but entirely because of her.

Mei Ju stared out over the tile roofs. "I knew he would love you. I thought I had prepared myself for it, but there is no way to anticipate the depths of pain… I thought he would always return to me… we have been such friends…."

"He will return to you," Lan said, her soft voice hiding her own pain at the thought.

"Of course he will. Hüi Wei is far too kind to ignore the mother of his children." Mei Ju put her hand over her mouth in dismay and turned to Lan'xiu. "I'm sorry, I had forgotten. The special physician said that you will never be able to bear Hüi Wei a child after what Ci'an did to you. I am sorry for you."

Lan covered her eyes for a moment. Mei Ju's sympathy was almost more than she could bear. "I will never give him a son," she acquiesced.

Mei Ju leaned forward and twined their fingers together. "Then you know how bereft I am, as I know your pain."

For a moment, Lan felt deep shame and guilt that this woman was so deceived as to what she was, but then the regret that she truly could not bear her lover children made her lips tremble. "At least he has your children. You have given him many fine sons and daughters."

"At least I have that. You are generous to say so." Mei Ju smiled through her tears. "I will always have that honor." She leaned forward to search Lan'xiu's eyes. "Do you truly love him?"

All grandiose thoughts of how to compare her love deserted Lan. "Yes," was all she said, but it satisfied Mei Ju.

"One cannot force a man to love where his heart is not engaged," Mei Ju murmured. "At least I had him for many years to myself." She looked at Lan'xiu again. "Forgive me for venting my anguish upon you. It is not your fault."

"Believe me, Mei Ju, I never wanted to cause you pain—"

"I know, hush, my dear." Mei Ju patted Lan's hand and sat back in her chair. "Will you come to see me and the children every now and then?"

"I would love to," Lan said sincerely. "Aside from my mother and Ning, you are the first person ever to be kind to me."

Mei Ju laughed regretfully. "Not so very kind today. But I shall become accustomed in time, I dare say. One can become accustomed to anything, even having one's heart rent asunder."

WHEN Lan'xiu emerged from the visit with Mei Ju, she felt that she wanted nothing more than to retreat to her bed and sleep for days, but she no longer had a bed within the household square, and it was not fitting behavior for a warrior princess anyway.

She stood upon the step of the house, wondering where she was to go and what she was to do. Fortunately, Ning came to greet her. Her lips twitched as he bowed obsequiously to her, knowing it meant they were under observation.

"Princess Lan'xiu, if you will accompany me."

She nodded and followed Ning, becoming aware that soldiers were falling into position around them. It would have made her nervous but for the fact that she recognized them as members of her guard. She gave them an almost imperceptible nod of acknowledgement and marched with Ning to the big iron gate where Captain Wen stood at attention.

"Open the gates for the princess!" he cried out proudly.

Two of the household guard unbolted and unlocked the gate, and Princess Lan'xiu retraced the steps she had taken her first day as a prisoner within these walls, except this time she walked as a woman of rank and consequence, surrounded by her own guard.

Captain Wen led the party to the same door by which Lan'xiu had the left the palace, an unimportant side door, rather than to the two grand doors at the front reserved for visitors of state. Lan'xiu was glad of it. She had lived most of her life trying not to attract attention, and now when she felt unsure of the future was not the time to boldly march in at the front door.

Once inside, Captain Wen spoke briefly with Ning who pointed up the stairway.

"Follow me, Princess," Ning said.

Aware of the men who never left them, Lan'xiu climbed the stairs and followed Ning down a hallway that curved to the back of the building, counting the number of doors they passed so she would not be totally lost on her own. The way her guard remained close to her, however, she was beginning to wonder if she would ever walk alone again. Then she recovered her sense of humor; as a woman and a princess, she had never been permitted to be entirely alone except within her bedchamber. The difference was that she was accustomed to Ning and he knew her secret.

Ning stopped before a tall door and opened it, bowing low, by which she understood he wanted her to go inside.

Once inside, Lan'xiu stopped short and smiled in delight. "Ning, did you do this?"

Ning smiled back at her. "It was my lord general's idea, but I saw to it that his intention was carried out properly."

Between them, Hüi Wei and Ning had had the furnishings from the bedchamber in the seventh house in the square brought here and installed in this much bigger room. The yellow curtains Lan had so loved hung at the windows and the same rosewood wardrobe and bed stood within the room.

A few more chairs were positioned about the room, and also another table, upon which stood a jade and silver casket with a lock wherein Lan found her jewels. The same bench stood at the foot of the bed, and Lan crossed the room to sit upon it, thinking about the time Hüi Wei had made love to her on it.

"Look, Lan'xiu." Ning pulled open the doors of the wardrobe to reveal many pretty new dresses hanging there.

She merely smiled. At this point, the thought of her new armor excited her more, but she was touched at the evidence that despite the fact Hüi had not visited her at all during the past week, she had yet been in his thoughts.

"Through here is the bathing room, and beyond—" Ning wiggled his eyebrows and gave a hastily concealed leer, as if he'd only just remembered Captain Wen's presence. "—you will find my lord general's bedchamber. If you wished to, ahem, speak with him."

Lan glared at her servitor with an expression that promised later retribution, but only said, "Thank you, Ning."

Captain Wen bowed and said, "Princess, two of my men will be stationed outside in the hallway, at a distance where they cannot overhear conversation. But if you need them, they will be there within calling distance. Is there anything else I can do?"

Lan'xiu stood up and smiled at him. It startled and touched her to see how pleased he seemed that she was speaking directly to him. "Captain Wen, I thank you. You have done much to keep me safe and comfortable, and I thank you for your allegiance."

"It is my pleasure, your Highness." Captain Wen bowed again.

"If you really wish to please me…."

"I do!" he assured her.

"Take this servant of mine somewhere and regale him with a good meal, much liquor, and a story of your great prowess in battle."

Captain Wen glanced uncertainly between Lan'xiu and Ning, but then a smile crept over his face. "Shu Ning-xiānsheng, would you care to accompany me?"

"Where?" Ning asked.

"Does it matter?" Lan'xiu demanded. "Go! You deserve a respite from watching over me, and I shall come to no harm here in the palace with two soldiers outside the door."

At last Ning smiled at Captain Wen. "Thank you, Lan'xiu."

Although he was wearing a different dress, having gone to Mei Ju more somberly clad in respect for her, Lan'xiu took up the same pose on the bench as he had the day he awaited Hüi Wei in the seventh house. His feet were planted square on the floor, his legs and knees together. His back was straight, and he placed his hands on his knees.

Remembering the occasion when he'd waited on this bench for Hüi before, Lan'xiu felt his palms start to flutter with anticipation. His cock was getting thicker, pushing against the silk of his panties. He could feel the fluid form at the tip and dampen the fabric. He moved his shoulders to feel the heavy embroidery of his corselet rub over his nipples. Lan liked that feeling, too, it added to the anticipation of waiting for Hüi.

His breath came shorter and his heart pounded when he heard the click of the door as it opened. Lan looked up, not realizing his face wore an expression of joyful anticipation.

To Hüi, the sight of Lan'xiu waiting for him reminded him of the beginning of their love, and he hoped the rush of emotion would never change.

Once the thrill of being master of such beauty excited Hüi Wei; now it was love that made his heart pound, and fear of what was to come. Resolutely, he pushed away the dread thought of what he was risking by allowing Lan'xiu to accompany him to war, knowing his young lover preferred to face danger with courageous laughter.

He paused to drink in the joy and love on the beautiful face. "Do you like the room?"

"It is beautiful, Hüi. I thank you for thinking of me."

"When am I not thinking of you?" Hüi came to Lan then and sat on the bench beside him. "I fear we have little time to enjoy being so near before we must depart."

"But at least we have tonight."

Hüi raised his hand to caress Lan's cheek, stroking down his smooth throat and working his way under the layers of silk to find a nipple, rubbing gently over it to feel the flesh harden beneath his fingertips. He loved watching the muscles in Lan's throat work, the way his lids veiled his eyes and his lips parted to catch his breath. "We have tonight, and we will have many more nights, my love."

"I never thought, when I was brought here to be a concubine, that this could happen to me," Lan said softly, arching into Hüi's touch.

Hüi withdrew his hand and stood up, sweeping Lan up into his arms to kiss him deeply. "The last concubine. I shall never take another, for all that I need I hold here in my arms, princess of my heart."

He bore Lan to the bed and laid him gently upon the mattress, sinking down next to him to take his lips in a tender kiss.

CHAPTER NINETEEN

"I LOOK like a boy," Lan'xiu said in a voice of displeasure.

"Good. You will attract no undue attention that way," Ning replied. "Battles are full of boys."

"I like it," Hüi teased from where he sat observing. "You look very fetching."

It was stunning to see how handsome Lan looked in his leather armor and dark trousers. His sword hung from his belt, and he wore gauntlets on his hands. His hair was braided into a long queue at the back, and his bronze helmet stood upon the table.

"It feels strange," Lan said. At Ning's insistence, he also wore men's undergarments and sorely missed the silk of his corselet.

"Dressed this way you will blend in with the troops," Hüi said firmly. "And that will be to your advantage. Can you doubt that if Wu Min comes to fight and spies you, dressed as a woman upon the field, that all his energy will be turned to destroying you?"

"You are right," Lan said. "I will wear a pretty dress when this battle is won."

"And I shall—" Hüi stopped and looked at Ning.

"Tear it off her, *I* know."

"Ning! When will you learn to hold your tongue!"

"Never!" Ning laughed. "That is what you value about me. I shall leave you alone for a quarter of an hour, but then we must be off." He bustled out of the room and shut the door behind him.

Lan turned to Hüi with sadness in his eyes. "Why must men fight? Why can they not embrace the beauty of our land and live simple lives in peace?"

Hüi stood and came to him, taking him in his arms for a chaste embrace. "Men are not made that way. They are meant to strive and compete."

"But to the death?"

"Tell me, my love, if your brother were here, would you let him do what evil he might desire?"

"I would fight him to the death before I let him give rein to his cruelty and evil!" Lan gritted out between clenched teeth.

"As all men do when pushed to their limit, good or bad." Hüi tightened his hold and then released Lan, stepping away from him. "You have a gentle soul. Perhaps it would be better if I forbade you to accompany me."

"I would like to see you try, my Lord." Lan straightened up and smiled gallantly. "To war, my Lord, and victory for us both."

IT WAS a matter of honor to Lan'xiu to ride his horse all the way instead of traveling in one of the supply carriages. He sometimes felt that Hüi forgot what he really was, with all his concern for his supposed delicacy, and he would ride like all the other men. He was glad to see the same mare he'd ridden when they visited the summer palace, and she seemed to remember him too, nuzzling at his fingers.

After the first strangeness of his new armor and men's clothing, Lan had gotten used to it quickly. Hüi Wei was much occupied, as a general must be, with directing operations, receiving reports from the scouts, and surveying their approach, and therefore he was not always by Lan's side, although they tried to sleep near each other on the ground when the column halted for the night.

Unlike some generals whose sense of condescension required grandiose tents and many servants, Hüi Wei lived as his troops did, deeming speed to be the essence of victory. He could not be bothered to be weighed down with the trappings of rank.

However, Lan was never left alone. For one thing, Ning stayed close, as he had all of Lan's life, making sure that he could not make a move without supervision. But now Lan's personal guard also rode ringed around him. They weren't obvious, but they didn't permit any of the other soldiers to come closer than twenty feet. It made him feel a bit safer. Despite his training, Lan was very aware that he had no actual experience in war. His most devout hope was that he would not disgrace himself, Ning, or worst of all, Hüi Wei with his conduct in battle. He invoked his gods and omens to grant him the courage to face death bravely if that was to be his destiny.

Silently, Lan listened to Hüi review plans and maps with his generals. It soon became clear to him that Hüi Wei had lied, either to her or to himself, about directing his troops from the rear, perhaps to dissuade her from accompanying him. Lan'xiu doubted that Hüi could forego the challenge and thrill of battle even at the cost of his own life. Jiang was there as well, refusing to be left behind at this critical moment and having left the reins of government in the hands of one whom he trusted above all else, his partner, Zheng Guofang. Between them, Lan felt humbly respectful at their ability to plan to meet different eventualities and strategize to turn them to their advantage.

However, there was a part that he was there to play. Only he could prevent what the omens had revealed to him. Carefully, he had tried to speak to Hüi Wei about his visions.

"You must keep to the flatlands," Lan said. "If you venture into the hills, it is easy to get lost."

"I have never been lost," Hüi boasted. "With the sun and the stars to guide me, how would I lose my way? I have never allowed an enemy to slip away and sit in comfort while he mocks me from the peaks."

"The weather in Liaopeh—"

"—is much like weather anywhere else," Hüi said firmly. "Do not be so fearful, my love. I will come to no harm."

Lan lay awake in his blankets late that night, long after Hüi Wei had gone to sleep. He wished he could edge closer and gain some warmth from being held in Hüi's arms, but he could not compromise the general's reputation that way. The rumor that the general had taken a young soldier as his lover was not one Lan wanted to generate.

He could feel the ground move beneath him, and at first thought he might be getting dizzy, but then Jiang and Hüi sat up, listening. "They are coming," Hüi said. And then he was gone, running for his horse.

Jiang stood and told Ning, "Get your horses. They probably won't attack until dawn, but better on horseback than on the ground."

Lan was already on his feet, rolling up the blankets while Ning went for their horses. Four of his guard stayed with him until his horse was brought to him. Servants collected the blankets and other items to load onto a cart while Lan sat astride his horse, pulling off the main roadway to allow the war chariots to roll past.

Captain Wen looked as calm as always, but his horse fidgeted, as if some excitement from the man was communicated to the animal.

"Captain Wen," Lan said. "Listen to me. I know what your orders are from the general, but in battle you will take your lead from me. Those hills over there—" Lan pointed to the dark mountains, visible only in the night by the mists that hovered within the passes. "Those hills lead into the mountains of Liaopeh, my homeland. Ning and I have covered every inch of that land and we know it well. If we move, stay close by."

"Yes, my—sir!" Captain Wen said, although a slight frown creased his forehead. He looked at Ning, who gave him a decided nod.

"I will try not to get any of us killed," Lan said with a wry smile. "I thank you for your loyalty." He stood in the stirrups and bowed to his guard. "I shall try to honor you by matching my courage to yours."

The guard raised their spears almost as one in salute. It moved Lan more than the loudest shout could have, and he was comforted, knowing they would have his back. He turned his horse to follow in the tracks the chariots had left behind. The heft of his spear was comforting in his hand.

"Do you think he will come?" Ning asked quietly.

"I know he will," Lan said. "He will not suspect I am here, so I am not his target. But Wu Min knows the hills as well as I. He has some snare devised to keep Hüi Wei facing the west. The mountains look impassable from here, and I have not been able to convince Hüi that there are ways through them. Very well, Hüi may face the west. We will guard the east."

"Your mother was a very wise woman," Ning commented.

Lan bit his lip as he always did when reminded of his beautiful mother, who died too soon. "Yes. She gave me you. I thank you now, Ning, if I never did so before, not only for your loyalty and love, but that you trained me as no princess has ever been trained before. Without you—"

"Ah yes, without me, you would be just the ordinary sort of princess, sitting at home and wringing your hands," Ning said, smiling. "It was my honor to have such a good student."

Lan stretched his free hand toward Ning and tapped his shoulder. "I will thank you again later, when we are free of this mess, but for right now, shut up."

Ning did so, but the pride that shone in his eyes as he rode at the side of his princess made Lan very happy that they were both alive to see this day, when Lan'xiu rode free as the warrior princess he was meant to be.

Lan'xiu could see that Hüi was keeping to the rear on the top of a bluff where he could survey the battle, at least for now. He had no doubt that, if necessary, Hüi would race into the melee to turn the tide. The infantry, cavalry, and chariots had swept down off the ridge and were upon Daji's forces before the first light of dawn, the sun rising behind them, taking him by surprise and forcing the battle to commence.

Lan could see that Hüi had not committed his entire force on one front, but sent forth enough men to lure Daji into a trap of his own choosing. But still Lan'xiu was uneasy. He and Ning increasingly turned to the east. The mists did not lift from the mountains, as they often lingered in early spring. The sun was not yet strong enough to burn the mists off, and mountains loomed, gloomily shrouded in gray.

The sound of the battle was fearful, and Lan could not catch any warning noises from the mountainside. He turned back to view the battle below and suddenly caught the flash of something metal on the field. He grasped Ning's arm. "Did you see that?"

"They signal for aid, Lan'xiu," Ning agreed grimly.

Both of them turned to stare into the mountain passes, but the mists were too thick to allow any sign to be seen. Or so Lan'xiu thought. All of a sudden, he caught sight of a feeble flash of light.

"There. We must go," Lan muttered. "Captain Wen, tell your men to ride softly and have their spears ready. No unnecessary noise. Take your cue from Ning and me."

"What are you doing, your Highness?" Wen asked urgently.

"Making sure that General Qiang Hüi Wei and his men live to enjoy their victory," Lan said.

CAPTAIN WEN quickly ordered his men to ride quietly, making sure to muffle the scrape and clank of their weapons. As a good commander, he took the lead behind Lan'xiu and Ning, not wanting to risk his troops where he dared not ride himself.

Although he had come to know Ning in the physical sense, there was much about his lover that yet remained a mystery. His body was like neither that of a woman nor a man, but an intriguing combination of both with strong muscle and smooth skin. He knew nothing of Ning's past or how he had come to be cut, but he had the idea that for Ning, the decision to be made eunuch had not been easy or even voluntary. And the princess; perhaps in Liaopeh, princesses were given a different sort of training than he knew of, but the way they handled their weapons awakened a new respect within him.

The princess was clearly at ease with a spear in her hand, and he had seen her facing Second Wife with a sword reddened with Ci'an's blood. But Ning! He could be no mere bedchamber servant! Clearly, he must be a warrior of the first order. Even Lan'xiu fell back to let him lead the way.

The sounds of the battle behind him seemed distant and haunting from within the alien, jagged shapes of the red rock that surrounded them. Where Wen would not have suspected a man could pass, Ning and Lan'xiu led the small group ever farther between narrow, twisting walls. Above them rock towered and shut the daylight away from them. Every now and then, they emerged into a clear area where the mists still hung low in spooky, ghostlike tendrils.

And still Ning led the way farther on the winding passageway that led higher into the peaks. Uneasily, Wen turned in his saddle, keeping watch behind them and peering up into the dim light, lest some lookout posted above drop down on them.

At last Ning raised his hand and Lan'xiu halted her horse. She turned to signal Wen silently, indicating that he range his men on either side of a narrow opening. He was unsure, but she was not satisfied until all his men were hidden from view, having urged their horses into narrow breaks in the jagged walls.

He positioned himself where he had a clear view. If any harm befell the princess, it would be his duty to bear this news back to his general, after which he would kill himself in an act of apology and contrition. Preferring to live, he decided he needed to keep a keen eye on whatever transpired to be ready to defend her.

The princess and Ning sat upon their horses, neither speaking nor looking at each other. The watchfulness in their bodies seemed to have communicated itself to the animals, for they also were still. Not even a snort or incautious movement marred the silence.

A man wearing the armor of the Liaopeh appeared suddenly within the narrow gap, and Wen was seized with suspicion. What did he actually know about Ning or the princess? He had admired her insistence that she not be left behind, but this clandestine meeting made him angry and uneasy, lest she betray the general. Yet something made him wait to see what would happen.

The young Liaopeh man was shocked into reining in, and his horse reared and whinnied. He hurriedly gained control over his mount again and stared at the two men who blocked his way. Without saying a word, he turned and disappeared back the way he came.

Still Ning and the princess did nothing, moved not a muscle, spoke no word. It seemed to Wen as if they could read each other's minds, and he wondered if they had given the Liaopeh soldier some sign imperceptible to him.

Wen was about to ride forward and demand some explanation when sounds beyond the gap caught his attention. As he waited, an older man rode into the small clearing. Judging by his armor, he seemed to be a Liaopeh general at least, and his cruel, angular face was alight with amusement.

"Princess Lan'xiu, you come to show me the way to your new owner. How very kind," the man said with immense confidence. "And your little toady still rides by your side. I can't think what your general can be thinking to permit you to scamper around unchained. He must be softer in the head than I supposed."

"I have come to show you the way to your new owner in the underworld," Lan'xiu said.

Her voice startled Wen. It seemed deeper and was filled with loathing and disgust.

"Very amusing. A sweet little girl raising her sword in contest with a real man," the unknown general jeered. "If anyone journeys to the underworld today, it will be you!" He drew his long sword with a snarl. "I shall enjoy this. And after I've given you what you deserve, I shall cut your little rat's head off and dispatch him to fetch your slippers for you in hell. That's all he's fit for."

Two soldiers appeared behind the general and charged toward Lan'xiu. Before Wen could shout an order, the princess had thrown her spear, skewering one man through the throat. He fell, clutching his throat and gurgling, to writhe in the dust until he died. His horse bolted through the opening on the opposite side of the clearing. The other soldier hesitated just long enough for Lan'xiu to snatch a spear from Ning. Wen noted that she seemed familiar with the weak spots in the Liaopeh armor as she jabbed the man in the armpit. He wheeled his horse and retreated back into the darkness beyond the gap.

The Liaopeh general did not move during the contretemps, the sarcastic smile still curling his thin lips. "You think to impress me with that little coup? Pah! They were mere soldiers, nothings. Their destiny is to die for me. One more or less will make no difference in the outcome."

"At least you will have a bodyguard to accompany you in your death, brother," Lan'xiu spat at him. "If you can still command their loyalty after you die."

"You forget, my dearest sister," Wu Min said, "your lamented mother read the omens for me. You cannot kill me. If you believe her oracles, my death cannot be caused by man or woman. You can stab at me all day with that toy sword, but in the end I will spill your blood in the dust and trample your broken body in my ride to victory."

"I remember," Lan'xiu said. "She also said that although I could never kill you, I would be the cause of your death. I wouldn't have blamed you for sending me away. Perhaps I might have done the same. But you didn't need to kill my mother."

"Old news, sister. Her bones have been dust in the wind a long time. As yours would have been, had events followed my plan. But I shall soon rectify that."

"You have no need to fear the hand of man or woman, but I have always found it amusing that you don't fear horses, for instance. I could spook your horse, and he might throw you onto those rocks and break your spine. It could be a long, slow death." Lan'xiu smiled.

Wu Min looked down uneasily at his horse. "My horse is too well-trained, and you would not harm him. You never could hurt an animal."

Then he dug his spurs deep into the horse's side, drawing blood with his wild strength, and charged at Lan'xiu, his sword raised to pierce her throat. She raised her own blade and sidestepped her horse, parrying his thrust and shouting like a clarion, "Neither man nor woman can kill you, Wu Min! Let a eunuch show us all who is the better man and warrior!"

Wu Min turned a stunned face toward Ning and raised his sword again. Wen urged his horse forward but stopped when Lan'xiu hurled a command to him.

Ning never even glanced at Wen, his concentration was so fierce. Wu Min had every advantage of size, height, and longer reach. His horse was taller and stronger, and yet from the back of one horse to another, Ning proved to be his master in swordsmanship. Every thrust, every slash from Wu Min was expertly parried and countered.

Wen was holding his breath, ready to ride forward to rescue his lover, but gradually he forgot to be afraid. Never had he seen such a fight! Brilliantly, Ning beat back the larger man with skilled finesse and superior strategy. He knew more tricks than Wen had ever seen!

Used to an easy life where he had only to command, Wu Min was tiring and his arm was dropping. His face was set in a desperate snarl, teeth exposed as he swung his sword at Ning frantically, hoping to best him with brute strength. Sweat rolled down his face from under his helmet, and he blinked quickly to rid his eyes of the sting.

Ning would not take advantage of those moments. He waited with a scornful smile at Wu Min's weakness before attacking again, but time and again his blade drew blood as he slashed at the general's exposed skin and pierced his armor between the leather plates.

"What do you want of me?" Wu Min finally roared, his heavy arm slowing as he slashed the air in vain.

"Something you cannot return to me!" Ning shouted in his altered voice. "You cannot give my balls back, so I will have yours this day!"

"No!" Wu Min roared. "I'll kill first you and then that unnatural spawn of the devil you serve!"

"You can try," Ning replied, a little smile lurking on his mouth.

Wu Min charged him and Ning stood his ground, keeping his horse under tight rein. Wu Min was so close Wen wanted to cry out and order Ning to move out of the way!

But Ning surprised him again. Just at the last possible moment, when Wu Min's sword thrust toward his chest, Ning crouched low, allowing the blade to pass over his shoulder, nicking his armor. But his blade took Wu Min under the arm, plunging deep into his side.

A screeching howl of pain erupted from Wu Min's throat, but he managed to hang onto his sword, though he was having trouble lifting it. "Five thousand men wait for my signal beyond that pass," he croaked. "They are coming to my aid even now. I am only wounded, but they will kill you and I will have the pleasure of watching!"

"No bandage will stop the spurt of life blood from your wound," Lan'xiu said in the coldest voice Wen had ever heard from her. "Do your fingers grow numb? Is darkness clouding your eyes? You are dying, my brother, and my mother's spirit waits to accuse you of the crimes you committed in this life. My death will bring you no comfort, for you will die long before I do."

"No, it cannot be!" Wu Min shrieked. "I will kill you!" His fingers opened and his sword fell to the ground. His eyes were empty as he stared about him. "The mists! The mists of death!"

"They come to claim you, brother. I wish you a pleasant journey, for at the end of it, you will pay for all the misery you wrought in this life." Lan'xiu stepped her horse forward, staring at her brother's face.

He looked about wildly, but death had stamped its claim upon his face and he was white with the loss of blood. Lan'xiu stretched out her hand and pushed him off his horse.

In a flash, Ning dismounted and stood by the fallen man. "The demons come to claim your soul and your body, but you will go to hell without the bits of flesh I claim as my just due. You will pay for your entertainment at my expense. I have waited a long time for this."

Wen flinched but forced himself to watch as Ning drew a dagger and sliced through Wu Min's trousers, severing his balls from his body. Wu Min howled with pain, but his voice was softer now, almost sobbing as the strength left him.

Ning tossed the dismembered testicles as far as he could throw them up onto the rocks, saying, "Let the buzzards have them for their dinner. That is all they are good for."

"Why would you do this, Lan'xiu, my dear sister? Why do you hate me so?"

Silently, Lan'xiu and Ning stood by and watched as Wu Min's blood clotted in the dust around him, turning black as the flow grew slow and ceased. When his body sagged into the laxity of death, Ning spat upon him, and Wen thought he might never plumb the depths of his hatred. Lan'xiu dismounted and grabbed her brother's boots, dragging his body to the side of the clearing. She looked up at Wen.

"We will make a stand here. Wu Min may have brought five thousand men, but they can only come by twos and threes through that gap. We must stop them here for the safety of the general and his force, your compatriots. Have your men ready with their bows."

"Five thousand—yes, your Highness." Captain Wen swallowed, feeling as if he was emerging from some bad dream. He whistled and his men appeared from their hiding places, their shocked faces showing him they were equally shaken by what had transpired.

Lan'xiu was atop her horse again, and she had her bow in her hand. "Soldiers of my guard, we are few and the enemy is many. My Lord Hüi Wei is down in that valley, fighting to defend our land and our honor. If his forces are split to face the men of Liaopeh, we may not carry the day. We will make our stand here and force the enemy from their hole." She pointed at the gap. "Five thousand may wait beyond that pass, but today twenty will stop five thousand. The Liaopeh forces must not march past us to surprise the general from the rear. Are you with me?"

"Yes," Captain Wen said. "We will stand and fight by your side."

Lan'xiu smiled, a smile in which courage, adventure, and amusement were combined. "I thank you for your service and your oath to me. If you die, I will die with you."

"We will not die," Ning said firmly. "We will fight."

Lan'xiu looked at him with an admiring gleam in her eye. "Ning, you were magnificent!"

"Thank you, Lan'xiu. And now, perhaps we'd better fight."

She turned to face the first of the soldiers bursting through the gap.

CHAPTER TWENTY

"JIANG, where is she?" Hüi was practically shouting in his panic. He was riding amongst the wounded and dead, looking for any familiar sight that would guide him to Lan'xiu.

"Gently, Hüi. I vow Ning and Captain Wen have kept her safely at the rear. And you have soldiers to attend to, be they wounded or dead. They have served you faithfully."

"You are right and I would do it, but I must know if Lan'xiu is alive!"

Jiang grabbed the General's arm. "Do not dishonor her by this demonstration of emotion. Even if she has died, the gods forefend, you will honor her as well as all the others who have fallen in your service."

Drawing a deep breath, Hüi tried to calm himself. "You are correct to reprove me. Have the field hospitals been set up? What of the prisoners?"

"The prisoners await your review. The hospitals are at the rear. I need your aid in transporting some of the wounded," Jiang said, knowing that what the general most needed right now was a task to take his mind off his worry. "I wonder whatever happened to Wu Min and his troops? I could have sworn the flash off that shield was a signal to a watcher on the hill."

"Perhaps he did as Lan'xiu suspected, lured Daji into making a stand and then abandoned him to his fate when he saw the size of our forces."

"Where is Daji?"

"He is being held apart from the prisoners," Jiang said. "Let us take care of our own first, and attend to the enemy last as befits his treachery."

"Very well." Hüi Wei tried to curb his rising fears and put his trust in the gods that Lan'xiu would not have come to any harm. When he bent to help a wounded man onto a litter, his mind was distracted from his personal fears by the suffering borne by his men. He turned his attention to them, knowing that a smile and word of commendation from him would ease their pain until the doctors could treat them.

All the rest of the day, he worked, giving water, calling a physician to a severely wounded man, talking to his men, while in the back of his mind, he wondered, why had he heard nothing from Lan'xiu, Ning, or Captain Wen? Could they all have perished in the conflict? If so, that was too great a sacrifice for him to bear. He saw Jiang watching him and was careful to school his face not to betray his emotions, but with every fiber of his being he longed to fling himself upon his horse and go searching for his love.

The sun was slanting low over the valley and painting it gold when at last his eye caught sight of a small band of armed men coming down from the mountains. Hüi froze, straining his eyes as he stared into the golden haze, willing it to be Lan'xiu and her guard.

"There she is!" Jiang cried out. "She is alive!"

The relief in his voice made Hüi decide to forgive Jiang for forcing him to keep to his duties. Apparently, Jiang had been equally worried but sufficiently in control to keep Hüi's honor and dignity first and foremost. For the first time, Hüi thought of Zheng Guofang, Jiang's partner and his own commander, worrying back in Yan over Jiang's safety. He resolved to send Jiang back to him before the rest of the troops.

He watched as the small band rode toward him and counted over and over again. One was missing. Surely it could not be Lan'xiu? No, he recognized her slim figure riding tall in the saddle, closely accompanied by the shorter figure of Ning. When the group reached the flatness of the plain, they spread out and he saw his count had been wrong. Lan'xiu was returning to him, whole and safe, with her entire guard having successfully defended her—against what?

Jiang spoke up in an amused voice. "Go on, go to her. You've done enough today. Reassure yourself that she is safe. And find out what happened with Wu Min!" He shouted the last words for Hüi had already found his horse and was galloping across the plain.

When Hüi saw Lan'xiu, his heart threatened to break out of his chest. There was blood on her face, but she smiled when she saw him.

Captain Wen and Ning rode close together, and the rest of the guard brought up the rear. There were a few makeshift bandages to be seen, but the men were all alive and looking rather proud of themselves.

"Princess Lan'xiu!" Hüi could not say more, he was panting for breath. By the look on her face—something of import had happened. "Where have you been?" he burst forth, aware that he sounded like a petulant child.

"Guarding the rear," Lan'xiu said. "We went up into the mountains. There was a signal from the plains. I was waiting for that, and the answering flash told me which pass my brother chose to ambush you."

"Wu Min is up there?" Hüi asked in astonishment. "I heard nothing and we had men keeping watch."

"We were up high enough that you would not have heard," Lan explained. "Wu Min is still up there, but he is dead."

"You—you killed him?"

"Not I. Ning did it."

Hüi turned astonished eyes upon the eunuch, who looked very proud of himself indeed and puffed up his chest, for he had met Wu Min, a man who stood at least a head taller than Lan'xiu and twice as broad, and vanquished him.

"I thank you, Ning-xiānsheng, for keeping Lan'xiu alive."

"Thank her yourself," Ning declared. "She kept herself alive. Even though I *am* the one who trained her."

"She is truly a warrior princess," Captain Wen declared, pride shining in his eyes. "It was a most magnificent fight, General! You should have seen Ning vanquish Wu Min! It was a good day for us. Many of the Liaopeh forces are dead and the enemy is in retreat."

"Behold, my Warrior Princess," Hüi said softly, pride and secrets in his smile.

Lan'xiu laughed happily. "I have men here who need their wounds attended to, my Lord. And then you must tell me what happened in your part of the battle."

AS USUAL, soldiers stood on guard through the night, although both upstart provinces had been well and truly defeated. The hospitals gave comfort to the wounded, and the dead had been buried with full honors and their belongings gathered to be returned to their families.

Hüi Wei had addressed his troops, thanking them for their brave fighting and assuring them of the rewards of victory. He never allowed his troops to loot and pillage, but tribute would be enforced and they would get their share of the treasure that way.

Food had been savored and alcohol had flowed freely among the men off duty, fires were lit and stories told around them, not the least the story of their own warrior princess, who had gone to meet the Liaopeh forces and vanquished them, saving them and the general from the ignominy of defeat—or at least more losses, because Hüi Wei's men could never believe anyone could best *them*. At least not with the general leading them.

Ning had made sure that members of the princess's guard had spread the story of the confrontation in the mountains, suitably embroidered, in order to win the acceptance and appreciation of the troops. They already thought her beautiful, now they knew she was brave as well.

Captain Wen had had his arm wound bandaged by the princess herself and told her all the while that her guard was sworn to her for life and would be proud to obey her orders in any battle. Then of course,

Ning had relieved her and given her to understand that she might safely leave his lover in his care.

Together, still dressed in their armor, although Lan'xiu had had a chance to wash the blood from her face, General Hüi Wei and the Warrior Princess went to the hospital to commend and comfort the wounded.

Jiang awaited them at a fire, round which some of the commanders and soldiers had gathered to cook a simple meal.

Lan'xiu was silent at first, listening to the stories of what had happened on the field of battle. She was glad she had missed it, certain that some of the risks Hüi Wei had run would have made her die of fright.

Of course, eventually Jiang and Hüi Wei demanded to hear what had happened in the mountains.

Lan'xiu was glad to praise her friend Ning. "If not for him, Wu Min would yet be alive, for I could never have killed him."

"He is truly dead?" Jiang asked thoughtfully.

"He is. We could lead you there tomorrow if you wish to see the evidence with your own eyes," Lan said.

"Why would his soldiers not simply bear his body away?" Jiang demanded.

"He made cruelty a sport and entertainment," Lan said simply. "Once his soldiers discovered he was dead, they would have no motivation to continue his fight."

"I thought you had piled the bodies so high that the gap is impassable?" Hüi asked, his eyes twinkling.

"We did," Lan said, her dimples showing. "But it is a very small gap. And they were easily discouraged."

"So Ning exaggerates?" Jiang laughed.

"Perhaps a bit. It was a short battle, but many men gave up their lives needlessly before they realized with Wu Min dead there was no point." Lan'xiu looked serious. "I am truly free now, thanks to you, my Lord. As long as Wu Min lived, I owed a debt to my mother to avenge her death."

Jiang drew a deep breath. "Do you wish to return to Liaopeh, to rule in your brother's stead? You have the throne, by right of birth."

"Of course not! That is, not unless my Lord wishes it." Lan'xiu peered at Hüi anxiously, dreading that she might be sent from his side.

"Your Lord wishes his warrior princess to remain by his side," Hüi answered. "Liaopeh will have to make do with a steward on the throne, one who answers to me."

As THE discussion wore on, Lan'xiu yawned and retired to the tent that had been set up for the general. Without Ning to help, she struggled a bit to free herself from the armor. Then she shivered as she bathed herself from a basin, hurrying because the water was cold and she didn't wish to be observed naked.

Nothing could be done about her hair, so she left it in the braid, but she donned one of her pretty cheongsams to wait for Hüi to come to her.

When the tent flap lifted, she was sitting within the golden pool of light from the oil lamp, waiting for him with a smile.

"My beautiful Warrior Princess, you have made me proud today, but never do so again! The idea of you going off into the mountains without telling anyone—"

"Ning and Captain Wen were with me, as well as the guard you provided me." Lan'xiu allowed Hüi to pull her to her feet and surround her with his arms, leaning gratefully against his strength.

"And both of them are boasting of your courage and skill with a bow," Hüi said. "If you wanted it, I would embrace you in front of my men and my people as a man. You could dress like a man and go into battle by my side. My men would follow you, they proved that today."

"But I don't want to. I will go to battle with you again, but I will go dressed the way I prefer," Lan'xiu said, laughing. "I like dressing like this. I love that you love me no matter what, but it makes me happy to be this way."

"What else can I do to make you happy?" Hüi growled, sliding his hand under Lan's robe.

"Take me, my Lord," Lan answered a bit breathlessly.

"Your order is my great pleasure, my Warrior Princess."

The cries and moans that came from the general's tent that night made his soldiers laugh with ribald merriment, but that belied their secret pride that their leader had found happiness with such a courageous warrior princess who pledged her loyalty to him.

AND so it was that General Hüi Wei, servant of the emperor and protector of the northern border and the provinces of Yan, Qui, Henan, and Liaopeh, ruled long and wisely upon his throne. He was accompanied every day of his life by his beautiful warrior princess, Lan'xiu; together they fought many battles and put down many rebellions to protect their borders. Lan'xiu led troops in numerous military campaigns, and General Hüi Wei placed great confidence in her. Although their union was never fruitful, due to the grievous injury inflicted upon her by the traitor concubine Ci'an, they lived a long and happy life together.

Lord Jiang and his partner, Zheng Guofang, were often guests of Hüi Wei and Lan'xiu, and fought in their command. Lan'xiu instituted reforms in the harem, by which the gates were kept open and the remaining wives were permitted to go shopping and to tea accompanied by their guards. The Sixth Wife Bai was released as a concubine, and rumor had it that Lan'xiu had found her a husband who accepted the two sons she had adopted. In the passage of time, Bai and her husband had sons of their own and lived happily in their own province.

The concubines Fen and Huan lived together in one house for the rest of their days, and it was noted that neither of them greatly missed Hüi Wei's presence. Their lanterns were never lit again.

It was otherwise with Mei Ju. Her lantern was faithfully lit once a week, when Hüi Wei would come to her, and what transpired behind their closed doors no one knew. However, it was seen that Lan'xiu and

Mei Ju sustained a great friendship, and First Wife was often within the palace with her children. Lan'xiu was beloved of them, although she insisted they mind their education, for she said if they were to grow up to govern as well as Hüi Wei, they would need to have knowledge of the world.

Mei Ju often was heard to say that Lan'xiu was their mother as much as she was. Inevitably she grew old, and when she died, she commended the care of her children to Lan'xiu, who guarded them carefully and with love. In the sequence of time as they came of age, each of the four sons was given the responsibility to govern one of the provinces their father ruled. The two daughters were permitted a say in choosing their own husbands and visited the palace of their father often with their children. After the prescribed period of mourning for Mei Ju, Hüi Wei married Lan'xiu in a small, private ceremony and made her First Wife.

When at last in old age, Hüi Wei died, Lan'xiu did not live past him more than one week. The legend went that she died of grief, so greatly did she miss him. They were buried in the same tomb, surrounded with food, armor, and swords. The aged eunuch Ning allowed none to prepare his precious princess for her journey to the heavens except himself, and he was heard to comment to his lover, Wen, that they had no need for treasure in the next world—they were each other's treasure and all they needed.

And so endeth the tale of Lan'xiu, the Great Warrior Princess of the North, and her lord, the General Hüi Wei, forever twined in love that lasted throughout life and beyond death.

CATT FORD lives in front of the computer monitor, in another world where her imaginary gay friends obey her every command.

She likes cats, chocolate, swing dancing, sleeping, Monty Python, Aussie friends, being silly, spinning other realities with words, and sea glass. She dislikes caterpillars, cigarette smoke, and rude people who think the F-word (as in faggot, or bundle of sticks) is acceptable.

A frustrated perfectionist, she comforts herself with the legend about the weavers of Persian rugs always including one mistake so as not to anger the gods, although she has no need to include a mistake on purpose. One always slips through. Writing fiction has filled a need for clever conversations, only possible when one is in control of both sides, and erotic romances, where everything for the most part turns out happily ever after.

Visit Catt's blog at http://catt-ford.livejournal.com/.

Also from CATT FORD

http://www.dreamspinnerpress.com

Also from CATT FORD

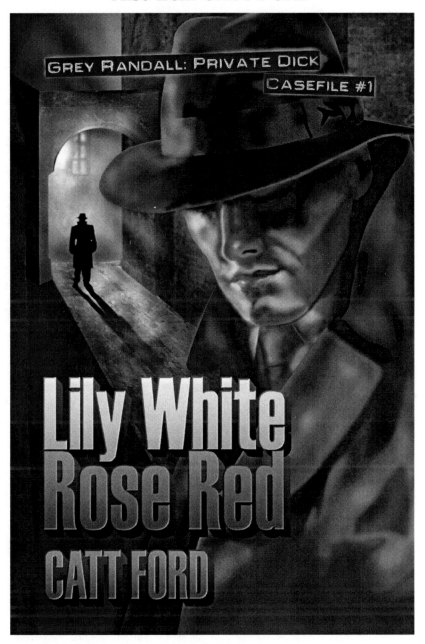

GREY RANDALL: PRIVATE DICK
CASEFILE #1

Lily White
Rose Red

CATT FORD

http://www.dreamspinnerpress.com

More Romance from CATT FORD

http://www.dreamspinnerpress.com

Also from DREAMSPINNER PRESS

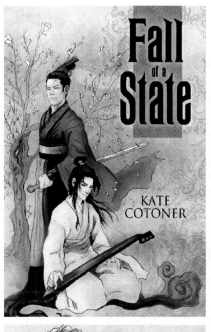

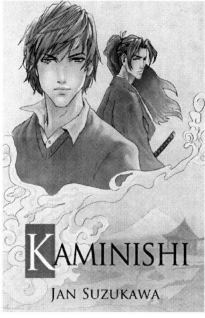

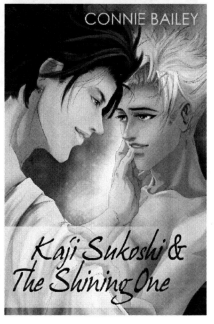

http://www.dreamspinnerpress.com

For more of the
best M/M romance,
visit

Dreamspinner Press

www.dreamspinnerpress.com

CPSIA information can be obtained at www.ICGtesting.com
Printed in the USA
LVOW091214250712

291460LV00003B/218/P